Praise for

"Renée Carlino's writing is c[...] [...]et power. You won't be disappoint[...]
—Joanna Wyl[...] [...]or

"*After the Rain* tore me up in the best way possible. Sexy, sweet, and sad, all woven together with an overwhelming undercurrent of hope, Nate and Avelina's story is one that goes straight to my list of all-time favorites."
—Amy Jackson, *New York Times* bestselling author

"I've come to think of Ms. Carlino's books as medicine for my soul. Her beautifully written words are not only healing but inspiring. This story put me through the emotional wringer, but I absolutely loved it. There is wisdom in this book, and it's an incredible talent when an author gives a reader something to think about and hold in their heart for the rest of their lives. . . . If you haven't already, please pick up a book by Renée Carlino today—your soul will thank you."
—*A Belle's Tales*

"Plain and simple, this book stole my heart. Between the compelling writing and the wonderfully well-developed characters I never stood a chance . . . *After the Rain* was an immensely touching and flawlessly written book that left a permanent mark on my heart."
—*The Book Enthusiast*

"A beautiful story . . . very true to real life . . . emotional, tragic, devastating, and bittersweet. . . . Be prepared for your heart to break, your eyes to tear, and your heart to quiver. *After the Rain* is an epic life story, as well as love story!"
—*A Bookish Escape*

"Renée Carlino has this writing style that just blows me away. . . . The writing was truly wonderful. . . . The story was beautiful and emotional. . . . This is a very well-written story that I would highly recommend!"
—*Book Babes Unite*

Praise for *Nowhere but Here*

"There is a certain 'magic' or 'spark' or whatever you want to call it that really makes a book come to life as you read it. As a reader, I'm on a constant search for that special spark and I absolutely found it here. *Nowhere but Here* was a unique and beautifully written love story. I laughed, I swooned, I wiped happy tears away, and I fell in love. This book warmed my heart and left me with the most wonderful feeling. I highly recommend it for all fans of romance!"

—*Aestas Book Blog*

"The story just consumed me, and all I know is how I felt during and after reading it. I felt hopeful. I even had that butterfly feeling in the belly that you get when reading something truly beautiful. . . . Would I recommend this one? I most definitely would."

—*The Autumn Review*

"The kind of romance that gives you butterflies in your stomach, that tingly feeling all over, and a huge smile on your face. . . . If you are looking for something emotional, where you can truly experience what the characters are feeling through the beautifully written words of an amazing author, complete with a wonderful epilogue that will give you a sense of completeness, then look no further."

—*Shh Mom's Reading*

"I will say this up front—almost no one writes swoony, realistic chemistry like Renée Carlino. Jamie and Kate fall in love in four days and I believed every minute of it. That's how good Carlino is at this. . . . If you're a fan of new adult, contemporary romance, or dare I say chick lit, you will enjoy *Nowhere but Here*. Carlino is officially on my auto-buy list, and I'd wager that if you check her out, she'll be on yours too."

—*Allodoxophobia*

"This is a story that has continued to stay on my mind, and my appreciation has continued to grow. Like *Sweet Thing*, I could feel Renée Carlino's passion for her characters and their story in every word. It's a wonderful feeling when you find an author who can translate that passion into an experience for readers."

—*The Bookish Babe*

"To say that I loved *Nowhere but Here* would be a dramatic understatement. . . . I don't know if I've been living under a rock or Renée Carlino has just been a well-kept secret. . . . I don't understand how everyone isn't shouting from the rooftops about this book! . . . *Nowhere but Here* is on my All-Time Favorites list, no question about it."

—*Nestled in a Book*

Praise for *Sweet Thing*

"Sassy and sweet, *Sweet Thing* melts in your mouth and goes straight to your heart!"

—Katy Evans, *New York Times* bestselling author of *Real*

"5 stars!!!! This is what I've been craving . . . one of my absolute favorites this year, and just one of my plain old favorites altogether."

—*Maryse's Book Blog*

"I have a new book boyfriend and his name is Will Ryan. I'm in love. . . . *Sweet Thing* was a sweet, heartbreaking, and romantic story that kept me up reading all night! . . . A fabulous debut novel. . . . I'll be watching out for more from Renée Carlino!"

—*Aestas Book Blog*

"This is 5 HUGE stars—a soul-searing, beautifully written book that now owns a piece of my heart . . . this book has made my all-time FAV list. . . . I cannot wait to see what's next for Renée Carlino."

—*Shh Mom's Reading*

"Surprisingly, this is Renée's debut novel because she writes like a pro with words flowing effortlessly and beautifully, totally hooking me from the beginning. There was something intangibly real and special about this book, which kept me reading until I finished it . . . one of my favorite stories of the year."

—*Vilma's Book Blog*

"When Will and Mia's story of self-discovery unfolds, it will fill you with love, it will crush you, it will frustrate you, it will lift you up and bring you down. You will share every heart-breaking moment and you will live every warm, tender, angry and funny exchange. . . . You will read *the end* with that warm book glow . . . you know, the one that lets you know you've just hung out with some wonderful characters who burrowed their way into your heart."

—*Totally Booked Blog*

"Sometimes—out of all the books you read—you come across one that stands out amongst all the other titles. Sometimes, you read a book that completely overwhelms your mind, your heart, and your soul. An all-consuming read that totally captures your senses and puts them into overdrive—but in the best possible way. There's just nothing better than the completely sated feeling you get from reading it. For me, that book was Renée Carlino's *Sweet Thing*."

—*Read This Hear That*

ALSO BY RENÉE CARLINO

Sweet Thing
Nowhere but Here
After the Rain

BEFORE
WE WERE
STRANGERS

A Love Story

RENÉE CARLINO

ATRIA PAPERBACK

New York . London . Toronto . Sydney . New Delhi

ATRIA PAPERBACK

An Imprint of Simon & Schuster, Inc.
1230 Avenue of the Americas
New York, NY 10020

First Atria Paperback edition August 2015

ATRIA PAPERBACK and colophon are trademarks of
Simon & Schuster, Inc.

For information about special discounts for bulk purchases,
please contact Simon & Schuster Special Sales at 1-866-506-1949
or business@simonandschuster.com.

The Simon & Schuster Speakers Bureau can bring authors
to your live event. For more information or to book an event
contact the Simon & Schuster Speakers Bureau at 1-866-248-3049
or visit our website at www.simonspeakers.com.

Interior design by Esther Paradelo

Manufactured in the United States of America

40 39 38 37

Library of Congress Cataloging-in-Publication Data
Carlino, Renée
  Before we were strangers : a love story / by Renée Carlino. — First Atria
paperback edition.
        pages ; cm (trade pbk. : alk. paper)
  I. Title.
  PS3603.A75255B44 2015
  813'.6—dc23   2015017238

ISBN 978-1-5011-0577-7
ISBN 978-1-5011-0578-4 (ebook)

For Sam and Tony, whom I'm blessed and lucky to know

Life goes not backward nor tarries with yesterday.
—KHALIL GIBRAN

FIRST MOVEMENT:
RECENTLY

1. Do You Still Think of Me?

MATT

Life was passing me by at high speed as I sat back with my feet up, rejecting change, ignoring the world, shrugging off anything that threatened to have meaning or relevance. I categorically disagreed with all things current. I despised the use of emojis, the word *meta*, and people who talked on their phones in line. Don't even get me started on gentrification. There were twenty-one Starbucks within a three-block radius of the building I worked in. Recording studios, film labs, and record stores were dying, if not already vacant corpses turned cupcake shops or blow-dry bars. They had stopped playing music videos on MTV and had banned smoking in bars. I didn't recognize New York anymore.

These are the things I pondered while sitting in my four-by-four cubicle at *National Geographic*. It hadn't felt National or Geographic since I had taken a desk job there a few years before. I had come out of the field, where I had seen everything, and I went into a hole, where I saw nothing. I was in the middle of the city I loved, back in her arms again, but we were strangers. I was still hanging on to the past and I didn't know why.

Scott smacked me square on the back. "Hey, buddy. Brooklyn for lunch?"

"Why so far?" I was sitting at my desk, fidgeting with the battery in my phone.

"There's a pizza place I want you to try, Ciccio's. You heard of it?"

"We can get good pizza on Fifth."

"No, you have to try *this* place, Matt. It's phenomenal."

"What's phenomenal, the pizza or the staff?" Since my divorce a few years ago, Scott—boss, friend, and eternal bachelor—had high hopes that I'd become his permanent wingman. It was impossible to talk him out of anything, especially when it involved women and food.

"You got me. You have to see this girl. We'll call it a work meeting. I'll put it on the company card." Scott was the type who talked about women a lot and about porn even more. He was severely out of touch with reality.

"I'm sure this qualifies as sexual harassment somewhere."

He leaned against the top of the cubicle partition. He had a nice-looking face and was always smiling, but if you didn't see him for a week, you'd forget what he looked like.

"We'll take the subway."

"Hey, guys." My ex-wife walked by, sipping a cup of coffee.

I ignored her. "Hey, Liz," Scott said and then stared at her ass as she walked away. He turned to me. "Is it weird to work with her and Brad?"

"I've always worked with her and Brad."

"Yeah, but she was your wife and now she's Brad's wife."

"I honestly don't care anymore." I stood up and grabbed my jacket.

"That's a good sign. I believe you. That's how I know you're ready for some strange." I often ignored these types of comments from Scott.

"I need to stop by Verizon first and get a new battery," I said, waving my phone.

"What *is* that?"

"A cell phone. Pretty sure you've seen one before."

"First of all, no one says 'cell phone' anymore. Second, that's not a phone; that's an artifact. We should ship it to the Smithsonian and get you an iPhone."

On the way out, we passed Kitty, the coffee cart girl. "Hello, gentlemen."

I smiled. "Kitty." She blushed.

Scott said nothing until we got into the elevator. "You should tap that. She totally wants you."

"She's a child."

"She's a college graduate. I hired her."

"Not my type. Her name is *Kitty*."

"All right, now you're just being mean." He seemed minimally offended on Kitty's behalf.

"I'm fine. Why is it everyone's mission in life to set me up? I'm *fine*."

"Clock's a-tickin'."

"Guys don't have clocks."

"You're thirty-six."

"That's young."

"Not compared to Kitty."

The elevator doors opened and we stepped into the lobby. A giant print of one of my photos ran the length of a wall.

"See that, Matt? That gets women wet."

"It's a picture of an Iraqi child holding an automatic weapon."

"The Pulitzer you got for it, genius, not the picture." He crossed his arms over his chest. "That was a good year for you."

"Yeah, it was. Professionally, anyway."

"I'm telling you, you have to use that to your advantage. You have a moderate amount of celebrity because of that photo. It's worked in my favor."

"How did it work for you, exactly?"

"I might've borrowed your name for a night. Once or twice."

I laughed. "That's disgraceful, man."

"Kitty's into you. You should give that little hottie what she wants. You know there're rumors about her."

"Even more reason to stay away."

"No, good rumors. Like she's crazy. A little animal."

"And that's good how?"

We made our way outside and headed for the subway station on West 57th to catch the F train. Midtown is always congested at that hour, but we were nearing the end of winter. The sun beating down between the buildings drew even more people out onto the street. I weaved in and out of the masses while Scott trailed me.

Right before we reached the station entrance he spoke loudly from behind.

"She'd probably be into anal."

I stopped and faced him at the top of the steps going

down. "Scott, this conversation is wrong in so many ways. Let's just end it here, okay?"

"I'm your boss."

"Exactly." I trotted down the steps toward the turnstiles.

There was an old woman playing a violin at the bottom of the steps. Her clothes were dingy and her hair was a gray, matted mess. The strings on her bow were hanging off, like floating foxtails, but she was playing Brahms flawlessly. When I threw five bucks in her case, she smiled. Scott shook his head and pulled me along.

"I'm trying to keep you happy and productive, Matt."

I swiped my Metro card. "Give me a raise. That will keep me happy and productive."

The station was crowded. A train was pulling up, but we were stuck behind a huge group of people who were pushing toward the front like they had somewhere important to be. Scott was content to hang back and stare at a woman who had her back toward us. She stood near the edge of the platform, rocking from heel to toe, balancing on the thick yellow line. There was something striking about her.

Scott elbowed me and then waggled his eyebrows and mouthed "nice ass." I wanted to punch him in the neck.

The more I looked at the woman, the more I felt drawn to her. She had one thick blonde braid running down her back. Her hands were shoved into the pockets of her black coat, and it occurred to me that, like a child, she was teetering joyously to the rhythm of the violin echoing against the station walls.

When the train finally pulled up, she let people rush past her and then stepped in at the last second. Scott and I stood on the yellow line, waiting for the next, less-crowded train. Just as the train doors closed, she turned around. Our eyes locked.

I blinked. *Holy shit.*

"Grace?"

She pressed her hand to the glass and mouthed, "Matt?" but the train was pulling away.

Without thinking about it, I ran. I ran like a crazy person to the end of the platform, my hand outstretched, willing the train to stop, my eyes never leaving hers. And when I ran out of platform, I watched the train fly into the darkness until she was gone.

When Scott caught up to me, he looked at me cautiously. "Whoa, man. What was that about? You look like you saw a ghost."

"Not a ghost. Grace."

"Who's Grace?"

I was stunned, staring into the void that had swallowed her. "A girl I used to know."

"What, like the one who got away?" Scott asked.

"Something like that."

"I had one of those. Janie Bowers, first girl to give me a blowie. I beat it to that image until I was, like, thirty."

I ignored him. All I could think about was Grace.

Scott went on. "She was a cheerleader. Hung around my high school lacrosse team. They all called her the Therapist. I didn't know why. I thought she was gonna be my girlfriend after that blowie."

"No, not like that," I said. "Grace and I dated in college, right before I met Elizabeth."

"Oh, like *that*. Well, she looked good. Maybe you should try to get in touch with her."

"Yeah, maybe," I said, but thought there's no way she'd still be single.

I LET BRODY, the seventeen year-old salesperson at Verizon, talk me into the newest iPhone. It actually costs eight dollars less a month to have a newer phone. Nothing in this world made sense to me anymore. I was distracted while signing the documents because the image of Grace, on the train, floating off into the darkness, had been running on a constant loop in my mind since we had left the station.

Over pizza, Scott showed me how to play Angry Birds. I thought that was a big step toward overcoming my technology phobia. The girl Scott was hoping to see wasn't working so we ate our pizza and headed back to the office.

Once I was back at my cubicle, I Googled Grace's name in every possible variation—first, middle, and last names; first and last names; middle and last names—with no luck. How was this possible? What kind of life was she leading that kept her completely off the internet?

I thought about what had happened to us. I thought about the way she looked on the subway—still beautiful, like I remembered, but different. No one would ever describe Grace as cute. Even though she was petite, she was too striking to be cute, with her big green eyes and massive mane of blonde hair. Her eyes had seemed hollow, her face a bit harder than when I last saw her. It had only taken one glance for me to know she wasn't the effervescent, free spirit I'd known years ago. It made me crazy wondering what her life was like now.

Cheers erupted from the break room down the hall.

I wandered over to witness the tail end of my ex-wife announcing her pregnancy to our co-workers. It wasn't long after my divorce that I became acutely aware of everyone around me carrying on, living life. I was static, standing on the platform, watching train after train go by, wishing I knew which one to be on. Elizabeth was already at the next stop, starting a family while I was slinking back to my shitty cubicle, hoping not to be seen. I was indifferent toward her and her pregnancy news. I was numb . . . but I shot her an email anyway out of some residual obligation still lingering from our failed marriage.

> Elizabeth,
> Congratulations. I'm happy for you. I know how badly you
> wanted a child.
> Best, Matt

Two minutes later, my email pinged.

> Best? Really? You can't say "love" after spending over a decade
> of your life with me?

I didn't respond. I was in a hurry. I needed to get back on the subway.

2. Five Days After I Saw You

MATT

I took the damn F train, an hour-long ride to Brooklyn from Midtown and back every day, at lunch, hoping I would run into Grace again, but I never did.

Things were bad at work. I had submitted a request to go into the field three months earlier but had been denied. Now I had to watch Elizabeth and Brad walk around in bliss as people congratulated them on the baby and Brad's promotion, which came right after the announcement.

Meanwhile, I was still rejecting any forward motion in my life. I was a stagnant puddle of shit. I had volunteered to go back on location to South America with a *National Geographic* film crew. New York just wasn't the same anymore. It held no magic for me. The Amazonian jungle, with all of its wonderful and exotic diseases, seemed more appealing than taking orders from my ex-wife and her smug husband. But my request hadn't been approved or denied. It just sat in a pile of other requests on Scott's desk.

I pondered the current state of my life while I stared at a blank wall in the office break room. Standing next to the water cooler, holding a half-empty paper cone, I tallied the insubstantial years I had spent with Elizabeth and wondered why. How had things gone so terribly wrong?

"What are you doin', man?" Scott's voice came from the doorway.

I turned and smiled. "Just thinking."

"You seem a little brighter."

"Actually, I was thinking about how I ended up thirty-six, divorced, and trapped in cubicle hell."

He walked to the coffeepot and poured a mug full then leaned against the counter. "You were a workaholic?" he offered.

"That's not why Elizabeth was unfaithful. She fell right into Brad's skinny arms, and he works more than I do. Hell, Elizabeth works more than I do."

"Why are you dwelling on the past? Look at you. You're tall. You have hair. And it looks like"—he waved his hand around at my stomach—"you might have abs?"

"You checking me out?"

"I'd kill for a head of hair like that."

Scott was the kind of guy who was bald by twenty-two. He's been shaving it Mr. Clean–style since then.

"What do women call that thing?" He pointed to the back of my head.

"A bun?"

"No, there's, like, a sexier name for it. The ladies love that shit."

"They call it a man-bun."

He studied me. "Jesus, you're a free man, Matt. Why

aren't you prowling the savannahs for new game? I can't watch you mope around like this. I thought you were over Elizabeth?"

I shut the break-room door. "I am. I was over Elizabeth a long time ago. It's hard for me even to remember being into her. I got caught up in the fantasy of it, traveling with her, taking photos. Something was always missing, though. Maybe I did work too much. I mean, that's all we talked about, that's all we had in common. Now look where I am."

"What about Subway Girl?"

"What about her?"

"I don't know. I thought you were gonna try to get in touch with her?"

"Yeah. Maybe. Easier said than done."

"You just have to put yourself out there. Get on social media."

Will I find Grace there? I went back and forth between wanting to do everything I could to find her and feeling like it was totally pointless. She'd be with someone. She'd be someone's wife. Someone better than me. I wanted to get away from everything reminding me that I still had nothing.

"If you care so much, why haven't you approved my request?" I asked.

He scowled. I noticed how deep the line was between his eyebrows and it occurred to me that Scott and I were the same age . . . and he was getting old. "I don't mean the actual savannahs, man. Running away isn't going to solve your problems."

"Now you're my shrink?"

"No, I'm your friend. Remember when you asked for that desk job?"

I walked toward the door. "Just consider it. Please, Scott."

Right before I left the room he said, "You're chasing the wrong thing. It's not gonna make you happy."

He was right, and I could admit that to myself, but not out loud. I thought if I could win an award again, get some recognition for my work, it would fill the black hole eating away at me. But deep down, I knew that wasn't the solution.

After work, I sat on a bus bench just outside the National Geographic building. I watched hordes of people trying to get home, racing down the crowded sidewalks of Midtown. I wondered if I could judge how lonely a person was based on how much of a hurry he or she was in. No one who has someone waiting for him at home would sit on a bus bench after a ten-hour workday and people-watch. I always carried an old Pentax camera from my college days in my messenger bag, but I hadn't used it in years.

I removed it from the case and starting clicking away as people flooded in and out of the subway, as they waited for buses, as they hailed cabs. I hoped that through the lens I would see her again, like I had years before. Her vibrant spirit; the way she could color a black-and-white photo with her magnetism alone. I had thought about Grace often over the years. Something as simple as a smell, like sugared pancakes at night, or the sound of a cello in Grand Central or Washington Square Park on a warm day, could transport me right back to that year in college. The year I spent falling in love with her.

It was hard for me to see the beauty in New York anymore. Granted, much of the riffraff and grit was gone, at least in the East Village; it was cleaner and greener now, but that palpable energy I had felt in college was gone, too. For me, anyway.

Time passes, life goes on, places change, people change. And still, I couldn't get Grace off my mind after seeing her in the subway. Fifteen years is too long to be holding on to a few heart-pounding moments from college.

3. Five Weeks After I Saw You

MATT

"Matt, I'm talking to you."

I looked up to see Elizabeth peering over the cubicle partition. "Huh?"

"I said, do you want to get lunch with us and go through the new slides?"

"Who's 'us'?"

"Scott, Brad, and me."

"No."

"Matt . . ." she warned. "You have to be there."

"I'm busy, Elizabeth." I was playing the Sudoku game printed on the brown paper bag from the deli where I buy my turkey sandwiches. "And, I'm eating. Can't you see that?"

"You're supposed to eat in the break room. I can smell those onions down the hall."

"That's because you're pregnant," I mumbled into my sandwich.

She huffed and then turned and walked down the hall-way, muttering something to herself.

Scott came up to my cubicle a minute later. "We need to go over those slides, buddy."

"Can't I just eat in peace? By the way, did you look over my request?"

He grinned. "You get in touch with Subway Girl yet?"

"I rode the subway to Brooklyn every day for a month and didn't see her. I tried."

It was true, I had been looking for Grace. After work, I would go to all of our old haunts in the East Village; I even hung out in front of the NYU dorm rooms where we had lived. Nothing.

"Hmm." He scratched his chin. "With all the technology out there, you're bound to find her. Maybe she wrote a Missed Connections ad. Did you look there?"

I set my sandwich down. "What's a 'missed connections' ad?"

He walked into my cubicle. "Get up, let me sit there." I rose from my chair. Scott sat down to pull up Craigslist on my computer, navigating over to the Missed Connections section. "It's like when you see someone in public and have a connection but don't know how to reach them. You can post about the experience here and hope they find it."

"Why wouldn't you just ask for their number when you see them?"

"It's one of those sensitive-guy, new-wave things. Like, if you don't have the balls to approach someone but maybe there's an attraction, you can post here. If they were feeling it too, they might see it and respond to your post. No harm, no foul. You write where it happened and what you were wearing and all that so the other person knows it's you."

I was squinting at the screen, thinking it was a stupid idea. "Yeah, but I actually used to know Grace. I might have said hello if I had more than a second before the train pulled away."

He swiveled the chair around to face me. "Look, you're not gonna find her on the subway. The odds are against you. Maybe she wrote one of these?"

"I'll look. Although, I'm pretty sure if she wanted to find me, she'd have no problem. My name hasn't changed and I still work at the same place."

"You never know. Just read them."

I spent the entire afternoon reading posts like, *I saw you in the park, you were wearing a powder blue jacket. We kept stealing glances at each other. If you like me, call me.* Or, *Where'd you go that night at SaGalls, you were talking about a cherry-drop martini and then you were gone. I thought you liked me. What's up?* And the-oh-so-common, *I want to do nasty things to you. I thought you knew that when you were droppin' it like it's hot and grinding on my leg at ClubForty. Gimme a buzz.*

Grace wasn't there, and I was relatively sure no one under the age of thirty could be found in the Missed Connections section. And then I read a post called "A Poem for Margaret."

Once there was a you and me
We were lovers
We were friends
Before life changed

Before we were strangers
Do you still think of me?
—Joe

I couldn't imagine twenty-year-olds named Joe and Margaret who spoke of the past in that manner. In an eerie way, it conveyed exactly what I felt for Grace, and I wondered for a moment if it was her. I called the number and a man answered.

"Hello, is this Joe?" I asked.

"Nope, that's the third time someone has called today asking that. Joe sure is a popular guy, but he doesn't live here."

"Thank you."

I hung up. Suddenly, the room darkened, with the exception of one set of fluorescent lights over my head and the desk lamp in my cubicle. From the hallway, Scott shouted, "I'll leave that one on for you, Matt! Get to it." He knew exactly what I was doing. Maybe Grace would find the post, maybe she wouldn't. Either way, I had to write it—if for nothing else, my own peace of mind.

To the Green-Eyed Lovebird:

We met fifteen years ago, almost to the day, when I moved my stuff into the NYU dorm room next to yours at Senior House.

You called us fast friends. I like to think it was more.

We lived on nothing but the excitement of finding ourselves through music (you were obsessed with Jeff Buckley), photography (I couldn't stop taking pictures of you), hanging out in Washington Square Park, and all the weird things we did to make money. I learned more about myself that year than any other.

Yet, somehow, it all fell apart. We lost touch the summer after graduation, when I went to South America to work for National Geographic. When I came back, you were gone. A part of me still wonders if I pushed you too hard after the wedding . . .

I didn't see you again until a month ago. It was a Wednesday. You were rocking back on your heels, balancing on that thick yellow line that runs along the subway platform, waiting for the F train. I didn't know it was you until it was too late, and then you were gone. Again. You said my name; I saw it on your lips. I tried to will the train to stop, just so I could say hello.

After seeing you, all of the youthful feelings and memories came flooding back to me, and now I've spent the better part of a month wondering what your life is like. I might be totally out of my mind, but would you like to get a drink with me and catch up on the last decade and a half?

M
(212)-555-3004

SECOND MOVEMENT:
FIFTEEN YEARS AGO

4. When I Met You

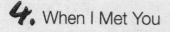

MATT

It was a Saturday when we met at Senior House. She was reading a magazine in the lounge while I struggled down the hall with my nineteen-year-old wooden desk. It was the one piece of home my mother had shipped from California, other than a single box, my camera equipment, and a duffel bag of clothes.

When she glanced in my direction, I froze awkwardly, hoping she'd look past me as I balanced the desk with little finesse.

No such luck.

Instead, she stared right into my eyes, cocked her head to the side, and squinted. She looked as if she were trying to recall my name. We had never met, I was sure of that. No one could forget a face like hers.

I remained still, transfixed, as I took her in. She had big, incandescent green eyes, alit with energy that demanded attention. Her mouth was moving and I was staring right at her, but I couldn't hear a word she was saying; all I could think about was how uniquely beautiful she was. The eyebrows that framed her big, almond-shaped eyes were darker than her almost white-blonde hair, and her skin looked like it would taste sweet on the tongue.

Oh my god, I'm thinking about what this girl's skin tastes like?

"Bueller?"

"Huh?" I blinked.

"I asked if I could give you a hand?" She smiled, piteously, and then pointed to the desk I had balanced on my knee.

"Sure, yeah. Thanks."

Without hesitation, she tossed aside her magazine, grabbed one end of the desk, and began walking backward as I struggled to keep up.

"I'm Grace, by the way."

"Nice to meet you," I said, out of breath. The name suited her.

"Do you have a name?"

"One more," I said, gesturing with a nod.

"Your name is One More? That's kind of unfortunate, but it does make me wonder how your parents came up with it." She grinned.

I let out a nervous laugh. She was stunningly beautiful but she was also kind of goofy. "I meant, we're one room away."

"I know, silly. I'm still waiting on that name."

"Matt."

"So Matty One More," she said after she stopped in front of my room. "What's your major?"

"Photography."

"Ah, so I must recognize you from Tisch?"

"Nope. This is my first year."

She looked puzzled. I reminded her of someone. I was hoping it was someone she liked. After we set the desk down, I moved past her to unlock the door. With my head lowered, I spoke to my Vans. "Yeah, I transferred from USC."

"Really? I've never been to California. I can't believe you left USC to come and slum it at Geezer House."

"It wasn't my scene." I turned around and leaned against the door before I opened it. Our eyes met for a few seconds too long, and we both looked away. "I had to get out of California for a bit." I was nervous-talking but I didn't want her to leave. "Do you want to come in and hang out while I unpack my stuff?"

"Sure."

She propped the door open with a stack of books and then helped me as I carried the desk inside to place in the corner. She hopped on top of it and sat, legs crossed, like she was going to meditate or levitate. I looked around my room again for the second time that day. It came complete with the standard dorm furniture: one metal extra-long twin bed, a desk that I could use for my camera equipment, an old stereo on the floor that the last person had left behind, and one empty bookshelf. The large box I had brought contained some of my favorite records, books, CDs, and photos. My best work from USC was matted inside a leather portfolio. Grace immediately grabbed it and began flipping through the pages. There were two long, narrow windows that bathed the room in sunlight, illuminating Grace's face perfectly. It was as if the light were coming from her.

"Wow, this one is amazing. Is this your girlfriend?" She

held up a photo of a gorgeous girl with devilish eyes, the curve of her naked body exposed.

"No, she wasn't my girlfriend. Just a friend." This was true, but it was also true that she had mouthed *Do you want to fuck me?* right before I snapped the photo while my friend—and her boyfriend—watched us silently. Like I said, USC wasn't my scene.

"Oh," she said quietly. "Well, it's a great photo."

"Thanks. The light in here is fantastic. Maybe I can take a couple of you?"

I saw her neck move as she swallowed. Her eyes widened and I realized she thought I wanted to photograph her naked. "Um, with your clothes on, of course."

Her expression lightened. "Sure, I'd be happy to." She continued to stare at the photograph. "But I think I could model for you like this girl, if it's done like this." She turned her green eyes on me. "Maybe someday, after we've known each other for a while. You know, for the sake of art?" She smirked.

I tried not to picture her naked. "Yeah, for the sake of art." And a work of art she was. She wore a man's white dress shirt, the sleeves rolled up to the elbow, with the top two buttons open. Her pink toenails caught my eye before my gaze moved up to the skin peeking out from a hole in the knee of her jeans. I watched as she began to braid her long blonde hair over her shoulder. I couldn't take my eyes off of her and she noticed, but instead of saying something rude she just smiled.

"So why did you call it Geezer House?" I asked as I turned to unpack the large box. I needed to distract myself so I'd stop staring at her.

"Because it's really fucking boring here. Seriously, I've been here a week and already I feel like my soul is dying."

I laughed at the dramatics. "That bad, huh?"

"I haven't played the cello once since I moved in; I'm afraid people will complain. Oh, by the way, you'll have to let me know if my playing gets too loud for you. Just bang on the wall or something."

"What do you mean?"

"I'm in the room right next door. The practice rooms are too far away, so I'll probably end up practicing in my room a lot. I'm a music major."

"That's really cool. I'd love to hear you play sometime." I couldn't believe she was in the room right next to mine.

"Anytime. So, not very many people choose dorm life their senior year. What's your excuse?"

"Couldn't afford anything else." I noticed she was wearing a badge with Greek symbols. "What about you? How come you don't live in the sorority house?"

She pointed at the badge over her breast. "Oh, this? It's fake. Well, it's not fake; I stole it. I live here 'cause I'm too dirt-ass poor to live anywhere else. My parents don't have any money to contribute for tuition, and it's hard for me to keep a job since I have to practice so much. I use this to get free meals at the dining hall on Fourteenth Street." She held her fist up and punched the air. "Pi Beta Phi, mac and cheese for life!"

She was adorable. "I can't imagine this place will be too boring with you here."

"Thanks." I looked up to catch her blushing. "I really don't have that much school spirit, but my music buddies will come over and liven things up for us once classes start and everyone is back in the city. I lived with a bunch of people in a crappy apartment over the summer and I got used to having a lot a friends around. It's been really quiet here. So far most of the residents keep to themselves."

"Why didn't you go home over the summer?"

"No space. My parents' house is small and I have three younger sisters and a brother. They all still live at home." She hopped off the desk and moved to the other side of the room to look through the items I had unpacked and stacked on the floor. "Shut up!" She held up *Grace* by Jeff Buckley. "He's practically the reason I came to NYU."

"He's a genius. Have you seen him play?" I asked.

"No, I'm dying to, though. I guess he lives in Memphis now. I moved all the way to New York from Arizona and then spent my first three months here searching for him in the East Village. I'm a total groupie. Someone told me he left New York a long time ago. I still listen to *Grace* everyday. It's like my music bible. I like to pretend he named the album after me." She chuckled. "You know what? You kinda look like him."

"Really?"

"Yeah, you have better hair, but you both have those dark, deep-set eyes. And you both pull off a scruffy jawline pretty well."

I brushed my knuckles over my chin and felt a tinge of insecurity. "I need to shave."

"No, I like it. It looks good on you. You have that thin build, too, but I think you're a bit taller than him. How tall are you?"

"Six one."

She nodded. "Yeah, I think he's much shorter."

I sat down on my bed and lay back, propping my hands

behind my head, watching her in amusement. She held up
A *Portable Beat Reader*. "Wow. We're soul twins for sure.
Please tell me I'll find some Vonnegut in here?"

"You'll definitely find some Vonnegut. Hand me that
CD over there and I'll put it on," I said, gesturing toward
Ten by Pearl Jam.

"I should go practice in a minute but will you play 'Release'? That's my favorite from this album."

"Sure, as long as I can photograph you."

"Okay." She shrugged. "What should I do?"

"Do whatever feels natural."

I popped the CD into the stereo, reached for my camera,
and began snapping away. She moved around the room to
the music, twirling and singing.

At one point, she stopped and looked grimly into the
lens. "Do I look lame?"

"No," I said as I continued pressing the shutter. "You
look beautiful."

She flashed me a shy smile and then her tiny frame
dropped to the hardwood floor, squatting like a child. She
reached down and picked up a button. I continued taking
picture after picture.

"Someone lost a button." Her voice was sing-songy.

She looked up from the floor, right into the lens, and
squinted, her piercing green eyes twinkling. I pressed the
shutter.

She stood, reached out, and handed me the button.
"Here you go." Pausing, she glanced up to the ceiling. "God,
I love this song. I feel inspired now. Thank you, Matt. I better
run. It was really nice meeting you. Maybe we can hang out
again?"

"Yeah. I'll see you around."

"I'll be hard to miss. I'm right next door, remember?"

She skipped out of the door and then a moment later, just as Eddie Vedder sang the final lyrics, I heard the deep strains of a cello through the thin dorm walls. She was playing "Release." I moved my bed to the other side of the room so that it would rest against the wall that Grace and I shared.

I fell asleep to the sound of her practicing late into the night.

MY FIRST MORNING in Senior House consisted of eating a stale granola bar and rearranging three pieces of furniture until I was happy with the tiny space I would call home for the next year. On one pass, I discovered a Post-it note stuck to the bottom of the empty drawer in the desk I had brought from home. It read: *Don't forget to call your mom* in my mother's handwriting. She wouldn't let me forget, and I loved that about her.

I found the payphone on the first floor. A girl wearing sweats and dark sunglasses sat in the corner, holding the phone receiver to her ear.

"I can't live without you, Bobbie," she cried, wiping the tears from her cheeks. She sniffled and then pointed to a box of tissue. "Hey, you! Will you hand that to me?"

I took the tissue box from the end table near a worn-out couch that smelled faintly of Doritos and handed it to her. "Are you gonna be long?"

"Seriously?" She moved the glasses to the end of her nose and peered at me over the top.

"I have to call my mom." *I sound pathetic. More pathetic than this girl.*

"Bobbie, I have to go, some dude has to call his mommy. I'll call you in fifteen minutes, okay? Yeah, some guy." She looked me up and down. "He's wearing a Radiohead T-shirt. Yeah, sideburns . . . skinny."

I threw up my hands as if to say, *What's your problem?*

"Okay, Bobbie, wuv you, bye. No, you hang up . . . no, you first."

"Come on," I whispered.

She stood and hung up the phone. "It's all yours."

"Thanks," I said. She rolled her eyes. "Wuv you," I called out to her as she walked away.

I pulled my calling card from my wallet and dialed my mother's number. "Hello."

"Hi, Mom."

"Matthias, how are you, honey?"

"Good. Just got settled in."

"Have you called your dad?"

I winced. I had transferred to NYU to put a whole country between me and my father's disappointment. Even after I had won photography awards in college, he still believed I had no future in it.

"No, just you so far."

"Lucky me," she said earnestly. "How are the dorms? Have you seen the photo lab yet?" My mom was the only one who supported me. She loved being the subject of my photos. When I was young, she gave me her father's old Ciro-Flex camera, which started my obsession. By ten, I was taking photos of everything and everyone I could.

"The dorms are fine, and the lab is great."

"Have you made any friends?"

"A girl. Grace."

"Ahhh . . ."

"No, it's not like that, Mom. We're just friends. I met her and talked to her for a minute yesterday."

Wuv-you girl was back. She sat on the couch, leaned over the arm dramatically, and stared at me, upside down. Her weird, upside-down face made me uneasy.

"Is she into the arts, like you?"

"Yes, music. She was nice. Friendly."

"That's wonderful." I could hear dishes clinking around. I thought idly that my mom wouldn't have to do the dishes if she were still married to my dad. My father was a successful entertainment lawyer while my mom taught art at a private school for a meager salary. They divorced when I was fourteen. My dad remarried right away, but my mom remained single. Growing up, I chose to live with my dad and stepmother, even though my mom's tiny bungalow in Pasadena always felt more like home. There was more space at my dad's for my older brother and me.

"Well, that's nice. Did Alexander tell you that he asked Monica to marry him?"

"Really? When?"

"A few days before you left. I thought you would have heard by now."

My brother and I didn't talk, especially about Monica, who was once my girlfriend. He was following in my dad's footsteps and was about to pass the bar in California. He thought I was a loser.

"Good for him," I said.

"Yeah, they're well suited for each other." There were a few beats of silence. "You'll find someone, Matt."

I laughed. "Mom, who said I was looking?"

"Just stay away from the bar scene."

"I went to more bars before I was twenty-one than I do now." Wuv-you girl rolled her eyes at me. "I've gotta go, Mom."

"Okay, honey. Call me again soon. I want to hear more about Grace."

"Okay. Wuv you, Mom." I winked at the girl as she stared me down a foot away.

"Wuv you, too?" She laughed.

5. You Were Like a Light

MATT

I killed time by rearranging my portfolio. At some point I knew I'd have to get out and make friends, but for the time being I was hoping to catch one person in particular, either on her way in or out. I'm not sure how obvious I was being by leaving my door cracked, but I didn't care, especially when I finally heard Grace's voice from the hall.

"Knock-knock." I got up to put on a shirt but she pressed the door open with her index finger before I had time.

"Oh, sorry," she said.

"No worries." I opened the door all the way and smiled. "Hey, neighbor."

She leaned against the doorjamb as her eyes fell from my face and traveled down my chest, to where my jeans hung below my boxers, and then further down to my black boots.

"I like your . . . boots." She looked back up to my eyes. Her mouth was open very slightly.

"Thanks. Do you want to come in?"

She shook her head. "No, actually I came by to see if you wanted to get lunch. It's free," she said quickly, and before I had time to answer she added, "They'll actually pay you."

"What is this free-paying lunch place you speak of?" I quirked an eyebrow at her.

She laughed. "You just have to trust me. Come on, grab a shirt. Let's go."

I ran a hand through my hair, which was sticking up in every direction at the moment. Her eyes fell to my chest and arms again. It was hard for me to look away from her heart-shaped face, but I glanced down to see her hands fidgeting at her sides. She was wearing a black dress with flowers on it, tights, and little black boots. She rocked back on her heels a couple of times. She reminded me of a hummingbird, one of those people who are always moving, always fidgeting.

"Give me one second," I said. "I need a belt." I rummaged through my belongings on the floor but couldn't find one. My jeans were practically hanging off at that point.

Grace plopped down on my bed and watched me. "No belt?"

"I can't find it."

She hopped up and went to a pile of my shoes near the closet. She yanked the laces out of one of my Converses and did the same to one of my Vans and knotted the ends together. "This should do."

I took the shoelace belt from her and fed it through the loops.

"Thanks."

"No problem."

When I threw on my black Ramones T-shirt, she smiled appreciatively. "I like it. Ready?"

"Let's hit it, G."

We jogged down the three flights of stairs and Grace shoved opened the glass doors to the building. Walking in front of me, she threw her arms open and looked up at the sky. "What a great fucking day!" She turned around and reached for my hand. "Come on, it's this way!"

"Should I be worried? How far is it?"

"It's about six blocks. And no, you shouldn't be worried. You're gonna feel good about this. Your heart will feel good, your wallet will feel good, and your tummy will feel good."

I didn't know anyone over the age of twelve who still used the word "tummy." We walked along, shoulder to shoulder, taking in the warmth radiating from the concrete. "I heard you playing last night," I told her.

She glanced at me nervously. "Was I too loud?"

"Not at all."

"My friend Tati came over and practiced with me. She plays the violin. I hope it didn't keep you up."

"I liked it a lot, Grace," I said, seriously. "How'd you learn to play?"

"I taught myself. My mom got me a cello from a garage sale when I was nine. We didn't have much money, as I'm sure you've gathered by now. There're no frets on a cello so it requires a lot of ear training. I just listened to a ton of records and tried to re-create the sounds. I got a guitar after that and then a piano when I was twelve. In high school, my music teacher wrote me an insane letter of recommendation. That's how I got in here. I struggled last year, though, and wasn't sure if I'd stay."

"Why?"

"I had no formal training outside of my high school orchestra, and this place is really competitive. I'm mostly trying to get good enough to be a studio musician."

"What kind of music do you like to play?"

"I like to play everything. I really like rock and roll, but I like the classical stuff, too. Even though it's a huge pain to lug around, I love the cello. I love how its texture can be growly or smooth. When I play the strings without a bow, it reminds me of skipping rocks, and I can't help but picture those flat little pebbles against the still water." I stopped. She walked a few feet ahead of me and then turned back. "What's up?"

"That was a really beautiful way to put it, Grace. I've never thought about music that way."

She sighed. "I just wish passion was enough."

"There's no right or wrong in art. My mom always said that."

I detected a slight nod and then she gestured toward the street. "Come on, we have to cross."

I was completely lost in New York and hadn't gotten my bearings, or even figured out how to use the subway, so having Grace there lessened the frightening newness of the big city.

"So, do you have a boyfriend?"

She continued looking ahead but didn't miss a beat. "No, I don't date."

"Just casual sex?" I grinned.

She blushed. "A lady never tells. What about you?"

"I had a girlfriend for a couple of years right out of high school but nothing serious since then. She's engaged to my brother now, so my track record is pretty awesome."

"You're kidding?"

"Nope."

"Isn't that weird? I mean, what happened?"

"She dumped me the week I declared my major. My dad, too." I said the last part under my breath.

"Did you guys have a good relationship?"

"Monica's dad and my dad are partners at the same law firm. We were kind of set up. I liked her at first but never really thought about a future with her. She wanted me to go into law but it wasn't my thing. We had different interests. It was for the best. We broke up, and then two weeks later she was dating my brother. I never talked to him about it. There are plenty of asshole things I could have said, but I didn't want to stoop to his level. He can have her."

"Were you heartbroken?"

"Not at all. I guess that's pretty telling. The hardest part for me is not laughing at the whole stupid thing when I'm around them. That's another reason I had to get out of L.A. My brother just graduated from law school and likes to rub it in my face. It takes everything in me not to remind him that he's going to have to live the rest of his life knowing I've fucked his wife."

"Oh." Grace looked shocked for a moment, and her cheeks flushed. I wasn't sure if I offended her.

We walked in silence as I berated myself for being so blunt until Grace pointed up to a sign. "Here we are."

"We're having lunch at the New York Plasma Center?"

"Yep. So here's the deal. For your first time you can only do plasma. Make sure you eat as many of the free pretzels and granola bars as you can and drink as much of the juice, too. Then you can hang out with me while I get my platelets sucked out."

"Wait . . . huh?"

"Yeah, it takes, like, an hour to do the platelets, which really gives us time to feast. Then you'll get twenty-five bucks and I'll get fifty."

I tried to process what she had just told me, but when she started laughing, I couldn't help laughing, too.

"You think I'm crazy, huh?"

"No, I think this a great idea. You're a genius."

She elbowed me playfully. "We're gonna get along."

Once we were inside the blood bank, everyone behind the counter recognized Grace and smiled or waved at us as we stood in line.

"You come here a lot?"

"That's such an old pickup line, Matt. I think you need new material."

"I'm really into girls with big platelets."

"Much better. Now you have my attention. You're in luck, because I'm really into guys named Matthew."

"It's Matthias, actually."

"No shit?" She cocked her head to the side. "I've never heard that name before. Is it biblical?"

"Yep. It means God-like."

"Stop."

"No, I'm serious. It means God-like appendage." It took her a second to comprehend what I was saying. I tried not to smile.

Her mouth opened in a perfect O. "You are . . ." She shook her head, and then seized my hand and pulled me toward the counter.

"What? What am I?"

"Shameless!" She turned her attention to the receptionist.

"Hi, Jane. This is my friend, Matthias. He has excellent blood and he'd like to sell you some."

"You came to the right place." She gathered some forms from under the counter. "What's your last name again, Grace?" she said as she riffled through a file.

"Starr."

"That's right, how could I forget? And you're giving just plasma today, Matthias?"

"Yes. And it's Matthias William Shore, if you need my full name."

Grace looked at me sideways. "Well, Matthias William Shore, I'm Graceland Marie Starr. Delighted to make your acquaintance." She held her hand out to shake mine.

I kissed the back of it. "Pleasure is all mine. Graceland, is it?"

She blushed. "My parents are Elvis fans."

"Lovely name for a lovely lady."

The woman behind the counter put an abrupt end to our courtly exchange. "Just blood, Grace, or platelets, too?"

"Today, I'll be selling my enormous, lush platelets." She leaned in and whispered in my ear. "Are you turned on?"

I laughed. She could be brazen, but that didn't mask her sweet, shy side. Something about her made me want to get to know her in every possible way.

After the forms were filled out and the blood checks done, they took us into a big room where there were ten other people getting their blood drawn. We lay across from each other on inclined beds. Grace watched me with a smile as they inserted a line into my arm. She was hooked up to a machine that took the blood from one arm, removed the platelets, and then returned the plasma to the other. I chomped on the pretzels and waited as my blood dribbled into the plastic bag. She held her juice in the air and said, "Cheers."

I started feeling lightheaded, almost drunk. Black nothingness began filling my vision from the sides. "Best date ever," I said woozily, holding my juice box up to her.

She smirked, but there was compassion in her eyes. "Who said anything about a date?" I gave her a lethargic shrug. "Let's make a deal. If you make it through this without passing out, I'll let you take me on a real date," she said, before everything faded to black.

Smelling salts work, apparently. My eyes opened to find a nurse who looked like Julia Roberts circa *Mystic Pizza* leaning over me. Her bushy eyebrows pinched together and her big hair bounced as she talked. "You okay, sweetie?"

I nodded. "I think so. Why are you upside down?"

She smiled. "The bed can be flipped so that if you pass out, we can get your feet elevated above your heart."

I was totally out of it. "Thanks, baby. You saved me."

"No problem, baby." She chuckled.

I looked across the room to Grace, who seemed listless. "You okay?" she asked quietly. I nodded.

After they removed the needle and loaded me up with sugary snacks, the nurse helped me stand. "You can stay as long as you need to," she assured me.

"I'm all right. I'm just gonna sit with my friend over there."

I shuffled over to Grace, who was beginning to look pale and tired. Sitting in the chair next to her bed, I noticed that goose bumps covered her arms and legs. Her dress was riding up on her thighs as she slumped against the headrest.

She noticed my gaze and discreetly tugged the hem of her dress down.

"Hey," I said as I looked above her and studied the machine of pinwheels and tubes. It looked like a Willy Wonka contraption.

"Hey yourself," she said in a low voice.

"Are you okay?"

"Yeah, I'm just tired and cold." She let her eyes close. I stood up and rubbed my hands up and down her arms.

With eyes just barely cracked, she shot me a tiny smile and whispered, "Thanks, Matt."

When the nurse walked by, I quickly caught her attention. "Excuse me, nurse. She's freezing and she seems kind of out of it."

"That's normal. I'll get her a blanket," she said, gesturing to a nearby chair.

I rushed over and grabbed it before the nurse even had time to turn around. I covered Grace all the way up to her neck and then tucked the blanket in at her sides so she was completely cocooned.

"Perfect," I said. "A Grace burrito."

She laughed silently and then closed her eyes.

I sat back down in the chair and watched my new friend. She didn't wear much makeup, if any at all. Her lashes were long, her skin flawless, and she smelled of lilac and baby powder. In the short time I'd known her, I could tell that as savvy as she seemed about the world around her, there was a poignant fragility about her, a childlike innocence I had detected immediately. It came through her eyes and shy gestures.

Glancing around the room, I noticed a few homeless-looking people and one grungy, obviously very inebriated man in the corner making a fuss over the fact that there were no more Oreo cookies left in the snack basket.

Resting my head back, I let my own eyes close, then drifted off into a light sleep, listening to the sound of the machine above me removing Grace's platelets and then pumping the blood back into her body. I wondered how often she had done this for fifty dollars.

I don't know how much time passed when I felt a delicate hand on my shoulder. "Matty, come on, let's go." I opened my eyes and looked up to find Grace, pink-cheeked and grinning from ear to ear. She handed me twenty-five bucks. "Sweet, huh?" She seemed back to normal and totally poised, with her small purse strung across her body. "Need a hand?" She reached out to me.

"Nope." I popped out of the chair. "I feel like a million bucks."

"You look about twenty-five short of a million."

A strand of hair had fallen out of her hair tie. I reached to tuck it behind her ear but she flinched. "I was just going to . . ."

"Oh, sorry." She leaned in, so I reached down again, and this time she let me tuck her hair back.

"You smell good," I said. She was mere inches from my face, looking up at me. Her eyes focused on my lips. I licked them and then leaned down an inch closer.

She looked away. "Ready?"

I didn't feel rejected. Instead, her reservation piqued my interest even more. I was curious.

"Seems like there were a lot of druggies in there," I said, once we were outside. "Do you think they use that blood?"

"I don't know. I've never really thought about it."

The sun was high in the sky, there were birds chirping, and Grace was standing stock still with her head down, her eyes trained on a line of ants heading toward a trashcan.

"What do you want to do now?" I asked.

She looked up. "Wanna get some weed and hang out in Washington Square?"

I laughed. "I thought you'd never ask."

"Come on, druggy." She yanked on my hand and we were off. A block down, she tried to pull her hand out of mine but I wouldn't let her.

"You have tiny hands," I said.

At the corner, as we waited for the crosswalk, she pried her hand away and held it up. "Yeah, but they're bony and ugly."

"I like them." When the walking sign lit up, I grabbed her hand again and said, "Come on skeletor. Let's go."

"Funny."

She let me hold her hand the rest of the way.

We stopped by Senior House so I could get my camera. Grace grabbed a blanket and the skinniest joint I had ever seen. On our way out, Daria, our RA, stopped us as we passed the registration desk. "Where are you two headed?"

"The park," Grace said. "What are you doing here?"

Daria popped the last bit of a fish stick into her mouth. "Lots of people movin' in today. I'm just gonna keep getting bugged. I might as well sit here. By the way, I wanted to talk to you, Grace. The cello-playing at night can get pretty loud. It was okay for the first few days, when no one was here, but . . ."

"I don't mind and I'm right next door," I interrupted.

Grace turned around and shook her head at me. "Don't. It's okay. I'll keep it down, Daria."

We turned and left the building. "Daria looks like a man, huh? Like David Bowie or something?"

She scrunched her face up. "Yeah, but David Bowie looks like a woman."

"True. Maybe you should learn some Bowie songs to keep Daria happy."

"Yeah, maybe I will."

At the park, she laid the blanket down near a big sycamore tree and sat with her back against the trunk. I lay on my stomach, facing her. I watched as she lit the joint, inhaled, and passed it over to me. "Do you think we'll get busted here, out in the open?"

"No, I come here all the time."

"Alone?"

"A bunch of people from the music department hang out here." She took a long hit and then looked up, startled, and coughed a puff of smoke out. "Oh shit."

"What?" I turned around to see a man in his early to midthirties coming toward us. He was dressed in khakis and had a severely receding hairline. "Who's that?" I asked, grabbing the joint and stubbing it out.

"That's Dan—I mean, Professor Pornsake. One of my music teachers."

"You call him Dan?"

"He told me to. I don't think he likes his last name."

"Understandably."

She nervously brushed grass from her lap and sat up straight. I turned on my side, propped my head on my hand, and looked up at Grace's face. She was high as a kite on just the small amount we had smoked. Her eyes were narrow, red slits, and she was grinning maniacally.

I started to laugh. "Oh my god, you're super stoned."

She made an attempt at a serious face, "Don't start!" she said, mock-scolding me. We both lost it and fell into a fit of silent, hysterical laughter.

"Grace!" Dan called out as we struggled to pull it together. "What a pleasure seeing you here." He had a bushy mustache that moved dramatically when he talked. I fixated on it and didn't realize that Grace had introduced me.

"Matthias?" She nudged me.

"Oh, sorry, nice to meet you, professor." I leaned up and shook his hand.

He smiled strangely at me. "So, how'd you two meet?"

"He lives next door to me at Senior House," Grace said.

"Oh." There was something in his expression that made me think he was disappointed.

"Well, I'll let you two get back to whatever it is you were doing." He looked directly at Grace. "Make sure you stay out of trouble."

Grace seemed far away, lost in thought as she starred at him walking away.

"He has a thing for you, huh?" I moved up on the blanket.

"I don't know, but I can't mess up here. I'm on thin ice already." I pulled off a string that was hanging from the bottom of her dress. "Thanks," she said, looking dazed.

"You're welcome." I blinked a few times and then yawned.

She patted her lap. "You wanna lay your head?" I rolled onto my back and laid my head on her thighs. She leaned against the tree again and relaxed before mindlessly running her hands through my hair. "Fast friends," she said lazily.

"Yeah. I like you. You're kinda weird."

"I was gonna say that about you, I swear."

"Did someone break your heart? Is that why you don't date? Please tell me you don't have a thing for Pornsake?"

She laughed as she dug around for the joint. "Why? Would that make you jealous?"

"Jealous? No, it's your life. I mean, if you want to be kissing that guy and potentially ingesting any food item lost in that absurd mustache, be my guest."

"Ha-ha. There's nothing going on with Pornsake . . . and gross! And no, I didn't get my heart broken. I just have to stay focused on school to keep my grades up."

I knew there had to be something more than the fact that Grace wanted to stay focused, but I didn't push her. We had only just met, yet she had spent the whole day with me and part of the day before *not* focused on music, so I knew there was another reason. I might have thought she wasn't into me and didn't want to send mixed signals, but I saw the way she looked me up and down and the places that her eyes would land.

I took my camera, turned it around to face us, and then clicked the shutter three times.

6. I Needed to Know You

MATT

Later that week, in the dark room, I studied the negatives. I couldn't fully make out Grace's expression in one picture so I enlarged it to make a print. When the image began to appear, I realized right away that instead of looking into the camera lens, Grace was looking down at me, adoringly. It made me smile the entire time I was in the lab that day. I took the print after it dried and waited for Grace on the steps outside of Senior House. I removed a cigarette from behind my ear and lit it as I waited.

A minute later, Grace walked up, carrying her large cello case. "You want me to carry that for you?" I asked as I got to my feet.

"No, sit down. You got another one of those?" She pointed to the cigarette and then sat next to me on the steps. It was late in the day but still warm. I had a T-shirt, jeans, and no shoes on. She was wearing a white V-neck and cut-off Levis. The skin on her legs was tan and smooth. She held two fingers to her lips, reminding me again that she wanted a cigarette.

"I only have this one, but I can share." I handed it to her and then held up the photograph I had developed that day. "Our first photo together." At the bottom I had used a grease pen on the blank photo paper. I had written "BFFs" on it so that when it developed, it stayed white.

She laughed. "Best friends forever? Already?"

"Wishful thinking." I shot her a big toothy grin.

"I love it. I will cherish it always. Thank you, Matt."

"Did you practice a lot today?" I asked.

"Yeah, I'm beat and hungry."

"Daria can probably warm you up some fish sticks if you want."

Grace scrunched her nose up. "Why does she always eat those? It's so nasty."

"Probably because they're cheap."

"Speaking of . . . on Wednesdays there's a diner that I go to that serves free pancakes if you wear your pajamas. You feel like breakfast for dinner?"

I laughed. "Sounds good."

She stood and stomped on the cigarette. "Cool, let's get our jammies on."

I put on flannel pajama bottoms but kept my white T-shirt on. I slipped on giant slippers that gave me Sasquatch feet and walked over to Grace's room. I pushed the cracked door open and inhaled sharply. She was in her underwear and bra, her back toward me. I swallowed hard and tried to will myself to turn around and walk out before she saw me, but I couldn't take my eyes off the round curve of her perfect ass. She had on white cotton panties with tiny flowers and a little ruffle at the top. The material rode up on one cheek. I felt an urge to drop to my knees and bite her there. My heart picked up and my dick twitched as I held my breath. *Fuck!*

Without noticing me, she lifted a pink T-shirt nightgown over her head and pulled it on. She turned to reveal white polka dots and a Hello Kitty logo on the front. I couldn't stop the grin from spreading across my face.

She froze when she saw me. "How long have you been standing there?"

"Just a second," I lied.

She glanced down at the front of my pants. I didn't follow her gaze; I just tried very inconspicuously to adjust myself enough so that she wouldn't notice what was going on down below.

"Oh." She looked further down at my slippers. "Dude, those are so rad."

I laughed, feeling a bit relieved that I wasn't caught. "How far is this place?"

"We have to take the subway—it's in Brooklyn." By that point she was on the floor, tying the shoelaces on her blue Converse.

As she walked toward the door, my hand naturally fell to the small of her back. She stopped and turned toward me, her face just inches from mine. "Do you wanna bring your camera? It's a pretty picture-worthy place."

"Good idea."

I went to my room, grabbed my camera, and then met her downstairs, where she was standing with a guy and a girl, also in pajamas. "Matthias, this is Tatiana. She plays the strings with me. And this is Brandon, her boyfriend."

I hadn't expected company, but I was excited to meet

Grace's friends. Reaching out, I shook Tatiana's hand first. She was wearing red footy pajamas and a baseball cap. Although pretty in general, she looked plain standing next to Grace. Brandon was wearing a typical pair of gray college sweats. Brandon was on the short side, with dark cropped hair and frameless glasses. We exchanged grins at our outfits and headed out the door.

The diner was a '50s-throwback type of place, with shiny red booths and little jukebox stations at every table. Grace scooted into the booth first and began flipping through the song pages. "I love these things."

Tatiana and Brandon sat across from us, almost on each other's laps. Tatiana reached into her bag and pulled out a flask. "Bailey's and rum for our vanilla shakes. It's to die for."

Grace and I made appreciative ooh-ing sounds.

"How long have you two been together?" I asked.

"Three weeks," Brandon said, before leaning in to kiss Tatiana. I noticed that Grace watched them with intense interest.

I instinctively rested my hand on Grace's bare thigh where her nightgown had ridden up. She didn't push me away but didn't respond either. When I moved my hand higher, she gestured to let her out of the booth. She got up and danced toward the bathroom, singing along to James Brown's "Please, Please, Please."

"So, Brandon, what are you studying?"

"Music, but more on the recording and business side of things. You?"

"Photography."

He pointed to the camera on the table. "I guess I should have figured that out."

"It seems like you and Grace have been inseparable the last couple of days," Tatiana said.

"She's literally the only person I know here. I just moved to New York."

"That's not what I meant," she said with humor.

"Well, who wouldn't want to be around her?"

"True."

Once Grace returned, we filled up on pancakes and Bailey's-spiked vanilla shakes while Grace sang along to every '50s song she knew. Meanwhile, I studied her every movement, her little habits.

"You smell your food before you eat it," I said with a laugh.

"What? No." Her eyebrows squished together.

Tatiana laughed as well. "Yeah, she does. Just for a split second."

"No, I don't," Grace protested.

"Trust me, it's cute." I winked at her.

"It's embarrassing. I've done it since I was a toddler."

I messed up the back of her hair. "I said it's cute."

She looked up at me, cheeks pink, and smiled.

On our way out of the diner, Tatiana and Brandon said their good-byes and then headed to a movie theater in the opposite direction.

"Your friends are nice," I said.

"Yeah. They were all over each other tonight, huh? Good for them, I guess."

"Wait, I have an idea before we get on the subway. I have color film in here," I said, pointing to the camera around my neck. "I want to try something." I grabbed her hand and pulled her up a flight of concrete stairs to the subway overpass. The traffic was fast on the street below us. I led Grace to stand on one side of the overpass while I rigged my camera to the railing on the other side, using the strap. Traffic lights shone behind her, silhouetting her. The bottom of her pink nightgown fluttered delicately in the wind. "I'm gonna set the timer and run over and stand with you. Just look right at the camera and don't move. The shutter speed is really slow so the exposure is going to be long. Try to keep as still as you can."

"What are you going for?" she asked as she watched me adjust the settings.

"The traffic lights will be out of focus behind us because they're moving, but if we stay really still, we'll be clear, along with the buildings in the background. It should look really cool. The timer is ten seconds long; you'll hear it ticking faster and faster until the shutter opens, and then that's when we have to be really still."

"Okay, I'm ready." Her legs were slightly parted, like she was about to start a jazz dance routine. I pressed the button and ran to stand next to her. Without looking over, I grabbed her hand in mine and focused on the camera lens. As the timer sped up, I could sense that she was looking at me. Right at the last second, I looked at her. The shutter opened and I said, without moving my mouth, "Kee stil." She giggled but continued staring up at me with wide eyes, watery from the wind. Three seconds doesn't seem like a long time, but when you're gazing into someone's eyes, it's long enough to make a silent promise.

When the shutter closed, she let out a huge breath and started laughing. "That felt like forever."

"Did it?" I said, still staring down at her. I could have looked at her like that all night.

On our way back to Senior House from the subway, we shared half a joint. "Did you have a lot of boyfriends in high school?"

"No. I didn't have much time. I had to get a job right when I turned sixteen so I could get a car to drive my siblings to school."

"Where'd you work?"

"The Häagen-Dazs in the mall."

"Yum."

"Well, at first it sucked because I gained, like, ten pounds, and then I got really sick after eating too much rum raisin. I couldn't stomach the stuff after that. I worked there for three years until I graduated from high school. I still have a really big right bicep from scooping ice cream. I'm all lopsided."

She made a muscle and held her arm up to me. I squeezed her tiny arm between my fingers before she pulled out of my grip. "Jerk."

"Spaghetti arms."

"I'm buff. Let me see yours."

I made a muscle. Her small, delicate hand couldn't even squeeze my arm. "Dude, that's pretty impressive. What do you do?"

"I have one of those pull-up bars. That's all I do, really. And I surfed a lot in L.A."

"Do you miss it?"

"The surfing, mainly."

She paused. "Shit, what time is it?"

I looked at my watch. "Nine fifteen. Why?"

"I wanted to be back by nine thirty."

"What happens at nine thirty?"

"This beautiful dress turns into a shabby rag." She

twirled around. I bent and threw her over my shoulder. "Oh my god, put me down!"

"No, princess. I'm getting you back by nine thirty."

I busted through the door of Senior House and ran up the stairs, with Grace hanging over my shoulder and punching my butt. I heard someone behind me say, "Dude, that chick's wasted."

I set her down right in front of her door, looked at my watch, and put my hands up. "Nine twenty-nine, baby."

She high-fived me. "You did it! Thanks, buddy."

I looked behind Grace to see a scantily clad girl in a jean miniskirt and heels. Grace turned around to follow my gaze. When she looked back, I smiled innocently at her.

"You like that? Is that your type?"

I leaned against her door and crossed my arms over my chest. "Not really."

"Were you a player in L.A.?"

"Not at all."

"How many girls have you been with?" Her expression fell serious.

"Is this a trick question?"

"I'm just curious 'cause you're a good looking guy and . . ."

"You're beautiful. Does that mean you've been with a lot of people?"

She huffed. "Fine, don't answer the question."

"I've been with a few girls, Grace. Not a lot."

"Have you ever been with a virgin?"

I jerked my head back and noticed that her lip was quivering and her eyes were wide and earnest. "No. I've never been with a virgin," I said. I lowered my head to meet her gaze, but she quickly looked down and stared at her shoes.

I was very close to asking Grace if she was a virgin but I already knew the answer and I didn't want to embarrass her.

"Well, I better get to practicing," she said.

"Hold on one second." I ran into my room and dug around before returning with *Surfer Rosa & Come on Pilgrim* by the Pixies. "This is a great album, one of my favorites. Track seven is the best."

She read the title, "Where Is My Mind?"

"That's the one."

"Cool. Thanks, Matt. Hey, tomorrow after class"—she was hesitant—"I was gonna go up on the roof and study."

"Uh-huh."

"Well . . . do you wanna join me? We can listen to music."

"Yeah, let's do it."

"Okay, I'll be done at three. I can make sandwiches?"

"That sounds great." I gestured for a hug. As she wrapped her arms around my waist, I kissed the top of her head and smelled her lilac hair.

She pulled away and squinted. "Did you just kiss the top of my head?"

"Just a friendly kiss. Like this." I bent and kissed her cheek. She stood still, her eyes wide. "Goodnight, Gracie."

"Night, Matty," she whispered as I walked back to my room.

GRACE AND I hung out practically every day after that, and a routine quickly formed. We would sell our blood and have pajama dinners and find other ways to save money. We studied together, and she played music while I photographed her. Her long blonde hair would fall across her face as she played with passion, tossing her head back and forth with the movement of the bow. It quickly became my favorite sight.

Throughout the fall and into the winter, Grace and I hung out a lot, mostly with her music friends. Brandon and Tati became our couple buddies, and though Grace and I weren't a couple at all, it felt that way. Grace and Tati found ways for us to get free admission to all the museums, and they even dragged me to a free symphony. I thought Tati and Brandon were a little overly enthusiastic about listening to classical music for two hours straight, and I definitely thought they were going to kick me out for wearing jeans, but I was surprised by how much I liked it and how cool everyone was.

But as much as Grace was into music, she was always looking for stuff for me, too. She'd slip newspaper clippings under my dorm room door about photography exhibitions around town. We did everything we could to get out of the crappy dorms and the pervasive smell of fish sticks emanating from Daria's room.

You know those frugal traveler books, like *The Rough Guide to Hawaii* or *New York on Five Dollars a Day*? I swear to God, we did it on two dollars a day. It involved a lot of ramen noodles and turnstile-hopping in the subways, but we managed to see the city inside and out.

New York has an energy that takes root inside of you. Even a transplant like me gets to know the different boroughs, like they're living, breathing organisms. There's nowhere else like it. The city becomes a character in your life, a love you can't take out of you. The mysteriously human element about this place can make you fall in love and break your heart at the same time. When you hear her sound, when you breathe in her scent, you share it with all the people walking beside you on the street, in the subway, or gazing from a tall building across Central Park. You know at once that you are alive, and that life is beautiful, precious, and fleeting. I think that's why people in New York feel so connected to each other; the city harnesses this collective love and admiration. Grace and I were falling in love with her together.

Almost every afternoon for the next couple of months, I would find Grace studying in the lounge, waiting for me. Our friendship had become so comfortable that brushing up against her, twirling her around, grabbing her hand, and giving her piggyback rides felt totally normal. Sometimes there would be quieter moments when it seemed like she wanted me to kiss her—and Lord knows I wanted to, but she would always break the silence or look away. I didn't care, I just wanted to be around her. I found myself less interested in dating or even looking at other girls.

"It's late, huh?" she remarked on one of many nights we spent together, just hanging out.

"It's two," I said, glancing at the clock.

"I should go back to my room." Grace was lying across my bed horizontally, on her stomach, with her head hanging over the edge. She was in sweats and a Sex Pistols T-shirt, with her hair twirled up in a messy bun. I knew she didn't really want to leave, even though we were both exhausted.

"Wait, let's play Never Have I Ever."

"Sure. You go first," she mumbled.

"Never have I ever stolen something."

She looked sad for a moment and then put a finger on her hand down.

"What did you steal?" I asked.

"Well, there have been a few things. The worst, I'm too embarrassed to tell you about." She rolled over and buried her face in the comforter.

"Come on, tell me. I won't judge you."

"I stole forty dollars from my neighbor," she mumbled into the blankets.

"For what? Come on, tell me. It's part of the game."

"I don't like this game anymore."

I rolled her over to face me. "What was it?"

She looked up into my eyes. "I stole it to buy my senior yearbook, okay? I feel like a total asshole and I have every intention of paying her back."

My heart ached for her. I had no idea what it was like not to be able to ask my parents for forty dollars. She had stolen money to buy herself a yearbook, of all things—something most kids take for granted. How sad. "Let's play something else," I said. "How about Fuck, Marry, Kill?"

She perked up. "Okay. Yours are . . . . let me think, um . . . Courtney Love, Pamela Anderson, and Jennifer Aniston."

"Ugh, kill, kill, kill."

"Seriously, you psychopath, you have to answer." She bonked me on the head with her palm.

"All right, kill Courtney—that's a given—fuck Pamela, and marry Jennifer. There! Your turn. Bill Clinton, Spike Lee, and me."

"Ha! That's easy. Fuck Bill, marry Spike, and kill you."

"You're a terrible, mean girl."

"You love me." She sat up to leave.

"Grace?"

"Yeah."

"Nothing." I wanted to ask her what was going on with us. I wanted to know if we could be more than friends. I turned back and looked out the window.

She plopped down onto my bed and wrapped an arm around my shoulder. "I guess I'd marry you."

"Really? I was hoping it would go more like, kill Bill, marry Spike . . ."

"Ha!" She leaned over and kissed me on the cheek. "You're a good guy."

I wanted an award for the insane amount of restraint I had shown so far. My lips flattened. "That's it?"

"What are you fishing for, Shore?"

"I'm not fishing for anything, Grace. I feel like sometimes this"—I waved my hand between us—"it's unnatural."

"This what? Us being friends?"

I laughed. "Yeah, kind of." I worked very hard to avoid the sex question but I would often catch Grace staring when I changed my shirt or when I put a belt on. It was hard for me not to think she wanted me as much as I wanted her. And I was becoming secretly possessive of her. I could see how men looked at her without her even knowing it, and I was terrified that she was going to give herself to some dickhead with no heart.

She stood and headed for the door. Just before she reached for the knob, she turned and leaned against it. Her eyes fell to her feet. "Don't pressure me." She looked up and met my gaze. "Okay?" She wasn't irritated. Her expression was sincere, almost like she was begging.

"I haven't."

"I know." She smiled. "That's why I like you so much."

"Did something happen to you? Is that why . . ."

"No, nothing like that. My mom had me when she was eighteen. I don't know, I guess in some ways I felt like I ruined her life."

"That's terrible that she made you feel that way." I got up and walked toward her.

"She didn't make feel that way. I just didn't want that life. I always felt like my dad resented her. I don't know, Matt, I guess I've been focused on school so I can stay on track. That's why I don't really date. I like what we have, though. There's no pressure."

"I get it."

She might say these words, but I knew she was feeling the increasing tension between us as much as I was. Half the time, I was trying to hide a raging hard-on while she tried to avoid staring at my arms. Who were we kidding?

"Thanks for understanding," she said.

"You're welcome." I bent and kissed her cheek. "You're a good girl." I felt her shiver, and then I whispered, "Maybe too good."

She pushed me back and rolled her eyes. "Night, Matt."

I watched her saunter down the hall and then I called out to her, "You're smiling! I know you are, Gracie."

Without turning around, she held up a peace sign.

7. You Were My Muse

MATT

In lab the next day, Professor Nelson scanned my proof sheet with a huge smile. "Matt, you have such a natural eye. Your composition is perfect and original, like nothing I'm seeing from your peers. I love the graininess and how much you're willing to push the film. What speed is this and what did you shoot it at?"

"It's four hundred. I pushed it to thirty-two hundred."

"Nice. Lots of agitation when you developed the negative, I take it?"

"Yeah."

"This one is fantastic. Is this you?"

I had set up the timer and taken a picture of Grace standing in front of me as I sat on the floor. The only thing in the frame was her legs, just below the bottom of her wool sweater dress. My arms were wrapped around her calves. You can't see it in the picture, but I'm kissing her knee.

"Have you thought about doing more color, more landscapes—documentary-style stuff?"

"Yeah, I actually shot a roll of color the other day but I haven't developed it yet. I just really like this subject." I pointed to Grace.

"She's stunning."

"She is."

"You know, Matt, I'd hate to see your skills and talent go to waste."

"I'm thinking about going into advertising photography."

He nodded but seemed unconvinced. "Your photos have this story-telling quality that I don't see often. We can talk about composition, framing, contrast, or even printing, but I think this is the true mark of an artist, when you can make a statement about humanity in a single two-dimensional image."

I was a little embarrassed by the praise, but I was relieved to finally hear what I knew myself: that I was good at it. "I'll never stop taking photos. I just don't know how it'll translate into a career."

"I have a friend who works for *National Geographic*. Every year he sponsors a student to shoot abroad with him. You have to apply, but I think you'd have a good chance. You've got the technique for it."

I was taken aback by the suggestion but more so by how crystal clear my goals suddenly became in that moment. I thought *National Geographic* was a pipe dream. It's one of those things you aspire to as a kid, like becoming a professional baseball player or the President of the United States. In my book, traveling the world and taking photos was the ultimate level of success, and I couldn't believe this chance was falling into my lap, even if it was just an internship.

"I'm definitely interested." I hadn't known what I was going to do once I graduated, but now everything was coming into focus.

I made an extra print that day and slipped it under Grace's door during my break. On my way back to class, I saw her crossing the street about a block away. I yelled to her but she didn't hear me. By the time I walked a block up, I saw her quickly enter a medical building. I got impatient waiting at the light and dashed across the street when the traffic was clear. Once inside, I scoured each floor until I found her on the fifth, standing near a table with coffee and donuts. She was wearing a hospital gown, stirring cream into a little foam cup. When I marched up to her, she looked up at me, startled. "What are you doing here?"

"What are *you* doing here?"

"Generally speaking, a person's medical history is their own private business." She held up a little dough ball. "Donut hole?"

"Don't try to distract me. Are you sick, Grace?" I felt sick myself at the idea.

"No, I'm not sick. I signed up to do a medical study. You wanna do it, too?"

"You're letting them use you as a guinea pig for free donuts and coffee?"

"I'm getting eighty bucks a day. That's a lot."

"Grace, are you crazy? What kind of study is this?"

"I just have to take this medicine and then they take me off of it and see if I have any withdrawal symptoms."

"What? No," I said, shaking my head in disbelief. I turned her by the shoulders and pointed her toward the curtain. "Go put your clothes on. You're not doing this." I looked down at the open hospital gown in the back. She was so damn cute with her little flowery underwear. I pulled the back closed and tied the strings tight so the flaps overlapped.

She turned around and looked up at me with her big green eyes full of tears. "I have to do it, Matt. I need to get my cello back."

"Back from where?"

"I pawned it for money to pay the rest of my tuition."

"What about your student loans and financial aid?"

"I had to give some of it to my mom because my little sister needed to get a tooth fixed and they didn't have the money." Tears fell from her eyes. When I reached up to brush them away, she flinched.

"Grace, I won't let you do this. We'll figure it out, I promise." Grace selling her cello seemed crazy to me, considering she was a music major. It was hard for me to understand her level of desperation.

"You don't understand."

"Explain it to me then."

She crossed her arms over her chest. "I've been helping my parents out. Their situation is more dire than I've let on, so I've been sending whatever I can from my student loan money. I'm almost out of cash for the semester and my mom called and said she and my dad were going to be evicted. They had the money to cover the rent but my little sister had a broken tooth that needed to be fixed and their credit is shot so they had to pay in cash. I couldn't stand the thought of my sister going to school in pain with a broken front tooth."

I was shocked, but that didn't mean Grace needed to participate in potentially dangerous medical studies. "It's not your problem."

"It's my family. I read about this study and I can make the money back before next week. They pay you every day. I'm going to get my cello back and everything will be fine. But I have to do this, Matt. It's not a big deal."

"It's a huge deal, Grace. You don't know how this medication will affect you."

"You still don't get it."

"I'm trying to. I have some money. I'll get your cello back for you."

She shook her head. "I won't let you. You need to buy photo paper and film."

"I have plenty. Don't worry." Grace hated letting me help her. She wanted to be independent. "Go change—it'll be okay."

She turned and shuffled behind the curtain. When she came back out, she was smiling uncertainly. "You must think I'm insane."

"I like your neuroses." I put my arm around her shoulder. "I'm just not going to let anyone use you as a lab rat."

As she walked by the refreshment table, she scooped a handful of creamers out of the bowl and shoved them into her bag. She would steal creamers everywhere we went, mix them with water, and pour them over her cereal. I smiled at her and shook my head. In a silly voice she said, "Just goin' grocery shoppin'." The mood suddenly lifted and we both laughed as we walked out the door. Still, it killed me to think Grace was sending her parents money that her dad was probably using for beer.

We went to the bank and I withdrew the last three hundred dollars I had. I didn't tell Grace that I actually had negative eight cents in my account after the withdrawal. She took me to the pawnshop where she had dealt her cello, and we were greeted by a middle-aged man behind the counter. "Hello, Grace," he said.

I shot Grace a disapproving look. "He knows you?" I whispered.

She pinched her eyebrows together. "Kind of."

"Here to pick up your cello?"

"Yep," Grace said.

I handed the man three hundred dollars. He went into the back and returned a moment later with the large cello case. Grace completed the paperwork and we left. Once outside the building, I turned to her. "Stay here. I'll be right back."

I went back inside the pawnshop and asked the man for a piece of paper. "Here's the number where I live. Please don't let Grace pawn her cello again. She's an extraordinary musician. She needs it for school. Just call me and I'll come down and straighten things out."

That night, after Grace went to bed, I snuck down to the lounge and called my father collect from the payphone.

"Son?"

"Hi, Dad."

"Hey there. You impressing everyone at NYU?" Sarcasm seeped through every syllable. He was never good at hiding his disdain.

"I called because I have a friend who needs help and I

was wondering if you could loan me some money to lend to her." My pride was completely gone. I closed my eyes and waited for his response.

"This is for a her? A girlfriend?"

"No, Dad. It's not like that."

"You get some girl in trouble? Is that what you're telling me?"

I took a deep breath. "She's my closest friend here, and she doesn't have any help financially. Not like me and Alex. She's putting herself through school almost completely on her own. She's a musician and needs a new cello, but she can't afford it." I had to lie a little; I didn't want to go into all the details.

"You know, I have your brother's wedding to pay for."

"Monica's parent's aren't paying for the wedding?"

"Well, we want to throw them a nice engagement party, and then we have the rehearsal dinner and open bar and . . ."

"Okay, Dad. No problem."

A beat of silence. "Well, at least you're starting to appreciate what we've done for you. How much do you need, son?"

"A few hundred dollars."

"I'll put it in your account tomorrow. You know, I'm willing to help you out, Matthias. Just because you've decided on the hardest possible future . . ."

I laughed. He couldn't help himself.

"I'll get a job and pay you back. Thanks, Dad." I hung up.

As painful as it was to call him, I didn't care; all I could think about was how hard Grace worked, all the sacrifices she made just to play her music. She believed in it, she had faith that it would all be worth it, and what is faith if it doesn't endure? That's what I was learning from her: how to have faith in myself and my art.

I felt it for Grace before I even had a name for it. I might have said the word a million times, but it sounded different now that I meant it. When I thought about what we had, it didn't matter that it was just friendship. I loved her.

8. You Changed Me

GRACE

Even though I had mastered the art of running while carrying a giant cello case, I was still late to class the next morning. Thankfully, Professor Pornsake liked me and his class was a breeze, though not because I was a teacher's pet, as Tatiana claimed. All I had to do was play my cello, the one thing I did well. On most days, I would close my eyes, forget about everything, and escape into the music. But that Friday was different.

"You're late again, Graceland."

"Grace," I corrected him as I pulled my cello and bow from the case. There were several broken hairs hanging from the bow, and I attempted to pull them off while Dan hovered over me in his khakis, belted too high, and his orange polo shirt two sizes too small. I shot him a peeved look to let him know I was irritated over the unnecessary attention. "What?" I said.

He grabbed the bow from my hand and studied it. "This is nylon."

"I know."

"You're first chair, Grace. Get a quality bow. Why are you using this crap?" A bit of his mustache stuck out over his top lip and wiggled as he spoke.

"I'm a member of PETA. I don't use bows made with horse hair."

I could see Tatiana's body shaking with laughter in the chair in front of me.

Pornsake smirked. "Come on. Really?"

I huffed. "I'll get a new bow this week." I knew I couldn't afford it, but he was right—nylon bows were crap.

"Good deal. Okay guys, let's start with Pachelbel's 'Canon.'"

Tatiana sighed audibly. We were so sick of playing that song. It was like every music teacher was preparing us to be in one of those string quartets that plays at weddings. Pachelbel's "Canon," Handel's "Water Music," and Mendelssohn's "Wedding March" were ingrained so deeply into our minds and muscles that I literally started to believe it was affecting my ability to play other songs.

Pornsake walked to the front of the room and started counting down from three. I kicked Tati's chair and whispered, "Irish style." We started playing the traditional way and then slowly picked up the pace, throwing off everyone in the room. Many of the others stopped playing and just glared at us as Tati and I turned the classic into an Irish jig. The music students with a sense of humor put their instruments down and started clapping to the beat; and some even tried to play along. We got a short round of applause at the end, but Pornsake stood still as a statue at the front of the room, his arms crossed over his chest.

"Really cute. Maybe you two can be street performers. God knows New York desperately needs more street performers."

I didn't say anything because I was already on thin ice, but Tatiana spoke up. "Professor Porn . . . Sake . . ." I slapped my hand over my mouth to hold in my laughter as Tati continued, completely straight-faced. "We just need to mix it up."

He nodded like a bobblehead for five seconds straight. "Fine. I'm not feeling it today anyway. You're all free to go. Practice in the park and get some fresh air. We'll get back into this tomorrow."

I reached down to open my cello case, celebrating for two seconds inside until I felt Pornsake hovering over me again. "Except for you, Grace. Stick around."

I froze in my chair with my eyes fixed on his beige Top-Siders. I had a sick feeling in my stomach, wondering if he was going to wait for everyone to leave the room so he could proposition me.

Crossing my legs and arms, I sat back in my cold metal chair and waited as the other students packed up. Tati turned around and looked at me blankly. Smoothing her frizzy brown hair into a ponytail, she whispered, "Why does he want you to stay?"

I shrugged. "No clue."

"Hey, do you and Matt want to hang out tonight? Brandon wants to get drunk."

"Why do you always assume I'll be with Matt? We're not dating."

She rolled her eyes. "I know, I know, you don't date. I assume you'll be with Matt 'cause you guys are always together."

"I need to study, actually. I'm staying home tonight. Matt can do whatever he wants, though." It seemed like everyone thought Matt and I were a couple. I was feeling the pressure to get my application in for grad school, which seemed like the logical next step, but it was like I had no self-control when it came to Matt. I wanted to be with him every second of the day, but my grades were suffering, and I knew I'd slip out of first chair with my stupid antics.

"Why don't you and Matt just bone and get it over with already?"

Pornsake walked up at that moment. "Well, Tatiana, it's a blessing, and quite frankly a miracle, that your vulgarity has not seeped into your craft." Pornsake was always blabbering about craft. Tatiana was a phenomenal musician, but once she put the violin down there was nothing classical about her. She had a tough exterior and a lot of Jersey girl in her.

"Thanks, Teach, I'll take that as a compliment. Bye, Grace." She picked up her violin case. As she left the room, she called back over her shoulder, "Come over tonight after you and Matthias bone."

Pornsake stared down at me, expressionless. "Take a walk with me?"

I figured being in public was a good option. "Sure." I stood and followed him out the door. He walked at a faster-than-normal pace, and I quickly ran out of breath, lugging my cello case behind me, trying to keep up. "Where are we going?"

"You'll see. It's just down here." We walked four blocks until we got to the corner of a small brick building. We were standing in front of a music store. There was no signage but I could see musical instruments through the glass door. "This is Orvin's shop. He's the best bow-maker on the planet."

I sucked air in through my teeth. "Professor . . ."

"Please, call me Dan."

"Dan . . . I don't have the money to buy a new bow. I was just going to have mine restrung."

He bobbed his head in understanding. "Grace, I don't normally do these kinds of things for my students, but I want to do this for you."

"What do you mean?"

"I'm going to buy you a bow because you're very talented. I love the way you play, and you have a great instrument there." He glanced down at my case. "You should have a great bow."

While he waited for my response, I looked at the way his eyes crinkled at the sides when he smiled, and for the first time I found charm in his good-humored face. "Okay," I replied.

"Come on, you have to meet this guy." He opened the door and motioned for me to go inside. Behind the counter stood a small man, at least seventy years old, with a bit of gray hair sprouting wildly from the sides of his head.

"Daniel, my boy," he said in a thick German accent. "Who have you brought to me?"

"Orvin, this is my most talented student, Grace." *Wow, really? I had no idea.*

I set my cello down, leaned over the counter, and shook his hand. He held my hand in his for a few seconds, inspecting it. "Small and delicate for a cellist, but strong, I can see."

"Yes. Grace needs a new bow, and I'd like for her to have the best."

"Sure, sure, I have something that would fit her perfectly." He went into the back room and came out with the most beautiful bow I had ever seen. He handed it to me, and the soft wood at the base felt like butter between my fingers. "Wow, this is so smooth."

"It's brazilwood and real silver, made with the finest horse hair," Dan said. Orvin nodded. A moment later, Dan pulled his checkbook out of his back pocket, looked over to Orvin, and arched his eyebrows.

"Eleven," Orvin said.

"Eleven what?" I said, my voice rising.

Neither answered me. "Be right back," Orvin said, heading into the back room and returning a moment later with the bow wrapped up.

Dan handed him a check, took the bow, and looked over at me. "Ready?"

I shot him my best hairy eyeball. "You're kidding me, right? You just bought me an eleven-hundred-dollar bow?"

"Consider it an investment. Come on."

Once outside, he tried to hand me the bow wrapped in paper.

"Really, Dan, I can't accept this. I seriously cannot pay you back. I barely have enough money to eat."

"Then let me take you to dinner," he said, instantly.

I starred up at him, blinking my eyes, while he waited for my answer.

"I . . ."

"It's not a date, Grace."

"It feels like a date." I was hesitant to agree; I still wasn't sure what Dan wanted from me.

"It's just a meal. We can talk about the orchestra I'm forming this summer. I was thinking I'd like you to be a part of it."

"Okay. Um . . ."

"Come on. Please?"

My college music professor was begging to take me to dinner. I looked around for other signs that I had been transported to an alternate universe.

"What time?"

"I'll come by Senior House at seven. You like Thai food?"

"Sure."

"There's a place about two blocks away from your dorm. It's pretty good."

"I know the place. I'll meet you there." The restaurant was right across from the photo store Matt had just started working at. I hoped we wouldn't see him.

By the time I got back to Senior House it was freezing out. I scurried through the lobby and up to my room and practiced for a few hours with my new bow. It was amazing how much it changed the quality of the sound. It amplified the music even more, filling the room with crisp notes.

By six o'clock I was starving, and frankly looking forward to dinner with Pornsake, even though I knew it would be uncomfortable. My plan was to eat the crap out of the free meal and try to keep the conversation light. I chose purple wool leggings and a long gray sweater with boots. I pinned my hair up into a bun on the top of my head and then wrapped a thick black scarf around my neck. I added a tiny bit of mascara and lip gloss for good form and then smoked half a joint, against my better judgment. I thought dinner with my music professor warranted a little chemical mind alteration. I trotted down the stairs and into the lounge, where I made a cup of hot chocolate.

Carey Carmichael and Jason Wheeler, two students who lived on my floor, were sitting on the leather sofa, whispering to each other.

"Hey, Grace, where's Matt?" Carey asked.

I fumbled through the stack of magazines on the console table behind the couch. "I think he's in the darkroom at school, developing prints."

I noticed Carey shoot Jason a questioning look.

Jason turned around to face me. "So, are you guys dating or what?"

Not this again. "We're friends," I said, cautiously. "Why?"

"Oh, good," Carey said, laughing. "We thought you guys were together-together."

"What if we were?" *And why does anyone care?*

"But you're not," Carey said. I shot her daggers. I'd never noticed she looked like the female version of Danny Bonaduce.

"What if we were?" I said again, trying to be nonchalant.

"The whole world knows that it's just a big party on Fridays in the campus photo lab. Everyone sneaks booze in and they all fuck each other in the film-processing rooms. It's like a giant celluloid orgy."

My mouth dropped open. Matt had been going to the dark rooms every Friday night, and he always came back a little drunk and stoned.

"Not like an orgy," Carey said, seeing my expression. "Everyone just goofs off. You know how tight those photography students are. There're rumors that people do it in the private dark rooms."

I had no idea what she was talking about. Matt hadn't mentioned anything like that to me. I also didn't know why I cared. It was his life, and I wasn't in a position to tell him what to do.

"Carey," Jason said, looking pointedly at her. "I'm sure Matt's not just developing prints in there."

I felt gut-punched. "Fuck you, Jason."

"What's your problem, Grace? You a goody-fucking-two-shoes or something?"

"Nothing." I looked at the clock. It was almost seven. "I have to go."

9. Why Didn't We Tell Each Other?

GRACE

The air outside of Senior House hit me like an arctic blast. Winter was settling in. I rushed to the stoplight, hit the cross-walk button, looked across the street, and then completely froze in my boots. Matt was standing on the other side, looking right at me. He was wearing a black T-shirt with a gray long-sleeved thermal shirt underneath, jeans, and his boots. It was coat weather, and as I watched him from across the street, his hands gripping the straps of his backpack, I thought I could see him shivering.

My heart skipped a beat; I swallowed. He smiled and I couldn't help but return it, even though I wanted to ask him a million questions I knew I couldn't. It was his life and we were friends. When it was time to cross, we walked toward each other and stopped in the middle of crosswalk.

"Where you headed?" he asked.

"Dinner."

His eyes flitted down my body and back up to my eyes.

In the three months I had known him, I had rarely worn anything nicer than sweats and ChapStick. There was a longing in his expression. "Let me walk you." His teeth chattered, drawing my eyes to his full lips and unshaven jawline. I wanted to rub my face against them.

The light was about to turn, and we had to get out of the middle of the street. "You're freezing, Matt. Just go home, I'll be fine."

We hurried across the street, shoulder to shoulder.

"Where are you going to dinner?"

"The Thai place around the corner."

His hands were deep in his pockets and his arms were pressed tight against his body. "I can walk you."

"I don't need you to walk me two blocks, Matt. I'm fine."

A subtle grimace flashed on his face and then he took a step toward me, reached his hand out, and caressed my cheek, our bodies inches apart. He released a weak, frustrated breath. "Who's taking you to dinner? . . . Grace?"

I peeked over Matt's shoulder and saw Dan standing there, an inscrutable look on his face. Matt turned around and then turned back to me, his eyebrows arched. "Pornsake?" I didn't like the humor in his tone.

I pushed him away. "Fuck you, Matt. I'm sure you can find something else to do. Isn't there some big darkroom orgy you need to attend?"

"What?"

"I can smell rum on your breath."

"So what? I had a shot with my photo buddies. I was coming home to see if you wanted to hang out."

"I can't. I have plans. Bye, Matt." I turned around and didn't look back.

Dan gave a halfhearted wave and shot Matt a friendly smile. I didn't want to see the look on Matt's face, so I tugged him by the arm and headed toward the restaurant.

Once inside, Dan pulled my chair out for me. He was kind and gentlemanly, offering to choose a wine for us. We made it through the first hour of dinner by making small talk about the orchestra he planned to form before the summer started. He was thinking about leaving NYU and following his dream of creating a fulltime traveling orchestra.

His teacher's façade slipped away, and his enthusiasm for music made him seem like a peer, not a professor. We laughed a lot, and there was an ease to the conversation. Something about him, his maturity and know-how, made him seem attractive to me for the first time.

"Are you and Matt dating?" he asked.

I had to make a decision in that moment. It wasn't like me to lie, but I didn't want to lead Dan on, and I knew why he was asking the question. "Well, it's complicated."

He looked down to his fidgeting hands. "I heard Tatiana this morning say something . . ."

"I like Matt," I blurted out. Which wasn't a lie at all.

"That makes a lot of sense."

"What do you mean?" I wasn't sure if he thought Matt and I would make a great couple or if he was making a general statement about dating in college.

"Girls like you always go for guys like Matt." That pissed me off. I didn't like that he assumed he knew anything about Matt, although at the moment my opinion of Matt probably wasn't much better than his.

"What, are we in elementary school, Dan?" I was suddenly extremely defensive. "Certain girls can only date certain boys?" I narrowed my eyes at him and leaned forward. "Wait, is this why you bought me a bow and took me to dinner. Did you think I would hop into bed with you?"

He put his hand out to stop me. "Hold on. Before you let your imagination get the best of you, the answer is no. I don't want to sleep with you." His eyes darted to the ceiling. He cocked his head to the side. "Well, actually . . ."

"Forget it." I started to get up.

"Stop, Grace. What I'm trying to say is that college guys like Matt usually have one thing on their minds, you know? I was like him once; I know these things. I bought you the bow because I wanted you to have it. I invited you to dinner because I like talking to you. Things are not always as black and white as we make them out to be when we're young. I'm less than a decade older than you, but in my time I've learned this much: there are lots of gray areas. Going to dinner at night with a man does not have to be about sex."

I swallowed but still found myself at a loss for words. He reached out and clutched my hand across the table. "Okay?"

"Okay," I said. We lapsed into awkward silence for the rest of the meal.

After dinner, he walked me back to Senior House and didn't even gesture for a hug. I thanked him for the bow and dinner and said I would see him tomorrow. When I opened the door to the lobby, I immediately heard Operation Ivy playing loudly on the lounge stereo, telling me to proceed with caution. I heard several voices laughing and talking, and when I turned the corner I spotted Matt on the couch with his arm around a girl who looked exactly like Rachel from *Friends*. He saw me, held up a shot glass full of brown liquid, and yelled, "Body shots!" He stuck a lime wedge in the girl's mouth, shook a saltshaker on her cleavage, and then—I kid you not—*grinned* at me before licking the tops of the girl's breasts. He took the shot and covered her mouth with his own.

The other people in the room became visible to me as I tore my attention away from the scene, which was making me nauseous. Everyone looked to be having a great time.

Matt, who had managed to pry his mouth free, was now watching me. "Want one?" He held up a bottle of tequila.

I flipped him off and walked toward the stairs, but he was behind me in an instant. "How was your date with Porn-sake?"

I didn't even turn around. "It wasn't a date. It was just dinner."

"Okay, Grace. Whatever you say."

I whirled around in anger at the top of the landing. "What if I told you that I had sex with him?"

"I'd say you're a liar." He had been drinking a lot. I could tell. Nothing was holding him back.

"He bought me a bow for my cello, so I sucked him off in the bathroom at the Thai place."

His lips flattened as he searched my eyes. "Oh yeah? Then why don't you come and hang out in the lounge with my buddies? You can never have too many girls around who like giving blow jobs."

"Okay, let's go." I walked past him and down three steps. He remained rooted on the stairs, looking puzzled for a few moments before catching up with me.

In the lounge, I grabbed the bottle of tequila and took a

couple of swigs, then went up to a tall blond guy with long hair. "I'm Grace." I stuck my hand out.

"Hey, Grace," he said, shaking my hand delicately. "You Matt's Grace?"

I huffed. "I'm nobody's Grace." I held the bottle out to him and looked over to find Matt back on the couch, except this time he was alone, watching me.

An hour of drinking and getting high went by. I was feeling really out of it. Rachel from *Friends* was back, and my blond buddy was inching closer and closer to me the longer we talked. Still, Matt hadn't taken his eyes off me.

"You want to go to my room?" my blond friend asked.

"Sure."

He pulled me away from the lounge toward the stairs. We got to the first landing when he pushed me against the wall and tried to kiss me. I turned my head. "No."

He laughed. "What did you think we were gonna do in my room?"

"Hang out?" I said, flushing pink.

He jerked his head back. "So you're just a little tease?"

"That's enough." Matt gripped the back of the blond guy's neck in a somewhat friendly way but clearly wanting to make a point. "She's fuckin' wasted, man. You really want to have sex with that? Dude, she's a mess."

I scowled.

Blond Guy looked over to him. "You're right." He rolled his eyes at me and then took off down the stairs and back into the lounge.

I fell into Matt's arms and crumbled from exhaustion. I just wanted everything to be normal with us. I wanted Matt to tell me everything and be my best friend again, but I worried something had changed between us in the span of a day. He held me close and whispered near my ear, "What are you doing, baby?"

I started to cry. I'll admit that crying was really lame, but the alcohol, pot, and my stupid behavior was wreaking havoc on my emotions. "Do I disgust you?"

"What are you talking about?"

"You said to that guy, 'Do you really want to have sex with that?' What was *that* supposed to mean?"

"Grace, your eyes are, like, almost all the way closed. You're super stoned and drunk. I know that guy and he probably wouldn't have cared if you passed out on him; he still would have taken advantage of you."

I planted my face in my hands and started to cry even more. The small amount of mascara I was wearing ran steadily down my face.

"Come on. Let's forget this shit." He pulled me up the stairs.

Inside my room, I dropped the keys on my desk and stumbled toward the bathroom. I heard Matt put a U2 CD on the stereo.

When it was just the two of us together, it was like everything was okay and we could be Grace and Matt. There was no need for discussion. But out there in the real world. . . .

I came out of the bathroom to find him tinkering with the thermostat.

"I'm roasting. What the fuck is the deal with the heater?" he said.

"Daria put in a work order. I asked her yesterday." The furnace in our hall was on the fritz and wouldn't work for three days straight, then it would suddenly start working but wouldn't stop. That's what you get when you live in an old building in New York City.

I started to shimmy out of my tights. "Turn around," I commanded, but he continued to watch me. "Turn around, I'm gonna change." He finally did. Begrudgingly. I threw on a summery flower dress that was sitting in a pile of clothes on my bed, then I sat down on the floor and watched as Matt kicked off his shoes. He slid across the hardwood in his socks and tried to pry open the window. "It'll get cold in here really fast if you open that."

He turned and eyed me, wearing next to nothing in my tiny spaghetti-strap dress. And then he took his shirt off. My breath hitched every time I saw him shirtless. His shoulders were broad but his waist was narrow, and he wore his jeans low on his hips, sometimes with boxers, sometimes without. That night he was sans boxers and wearing the shoelace belt I'd made for him.

"Whatchya lookin' at?" He walked toward me, smirking.

"Don't flatter yourself. I was looking at your cool belt."

"Sure you were." He grabbed the bottle of tequila from my bookshelf, took a swig, and handed it to me, but I waved it off. I couldn't drink another drop. "My other belt broke. My mom's going to make me a new one when I'm there for break."

"She makes belts?"

"Yeah, she's crafty."

"How does she do it?"

"She uses little metal tools to create designs in the leather." He pointed to the leather strap on his camera, which was resting on my nightstand, where he had left it the day before. I didn't look over. I was still busy staring at his happy trail . . . which didn't escape him. When I looked up at his face, I saw that his eyes were on me, unblinking.

I shook myself out of the daze and reached over to pick up the camera. There was an intricate pattern of circles and triangles perforated into the leather. "That's really cool."

Hovering over me, he held his hand out. "Come on, dance with me."

"What? No."

"Get up here and dance with me, chicken."

"I'm not a very good dancer and I'm too tipsy."

"You seemed to be pretty good at that little flirty thing in the lounge with what's-his-face."

"I feel stupid about that. Please don't bring it up. Anyway, you were the one doing body shots with Jennifer Aniston."

"She does kind of look like Jennifer Aniston, huh?"

I rolled my eyes.

"Come on, get up here. I'll lead. All you have to do is follow."

I took his hand and stood up. I laughed nervously but he didn't hesitate; he pressed one hand into the small of my back, grabbed my other hand in his, and pulled me into his bare chest. "Hand on my shoulder, Gracie."

The song "With or Without You" by U2 came on. Matt swayed to the beat then pushed me back and twirled me around. When he brought me back in, our bodies were even closer than before. He dropped his head down and kissed my bare shoulder. My heart was racing. His skin was hot against mine. We stopped moving and stepped away from each other, just a few inches. I ran my index finger down the indentation of his obliques and admired the sculpted muscles of his lower abdomen. The deep V of his abs seemed to point down, sending my eyes on a little trip south. I could see from the way his chest was moving that his breathing had picked up, too.

"What are you doing?" His voice was low.

"Sorry . . ." I tried to pull my hand away from his stomach, but he grabbed it and put it back.

"You don't have to stop."

I put my hands on his waist and slid them up his hard sides to his chest and the soft tuft of hair in the center before they came to rest behind his neck. We began to sway, like we were slow dancing. His eyes were closed but he was smiling. "Mmm. My turn."

"You don't take me seriously, do you, Matt?"

His eyes shot open. He pulled me flush to his body so I could feel him hard against me. "Is that serious enough for you?" he said, roughly.

I pushed him away and staggered sideways. He sat down on the bed and tapped his foot on the CD player to stop the music. Leaning over, he set his elbows on his knees, letting his head fall between them. "I'm sorry."

"I'm sorry, too." I shuffled across the floor, feeling embarrassed for the first time in a long time. I plopped down next to him and threw my arm over his shoulder. We lay back across the bed and stared up at the ceiling. I rested my head on his arm like we had done so many times before.

"It's not fair for me to do that. I'm really sorry, Matt."

"It's fine," he said, but I don't think he meant it.

I had thought over and over in my head how I would say what I wanted to say to him, but it came out all wrong. "Do you want me to get naked so you can . . . I mean, do you want to take a picture of my, of me . . . you know, like the naked girl in the . . ."

He chuckled. "Do you think that's gonna help my situation, Grace?" He lifted his head and glanced down at his crotch.

I could feel that my face was hot and completely red. "No, I mean . . ." I swallowed, and tears began to cloud my eyes. My voice didn't sound like my own. I sounded so weak. "I'm a virgin, Matt."

There weren't many virgins my age at NYU, and I was beginning to wonder if I had missed my window. That's what happens; as you get older, it gets harder and harder to pursue an intimate relationship with someone. I had avoided it because I was so laser-focused on school and music. By sophomore year, I was literally the only person I knew who was still a virgin. I felt like a joke. And I was scared guys would think I was weird or inexperienced.

Matt's face was penitent and his eyes were wide. He brushed my cheek with his palm. "I know, Grace. I've known since, like, the first day we met. You don't have to do anything. I'm sorry I made you feel that way."

"You knew?"

He nodded. I guess it was that obvious. Did I have "VIRGIN" tattooed on my forehead?

"I just thought maybe you would want to take a picture of me, like the other girl?"

I could see in that moment that Matt knew it would mean more to me than to him. "I would love to photograph you, Grace. I will always want to photograph you."

He stood from the bed and took a deep breath to collect himself before grabbing his camera. Looking back at me, curled up in my dress, he said, "I'll just take the pictures. You do whatever makes you feel comfortable, okay?"

"Okay. Can we have music?"

"Of course." He changed the CD and put on Jeff Buckley's "Lover, You Should've Come Over." I moved to the edge of the bed and lifted the dress over my head, tossed it aside, and then I slid my panties down to my ankles and kicked them off, never once looking up at Matt. Holding my hands over my bare breasts, I heard him snap a few pictures while I sat there, very still, looking down at the ground. He walked over to the lamp and put some thin material over the shade, dimming the light. I turned and pulled the bedspread back, revealing the white sheets before lying back on the pillow. I looked up at him finally but kept my body covered with my hands as best as I could.

His head was cocked to the side, like he was studying the composition, while he held the camera by the lens in his left hand. As he walked toward me, I could tell he was trying to read my expression. He stood over me at the edge of the bed and ran his right hand over my propped-up knee before skimming it down my calf. "Try to relax, okay, baby?"

I nodded nervously. "My boobs are really small."

He shook his head and smiled. "Take your hands away, Grace. You're beautiful." Something about Matt's confidence and the way he took photography so seriously made it easier for me to pose for him. When he pulled the camera away from his eyes, I could see the beatific expression on his face. It reminded me of the way I felt when I played music. It was like something transcendent happened to him when he took pictures. Closing my eyes and breathing shallowly, I put my hands above my head and then heard the shutter clicking away as Jeff Buckley promised me that it would never ever be over.

Later, as I lay wrapped in my blankets, I watched Matt scouring the room. "What are you doing?"

"Looking for my shirt."

I yanked it out from underneath the bed. "Found it. But it's mine now." I pulled it over my head. I loved the way Matt's clothes smelled, like fabric softener and man soap.

"Holding my clothes hostage?"

"Stay with me?"

He stared at me for an uncomfortably long time.

"Matt?"

"All right," he said, quietly. He slipped his jeans off and came toward me in his boxers. When I yanked back the old quilt, he slid between the blankets. "Come here, Gracie," he said, pulling me toward him. I passed out in his arms.

Would I ever be able to stop thinking about how it felt to be wrapped up in him like that? Our bodies merged into one. Sleeping alone would never feel normal again. The way he moved was confident. Male. Slipping into his embrace was the most natural thing. Maybe it was because of all the months we'd been studying each other, waiting for this moment. Or maybe it was because he had done this before.

10. That's When You Had Me

GRACE

Matt was gone in the morning. There was no question I was putting his self-control to the test.

Pornsake acted normal in the practice room on Saturday but Tatiana looked at me strangely. "You're kind of glowing, Grace. Oh. My. God!" She leaned over her chair to get closer to me. "Did you bone Pornsake after class yesterday?"

"God, no! And be quiet." I looked around to the other students, who were watching us.

Dan made an announcement, which saved us from the uncomfortable attention. "To those of you who are interested in going abroad next year with me as part of an orchestra I'm putting together, please stick around after practice. We'll be doing tryouts this afternoon."

I packed up my cello and followed Tatiana toward the door. Dan grabbed my arm. "Grace, you're not trying out?"

I looked down at his hand at my elbow. Dan was getting a little too close for comfort. "I should have told you. I'm applying to grad school. I turned in my applications this morning."

"But we talked about the tour last night . . ."

"Dan . . . Professor, I've been planning to go to grad school since my freshman year. I'm not sure that I can just up and leave for a year and a half."

"Grad school will always be there, Grace. I regretted not doing more things like this when I was your age. That's why I'm taking the time off now." He seemed frustrated.

"This isn't about . . ."

"What?"

"Never mind." I sensed jealousy from him. I tried to clarify. "The sooner I'm finished with my education, the sooner I can start making money."

"It shouldn't be about money, Grace. We're talking about music here. You have more passion than any other student I've come across." I glanced at Tati, who was standing in the doorway, listening.

"It's about money for me because I have none." I laughed bitterly. "And I have a shit-load of student loans to pay back." I pulled out of his grip.

"I see," he said in a biting voice. He nodded and I hurried toward Tati.

Once we were outside the classroom, Tati bumped shoulders with me. "I think you just broke Pornsake's heart."

"He's so nice but he doesn't understand."

"I guess I don't really either."

"What do you mean? I have no money and no support. Do you think traveling Europe is free?"

"I don't think that's the only reason."

I knew she wanted to mention something about Matt.

"Don't even say it. If you think it's such a good idea, then you go try out."

She stopped abruptly. "I think I will." She turned around and headed back into the class. "See ya, Grace." Tati didn't have to try out for anything. She was that good. I knew Pornsake would take her but I think she wanted me to go, too. It was frustrating that she didn't understand my situation.

On my way back to the dorm, I passed by Orvin's shop. He was sitting on a bench outside.

"Hi, Orvin." He looked up at me and squinted. "It's me, Grace. Remember? I came in with Dan?"

"Oh yes." He patted the bench beside me. "Sit down, sweet girl."

It was already getting late and cold and it was especially windy that day as taxi after taxi zoomed by. "The new bow is fantastic, by the way."

He grinned up to his eyes. "I'm so glad to hear it, Grace."

"I can't believe the difference in the sound."

He continued looking forward but he put his hand over mine. "Don't forget, those are just tools. The music travels through the instruments, but it comes from you, from your soul."

Wow. "Yes," I whispered, full of complete understanding.

"Dan has a lot of faith in you."

"He does. But I get tired of the classical stuff, and that gets me into trouble."

"Ha!" He chuckled. "I get it, dear. The best musicians are rule-breakers. The thing is that you have to know the rules before you can be any good at breaking them."

We sat there in silence for a long time. I closed my eyes and then he said, "There's music all around us, isn't there?"

I could hear cars screeching, horns honking, children laughing, and the constant clanking of pipes emanating from the manhole covers. And then, suddenly, all of the muddled sounds became clear and merged together into the most beautiful symphony. The score to my life.

Opening my eyes, I looked over and noticed that Orvin was watching me. "See what I mean? It's within you."

My eyes were misty from the wind but more from the emotion. "Yes."

"You have to learn to fly before you can soar."

I thanked Orvin over and over. Each day, I was learning how to simplify my life. Maybe that's what growing up was really all about. Adults always say how complicated life gets as we age, but really, I think we just look for bigger challenges to overcome. Our biggest fears stretch from sleeping without our beloved teddy bear to finding out that we have no purpose in life. Did time, maturity, and overcoming obstacles offer the kind of contentment so evident in Orvin? Or did we just simply give up and surrender to the life we were already living?

"Come back and see me soon," he said as he rose from the bench.

"I definitely will."

In my wallet, I had a calling card I had won in the monthly dorm raffle. I found a pay phone and called my mom.

"Grace, how are you, darling?" She sounded busy. I could hear my father yelling at my siblings in the background.

"How is everyone?"

"Your father lost his job again."

"Oh no, not again," I said, though I wasn't the least bit surprised.

She gave an exasperated sigh. "Yes, again."

"I really wanted to come back for Christmas. I can get a seasonal job at the mall and help out."

"Oh, Grace, that would be wonderful. Can you afford the flight?"

"I thought instead of getting Christmas presents from you and Dad, I could get a flight home instead?" A tiny glimmer of hope flickered within me.

Her next words snuffed it out. "We can't afford it, honey. I'm sorry."

I hadn't been home for almost a year. I felt sorry for my mother and I didn't want to burden her, but I was sick for home and I missed my siblings, their chatter, and the energy that I felt in our house, even when times were tough. The thought of spending the holidays in Senior House by myself was frightening. It was like the last weeks of summer when I was alone. Before Matt had arrived.

Cue long, uncomfortable silence. "Okay, Mom. Hey, I need to save the minutes on this card."

"Okay, I understand. We love you, sweetheart."

"Love you, too, Mom."

I spent the afternoon alone in my room, drinking cheap wine and feeling sorry for my mother, but mostly for myself. My door was cracked when Matt came down the hall after work late that night.

He pushed it open. "Knock-knock."

"Come in. Hang out." I was playing my cello near the window, wearing Matt's Ramone's T-shirt.

He came in and set down his messenger bag. "Guess I'm never getting my shirt back."

I looked at him smirking near the door. Something

came over me. I stood up and walked toward him, brazenly pulling his shirt over my head. I was wearing nothing but a bra and underwear. I handed him the shirt. "There you go."

He blinked. "Um . . ."

"Kiss me, Matt."

He kicked the door shut with his foot. "Are you drunk?"

"Kiss me."

I wrapped my arms around his neck. His hand went to my lower back as he leaned in and then, finally, he kissed me.

At first the kiss was slow and delicate, but then we moved faster, tongues twisting, hands roaming. Our skinned burned with heat, and everything felt more urgent. We kissed and kissed, and soon I was aching for him to touch me everywhere.

I fumbled with his belt.

"I got it," he said, kicking his shoes off. While I removed my bra and panties, he took off his jeans. I moved my hand to the front of his boxers "Will you?" I asked.

"Will I what?" he said, breathlessly.

"Have sex with me?"

He cupped my neck and tilted my head up to look him in the face. There was pure reverence in his eyes. "You want it to be me?"

I nodded.

He leaned in and kissed me again and then his mouth moved to my ear. "Grace, I have never wanted anything more in my entire life than to be inside of you right now." Nerves shot through my legs and arms just thinking of him inside of me. "But we're not going to do this when you've been drinking so much. Trust me. Okay?"

"I feel brave, though."

"I know, but you don't want to be numb."

"Don't I?" I whispered.

"No, baby."

I knew he was right. "Okay."

He held me to his chest for a few seconds before breaking away. I reached out and touched him through his boxers. "We can do other stuff."

I saw the muscles in his neck move as he swallowed. "Get into bed," he said, and I did. He slipped his boxers off. It was the first time I saw him like that, naked and vulnerable, and so painfully turned on that I actually felt sorry for him. It wasn't the first penis I had seen, but under the circumstances it was definitely the most shocking. It scared me a little. I couldn't believe I was practically begging him for it a second earlier.

When he saw my terrified expression, he said, "Don't worry, it'll feel good when you're ready."

He slid into bed behind me, spooning me. Our bodies were hot as we pressed against each other. He brushed my hair to one side and kissed my shoulder. I shivered and then relaxed into his arms and closed my eyes.

He held one hand around my waist and the other caressed the sides of my breast as he continued trailing kisses across the back of my neck.

"Why were you upset with me the other day? I meant to ask you," he whispered. I shrugged. "Tell me."

"Because Carey and Jason said everyone in the photo department has an orgy in the dark room on Fridays."

His chest rumbled with laughter. "That is ridiculous. I'll take you to the darkroom this Friday. There's no one in there except a couple of art nerds, like me."

"Why would they say that?"

"I don't know. Maybe it's a campus urban myth."

I relaxed further into his body. The hand around my waist gripped my hip and squeezed. "You have to tell me what's going on in your head."

"At the moment, nothing. Your hands are making me brain dead." I giggled, but Matt wasn't laughing.

"What's going on with Pornsake?"

"His name is Dan."

"What's going on with Dan the man?"

"Nothing. He's nice. He's my teacher. He bought me a bow and offered to buy me dinner. End of story. Oh, and he's forming this orchestra to go abroad, all over Europe. He wants me to do it."

I felt Matt stiffen. "For how long?"

"A year and a half . . . but I'm not going. It's too long and I don't want to postpone grad school."

He kissed my ear. "Okay." I felt him relax again.

His hand snaked down farther and I gasped when he made contact with the most sensitive part of my body. He made slow, deliberate circles at first, gently, and then he added more pressure. I felt the air on my nipples and tingles down my spin. My legs jittered.

"Has anyone ever touched you like this?"

"No." The word came out in a rush of air.

He kissed my ear. "Have you ever touched yourself like this?"

I nodded.

"Tell me what you like."

"What you're doing?" I moaned.

"I want you so bad, Gracie."

With all the tension that we had built up for each other over the last few months, and after several minutes of Matt's handiwork, I felt it happening. He never changed his motion; he knew exactly what he was doing to me. It was almost painful how worked up I was, but I knew I needed it for the release. I put my hand over his so he wouldn't stop. My stomach clenched and cold surges of electricity shot through my legs. I thought for a minute about what Matt was witnessing and the good feelings started to subside.

He whispered, "Relax. Let go." And then I did, and everything built up again, more quickly this time, until there was no stopping it. My body pulsed over and over. He held his large, warm hand against me as he kissed and sucked at my neck until the quaking stopped.

My head pressed back hard against his shoulder. "God," was all I could say.

He ran his hands up and down my arms. "You're so beautiful."

I had experienced that feeling before, but only alone, and I never expected to feel comfortable enough with anyone to be able to let go like that. Matt knew exactly what to do.

I turned to face him, and we kissed. "Thank you," I said near his ear. I tried to deepen the kiss, but he stopped and said, "Bedtime, young lady." He pinched my butt.

"Ouch, jerk!"

"Go to sleep, Grace."

"Don't you want me to do stuff to you?"

"Yes, soon, before I die. But not tonight."

"Where did you learn it?" I asked, my voice raspy.

He was on his back and I was on my side, lying in the crook of his arm, looking up at him.

"Where'd I learn what?"

"What you did to me. Do all guys know it?"

He was quiet. I could see his eyes blinking as he stared up at the ceiling. I think he was trying to figure out how to answer the question. A faint glow came through the window from outside. There was just enough moonlight peeking through the shade for me to see Matt's lazy smile. "I don't know if all guys know how, but if I told you how I learned it, you'd laugh."

"Oh, you *must* tell me now." I bit his arm. "What, are you like a porn connoisseur?"

"No. Men learn nothing from porn. I think porn is more about pleasing men." Matt was wise beyond his years.

"Hmm, maybe *I* should watch some then."

"You'll be fine. Your mere existence is pleasing enough. Trust me."

Pushing myself off his arm, I rolled onto my other side, facing away from him. "Oh please, Matt. I know nothing and I'm going to embarrass myself when we do it."

He rolled over and tucked me against his body, spooning me. His voice was low. "Don't think about doing it anymore, okay, Grace? Let's just let it happen naturally."

"Fine." I said through a yawn.

We lay in the hazy light, teetering on the brink of sleep. "My mother taught me."

"What?" That woke me up. "Your mom taught you what?"

"Well, she's kind of a hippie-feminist. It's not that she showed me what to do. She was always trying to teach my brother and me how to treat women equally, and I guess this was just part of it."

"And so . . . ?"

"She gave me a book on the female orgasm and basically said, 'Don't be an asshole.'"

I laughed so hard that my body curled into a little ball. "Wow!" I chuckled. "I really like your mom, Matt."

"You two would get along."

"So you read the book?" I asked.

"Every goddamn page. Many times."

"Well, you certainly aced the practical test, although I'm sure it wasn't the first time you've taken it."

"No more talking, Gracie. Close your eyes."

"Maybe I'll get to meet your mom sometime."

"Yeah." It was quiet for few minutes. "I hope."

I woke up alone the next morning. On my nightstand sat a bagel, coffee, and a note.

G-

I had to run. Daria had bagels so I snagged one for you. Just eat it, don't smell it first, or else you'll catch a whiff of fish sticks. ☹ What is wrong with her?! I have to work tonight, but you should come to the PhotoHut so we can talk and figure things out. I'm going home to California for Christmas. You want to come with? You can meet my mom and thank her for my mad skills. Peace, M

The thought of spending Christmas with him put a huge smile on my face.

11. We Made Unspoken Promises

GRACE

I hung out with Tati in Washington Square Park all afternoon. We were supposed to practice but we ended up smoking a joint, and I gave her the details about last night. I believe her reaction was, "I can't believe you experienced the big O. That's like skipping ten steps and going straight to boning-for-years status." I blushed about ten shades of pink.

The weather quickly got cold and gloomy, and when I left Tati at the park, I felt the first drop of rain hit my cheek. *Fuck.* I had six blocks to go, no umbrella or money to spare for a cab, and an enormous cello.

In the time it took me to get to the PhotoHut, the skies opened up and I was soaked within minutes. As I ran into the store, the door jingled but Matt wasn't behind the counter.

"Gracie, I'm in here!" he yelled from the back room.

"How'd you know it was me?" I yelled back.

I turned the corner and found him sitting at a desk with

one small desk lamp on. He looked over his shoulder and smiled. "I could just tell."

"Prove it."

Matt laughed. "You swing the door all the way open to accommodate your cello case, even when you're not carrying it. The bell jingles a second longer with you than the average customer."

He looked up from his dimly lit desk and saw me. "Jesus. You're freezing, Grace."

He stood and hurried toward me, taking the cello from my hands. "It's pouring," I said, and then a visible shiver snaked through my body. My numb fingers made it impossible to unbutton my jacket. Matt quickly undid the buttons for me and pushed my peacoat off my shoulders, letting it fall to the ground. He wrapped his tall body around me, and within seconds I was warm.

"I was in the park with Tati and then it started raining."

"Shh, you're drenched, you should get out of these clothes." He let go of me and began searching the cabinet for something while I checked to make sure my cello case wasn't wet on the inside.

He came toward me with a towel. "I knew these were in here somewhere. Do you want to take your sweater off and I can throw it in the dryer?"

"There's a dryer here?"

"Well, it's a print dryer. It's like a big hot roller, but at least you won't be freezing while you're here."

"I can just go home."

His brow furrowed.

"Don't look at me like that."

"Don't you think we should talk?"

"I guess we should talk," I said, hesitantly. I went to lift my sweater over my head and noticed his eyes were fixed on me. "Turn around." I said.

"I've seen you really naked, Grace."

"So what? Turn around, creeper."

He obliged but laughed. "You're a dork."

I threw the sweater at the back of his head and then quickly wrapped myself in the towel. Matt went to the corner and fidgeted with the dials on the rolling dryer while I wheeled around in one of the office chairs, propelling myself in circles, faster and faster.

When he was done, he found another chair, pushed off, and came sailing at me across the linoleum floor. "Bumper cars!" he shouted, right before he knocked into me and sent us both falling to the ground.

"Is this your definition of us *talking*?" I said as he hovered over me, a mischievous grin on his face.

He leaned down, kissed the tip of my nose, and then popped up to his feet, offering a hand to help me up. I clung to the towel as I found my seat again. There was nothing clumsy about his movements, and he was always self-assured. I found that incredibly sexy.

Rolling his chair up to me so that we were face-to-face, he grinned again. "You gonna go to California with me for Christmas, or were you planning on going home to your parents?"

"I can't really afford either one." I looked down at my hands in my lap. Even though he knew my circumstances, it was still hard not to feel embarrassed.

"I'll pay for your flight to go home and see your parents. I'd love for you to come with me, but I don't want to be selfish."

I wanted to be with him, and even though I missed my family, I felt like I was going to miss him more if we were apart for three weeks. "You really want me to meet your parents?"

"Yeah, Grace. I do."

"It'd be awesome to see California. I've never been."

"Then it's settled. Oh, one other thing"—he gave a cocky sideways smirk—"you asked me to have sex with you last night. Do you remember?"

Instant blush. "Of course I remember. I wasn't that drunk."

"So . . . what does that makes us?"

"What do you think?" I came back quickly.

"Do you want to date? Or were you just looking for someone to lose your virginity to?"

I tucked the towel under my arms, leaned back, and glared. "Well, isn't there a word for friends that mess around?"

"Yeah, it's a called girlfriend and boyfriend." There was a strange expression on his face, like he was waiting for me to react.

"But we should keep it casual, right?"

"Well, we both have to study a lot, plus I'm going away this summer and you're gearing up for grad school."

Everything froze. "You're going away?" *How the hell did I not know that?*

"Yeah." He stood and walked to the counter to retrieve a piece of paper and handed it to me. It was a letter from *National Geographic* informing Matt that he had been chosen for an internship.

I reread it twice and looked up to see him wearing a huge, proud smile. Even though my eyes were selfishly tearing up, I stood and hugged him. "I'm so happy for you! Congratulations, Matt, I can't believe it. I mean, I can because you're amazing, but this is such an opportunity. Gosh . . . to be the only undergrad student they picked."

"I know, I was shocked. It's a once-in-a-lifetime opportunity. I'm sorry I didn't tell you about it sooner; I was just nervous about jinxing it."

I kept looking down at the letter. "It's so great! I'm really proud of you."

"I'll be gone this summer, and when I come back you'll be in grad school. Hopefully I'll have a job, if everything goes as planned."

I couldn't believe Matt was leaving. I had such mixed feelings, but I knew it was the best option for him. "So for now . . . we just keep it casual?"

"I don't want to date anyone else and I don't want to find you getting accosted in the hallway either, but we can call it casual if you want," he said.

"Okay."

"Okay what, Grace?"

"I don't want anyone else either." *Ever.*

An odd smell wafted into the room just then. I sniffed the air and my eyes widened. Burnt wool. "My sweater!"

"Shit!" Matt jumped up and ran over to the dryer. He hit a button and then pulled out what was left of my favorite article of clothing. "Oh, man, guess you'll have to stay here naked." He tried to hold back the laughter.

"That's not funny, Matt. That was my favorite sweater."

He threw it onto the desk and pulled me up into his arms. "You don't need this." Tossing the towel aside, he began kissing my shoulder and neck. I tilted my head, giving him full access, just as the bells on the front door jingled.

"Crap!" I jumped out of his arms and grabbed the towel

off the floor while he made his way to the storefront. I heard a familiar voice. It was Dan.

I stood by the wall and listened to the conversation.

"Hi, Matthew."

"It's Matt."

"Hi, Matt. Tatiana told me I could find Grace here."

"Yeah, um . . . she's kind of busy at the moment."

"I just need to talk to her for a minute."

I couldn't tell what Matt's face looked like, but if I had to guess, I'd bet he was amused.

"Dude, she's in the back room half naked."

"Um . . .what . . ." Dan fumbled for words.

Matt took pity on him. "She came in here drenched from the rain so she's sitting in the back in a towel until her clothes dry."

I raised a brow. *Never mind that we were about to make out.*

"Oh."

"Hi, Dan!" I yelled.

"Hi, Grace. I think we should talk."

"Can it wait until class on Friday?"

"Yeah, I guess." There was long pause. I wondered if Matt was staring him down. "Let's do that. See ya."

They said good-bye to each other very kindly and then I heard the door jingle once again. A minute later Matt was back and I was still standing in my damp jeans with a white towel wrapped around my shoulders like a spiffy shawl.

"I have to close up in a few." He clapped his hands once. "So what did we decide again?"

"I think we decided that we're just going to do what feels right." He nodded as I spoke. "Just with each other . . . until you leave."

All the sounds from the machines stopped. It was completely silent and still.

"Friends forever, though, right?" He studied my face carefully, and it looked as if he were cataloging the memory.

It was impossible to look away from him.

Friends forever might have been a tired expression, but when he asked, it was like music or poetry. I knew it meant something else. I knew it meant *I need you in my life*. I tried to detect some humor in his voice, but there was nothing . . . just a request. We stood there, so young and so sure about each other. The cold, dank room suddenly filled with light. Matt's eyes twinkled and I felt dizzy as warmth spread from my head to my toes. His hands were open, reaching out to me, inviting me in for a hug, but I couldn't move; I had been reduced to a puddle of emotions just from the look on his face.

You can't re-create the first time you promise to love someone or the first time you feel loved by another. You cannot relive the sensation of fear, admiration, self-consciousness, passion, and desire all mixed into one because it never happens twice. You chase it like the first high for the rest of your life. It doesn't mean you can't love another or move on; it just means that the one spontaneous moment, the split second that you took the leap, when your heart was racing and your mind was muddled with *What ifs?*—that moment—will never happen the same way again. It will never feel as intense as the first time. At least, that's the way I remember it. That's why my mother always said we memorialize our past. Everything seems better in a memory.

"Yes, forever," I said, finally.

12. Everything Seemed Right

GRACE

Two weeks later, we were packing to go to California for Christmas break. We had seen little of each other since the night at the PhotoHut, with both of us totally drowning during finals and Matt working overtime to pay for my flight to California.

"Where are we staying when we get there?"

"We'll stay at my mom's. She has a tiny house in Pasadena, but there's a spare bedroom. It's better than my dad's; they actually have staff there. It's ridiculous." He was sitting on a big purple beanbag in the corner of my room, flipping through *National Geographic*, his jean-clad legs spread wide and his shoes kicked off. He looked comfortable and relaxed in his Sonic Youth T-shirt and paperboy hat.

"What do you mean by 'staff'?"

He waved his hand around vaguely. "Like maids and shit."

"Oh." I suddenly felt nervous. Even if we weren't staying

there, I knew we were going to have to meet his dad, brother, and stepmom at some point, and I wondered what they would think of me. Poor, pathetic Grace in her piecemeal, thrift-store wardrobe.

"Don't freak out Grace, it's all an act with them. Just be yourself. You're perfect." He put down the magazine and looked up at me. "By the way, what did Pornsake want the other day when he came looking for you at the store?"

"He's still trying to talk me into going abroad. Now Tati's going, so he's dangling that carrot."

"Oh," he said quietly. His eyes were distant for a few moments. "He acted like it was urgent."

"He's just like that," I said.

"He's pushy." Matt looked down and continued flipping through the magazine without looking up at me.

"He cares."

"He wants to get in your pants."

"So do you." I walked over, grabbed the magazine, and tossed it aside.

"That's true," he said, with a twinkle in his eye.

Standing between his knees, I bent and kissed the top of his head. He ran his hands up and down the back of my bare legs.

"Do you wear short dresses like this to make me crazy?" His voice was raspy. We hadn't done anything but kiss since the night Matt had proven his skills. We had slept in the same bed a few nights, curling up into each other, exhausted after marathon study sessions, but nothing beyond that. Frankly, his self-control was saintly. We were ready, I was ready, and Matt knew it. Now that the stress from finals had been relieved, the only tension left was the kind that wracked our bodies and begged to be released every time we touched each another.

"I'm almost done. I'll come over after I shower. Do you have wine in your room?" I asked.

"A little, I think," he mumbled into my stomach as I continued playing with his messy hair.

"I just want a tiny bit to take the edge off."

He gripped my legs harder and looked up at me. He understood. "I'll pick up some wine."

I nodded. "What time is our flight tomorrow morning?"

"Six fifteen."

"Yikes, that's early." I looked at the clock; it was already eleven p.m.

Matt stood up and held my face with both hands and kissed me softly. "Just come over when you're done. We can sleep on the plane."

I swallowed and nodded.

Before he reached the door, he turned around. "Hey, Grace?" He gripped the molding above the door and leaned in, his gaze on the ground. I could see his triceps flexing as he rocked forward a couple of times.

"Yeah?"

"Before you come over tonight . . . be sure . . . okay?" He looked up and narrowed his eyes. "And wear that dress."

His shirt had ridden up, revealing the muscles of his lower abdomen. I couldn't help but stare. When I looked back up to his face I expected to see a cocky smile, but his lips were flat. Serious.

"Okay." I said.

After he left the room, I ransacked my closet for something to pack that I could wear to his rich father's house.

I basically threw all of the clothes I owned into my suitcase, then I took off my dress, laid it out on the bed, and got into the shower. A million insecurities ran through my mind as I groomed every inch of my body.

I closed my eyes and took deep breaths, letting the hot water pour down on me. My hand instinctively moved lower as I ran through images of Matt touching me over and over again in my mind. I touched my breasts, trying to imagine what they would feel like to him. I wondered if I had sex appeal. I tried to imagine how I would pose or move my body. I didn't have a clue.

After the shower, I dried my hair quickly and put on a tiny bit of lip gloss. I had one matching bra and underwear set. It was cheap black lace, and the panties were unraveling a bit at the hip. I put them on and stared at myself in the full-length mirror. Cupping my breasts over the lace and smoothing my hands down my sides to my hips, my nerves began to calm. I needed to know how I would feel to him. I was smooth and warm, and when I reached lower, I was wet. I slipped my red dress with black flowers over my head.

Everything was ready and sitting by the door for the trip. The only thing left on my agenda that night was to lose my virginity. I was more nervous than I had ever been, but I was ready.

I knocked on his door a moment later, and when I heard him shuffling across the floor, my stomach dropped. He had told me to be sure, but now I was having doubts.

He swung the door open wide, already armed with a glass of wine, and handed it over to me. "I figured you'd need that right away."

In my typical, dorky way, I started blabbering. "Yeah,

I mean, I don't know what the heck I'm doing or what to expect, or what you like or . . . like, how I'm supposed to do it . . . or look or feel . . ."

"Stop, Grace. We don't need to talk about it. Just drink your wine and we'll hang out. Just relax and be us."

"Good idea." I went to his CDs and found Radiohead and put on *The Bends* album.

"Nice choice, lady," he said from the other side of the room as he threw a few things in his bag.

He was shirtless, and his unbelted black jeans were hanging below the line of his boxers.

I lay across his bed, set my wine on the floor, and picked up his camera. "Say cheese."

He turned around and smiled as I stared at him through the viewfinder. "You're much better on the other side of that thing. Here." He reached for it and I happily handed it over.

I rolled onto my back and put my knees up, letting my dress fall to the tops of my thighs. He started snapping away. "You're so beautiful, Grace."

"But do you think I'm sexy?"

"Yes. Very."

I sat up at the edge of the bed as he set the camera on the nightstand. I took the last sip of my wine just as the song "Fake Plastic Trees" came on. "I love this one."

He reached down for the hem of my dress as I went for the button of his jeans.

"Stand up, baby."

"I don't know what to do, Matt."

"You will."

He lifted the dress over my head and then braced the back of my neck and kissed me like it was his only purpose in life. The temperature around our bodies tripled. His other hand ran down my back, to my bottom, and then slipped under the lace. I could feel him hard against me.

Breaking the kiss, I stepped back. His chest was pumping in and out. I watched as he took me in, standing there, waiting for him, wanting him.

He nodded with wide eyes. "I like this."

Something came over me, and I felt encouraged and confident, for once. I closed the distance between us, pulled his jeans and boxers down, and dropped to my knees.

"Wow." *Wait, did I just say "Wow"?* I felt so silly. I was incapable of being the hot girl; I couldn't just act like I knew what I was doing, especially now that I was staring that thing down. All the unabashed confidence disappeared in an instant. I heard Matt chuckle.

"Stand up, Grace."

"Why?" I whined as he lifted me from under my arms. I looked up at his face and he was smiling, teeth and all.

"You are the cutest fucking thing in the world, do you know that?'

I crossed my arms over my chest and made a pouty face. "I was going for sexy, dammit."

"You're that, too. Let's just lie down and take it slow."

People never tell you that these moments can feel really awkward. When you're trying to do what you see on TV or read about in books, everything feels strange. I reached for the bottle of wine and took a swig. Matt was completely naked as he fell back onto the bed. His quiet self-assurance was a blessing in disguise; he wasn't "that guy," trying to be hot and smooth. He didn't *have* to try to be hot or smooth— he just was. I took off my bra and underwear with little ceremony and lay down next to him as he stared up at the ceiling.

Rolling over onto his side and propping himself on his elbow, he leaned in and said, "Close your eyes."

He kissed me, the heat spreading and the urgency building. When he used his teeth to tug on my bottom lip, I thought I was going to lose it. His hand moved between my legs and then he touched me down there. My breath didn't hitch, I didn't gasp, and I didn't stop him. I wanted more, more pressure, more contact. I placed my hand over his and pressed. Just like he said, I knew what to do. The awkwardness was gone.

His lips traveled all over my body, stopping at my breasts, his tongue toying with one nipple as his hand went to work on me. I could hear myself making noises, quiet little "ahhh" sounds. Not the way women do in the movies, just in the involuntary way that comes with pleasure. He gripped my hip hard and kissed me even deeper on the mouth. He went to my neck and ear and sucked and kissed until I was writhing underneath him. Pure. Bliss.

"Just feel me," he whispered. How could I not? I felt so ready for him. I wrapped my hand around his length and pulled him toward me with my other hand. "Not yet," he said.

He sat back on his heels and ripped a condom wrapper open. "I'm on the pill!" I shouted awkwardly. He jerked his head back in surprise. I stared at him, unblinking. There was just enough dim light in the room for us to see each other's faces. You have to admit that comic relief isn't always a bad thing right before you're about lose your virginity.

When Matt laughed, I brazenly leaned in and wrapped my hand around him again. "Just do me, okay?"

He was smiling but there was something else in his expression that looked like reverence. "You're so unexpected, Grace." He moved his body so that he was hovering over me with his weight on his elbows. He kissed me tenderly, sucking my bottom lip into his mouth. Everything slowed down in a good way, and then he moved his hand to the space between my legs and touched me again, more gently than before.

"Ahhhh," I whimpered.

He made a satisfied sound, then gripped the back of my thigh, hitching it up. My body was open to him. I waited. The anticipation increased everything, the heat, the intensity, the throbbing inside of me. I knew it was right.

"I love you," he said near my ear, and then he was inside of me. There was a moment of pressure, but it wasn't as painful as I had expected. His pace was slow until it felt completely normal, like something I had always been missing. We moved faster together, our quiet moans unstudied and real. It was such a strange idea knowing he and I were moving for our own pleasure while giving it back to each other, equally. Like nothing else in life, sex is perfectly selfless and selfish all at once. Hot and cold, yin and yang, black and white, and all of the shades in between. Finally, the whole world made sense. I was in on the secret now.

The echoes of his voice kept playing over and over in my mind as we moved together. *I love you. I love you. I love you.*

I love you too. Always. Forever.

13. Did Things Change?

GRACE

Matt and I slept a total of twenty minutes before his alarm buzzed. After turning it off, he rolled over on top of me, our naked bodies pressed together. My hands went into his hair as he sank down and took my nipple into his mouth, grazing lightly with his teeth and tongue. The room was still completely dark but totally charged with electricity. "Are you sore?" he whispered.

"No." I wanted Matt everywhere . . . again. I fully expected some residual pain or blood or a nightmarish reminder that a few short hours before, I had been a virgin. But there was nothing, just two insatiable, hungry young people aching for each other.

He moved back up to my neck and kissed and sucked from the hollow up to my ear. I was panting, and the two days of growth on his face tickled my neck in the most exquisite way. I could feel him hard and hot against my thigh as he pressed his body into mine. "Ahhh, Matt."

"I love that sound."

His voice near my ear shot jolts down my legs. My whole body quivered. There was no stopping us at that point. The intensity left me totally breathless. Our bodies were a blur, gripping, tugging, kissing, sucking, moving up and down, rolling over and back, every motion somehow perfectly fluid on Matt's tiny twin bed. He pulled me on top to straddle him. "Like this," he said, and then he lifted my hips and guided himself inside of me. I arched my back, pressing my hands against his taut stomach.

I could hear my tiny mewling sounds mixed with the deep, quiet, satisfied sounds rumbling from his chest.

"Do you feel it? Do you feel it, Matt?" I started moving faster.

"Yes, baby," he said, his voice strained. His eyes were drowsy with desire and his lips slightly parted.

I moved harder against him and then leaned back, putting my hands behind me on the tops of his thighs, making the friction even more intense. He pressed his thumb to the bundle of nerves right above where we were connected. His small, subtle movements shut the rest of the world out to me. The walls could have been crumbling, my cello could have been on fire in the corner, and I would have stayed right where I was until the very end, moving above Matt, our bodies connected.

When the quickening began, he gripped my waist and tensed. I felt my mouth fall open but no sound was coming out. I couldn't breathe at that moment for fear that it would all go away. I closed my eyes and let go. It was strange; it wasn't that I forgot that Matt was there—how could I?—but I had very little self-awareness and self-consciousness. It was like I forgot that *I* was there when the buildup began and the tingling waves of hot and cold shot through my body. Down below, the pulsing began, harder than it ever had before. Matt made a strangled sound from his chest.

The word "Yes" inched from my throat, almost painfully. It wasn't triumphant, like you see in the movies. It was quiet. Euphoric.

One last thought ran through my head before I collapsed on top of Matt. *I've got to get my hands on that book his mom gave to him.*

Moments later, he stirred under me as I lay splayed over his body. He kissed the top of my head and took a deep breath.

"We have to go, huh?" I grumbled into the smattering of hair on his chest.

"Yeah, we better get going, although staying in bed with you all day and spending Christmas in New York doesn't sound bad at all."

"Won't you miss Christmas with your family?"

His expression was inscrutable. "No."

"No?"

"Seeing my mom, maybe. But I'm definitely not going to miss stuffy dinners with my obnoxious brother."

"What happened that made you two so different?"

He rolled me over onto my back and pushed himself off the bed. "I just got lucky, I guess," he said with an arrogant smile. "I've gotta take a shower."

I stared at his glorious backside as he walked away. Even in the hazy early-morning light, I could see the fine, cut muscles of his back.

ON THE WAY to the airport, I fell asleep in the back of the cab with my head on Matt's shoulder. "Wake up, baby. We're here." Matt looked at his watch. "Shit, we gotta hurry."

He pulled his bag and my small rolling suitcase from the trunk. We sailed through the check-in line, and before I knew it, we were boarding the plane. I sat in the middle seat and Matt had the window. I was asleep on his shoulder again before we even took off.

About halfway through the flight, there was a little turbulence that woke me up. Matt was asleep with his headphones on. I made my way to the bathroom, and by the time I came back, Matt had ordered us both Bloody Marys. He looked up at me, eyes beaming, as I scooted in toward him.

"Gracie," he said, handing me a plastic cup.

"Matthias," I replied. There was a current of electricity in the air between us.

"I got you a double."

"I've never had one before," I said, buckling myself in. "But I'll try anything once."

I took a sip and was immediately surprised by how much I liked the spicy and salty tomato flavor. "You can't even taste the alcohol."

He laughed. "That's the point."

I turned my head to look Matt in the face. He had dark circles under his eyes, and his brownish black hair was sticking out in every direction. Somehow he still looked gloriously sexy. He took a sip, looked over at me, and grinned all the way up to his eyes. "Good, huh?" His voice was low and just rough enough to send shivers down my spine to the space between my legs.

"Uh-huh," I said, breathlessly. I thought about what Matt

and I had done hours before and what that meant for us . . . what that made us.

As if he could read my mind, his expression changed and his smile faded. "You okay?"

"Yeah." I was okay—happy, even, and bubbling with anticipation—but I still felt a tiny bit of trepidation. Why? My first time had been perfect—almost too good to be true. After hearing so many horror stories from girls in high school about how awkward, painful, and messy their first times were, how could I not memorialize what we had done? Every single moment with him had been amazing. He hadn't pushed me and he'd been totally patient and respectful. He'd been gentle but in control, and then afterward he'd been sweet and attentive. All the thoughts and memories started swirling around in my head . . . the way his hands touched me under the covers of his tiny dorm-room bed . . . his mouth everywhere . . .

Matt watched as I stared, blankly. His eyes dropped down to my open mouth. He knew what I was thinking about. He blinked. "I love that mouth."

Leaning in, I touched my lips to his, seeking comfort. We surrendered to the charged energy between us, almost like we were feeding it, trying to satisfy it. We kissed slowly and softly, our tongues dancing around, until I heard the unmistakable sound of an intentional throat-clearing. I looked over my shoulder to see the woman in the aisle seat, watching us intently. She seemed like a jovial southern woman, with lots of makeup and big, white-blonde hair.

Were we being rude twisting tongues in the cramped seats of an airplane? Probably, but I didn't care. I was almost willing to strip naked right there, if Matt asked me to.

I smiled at the lady. With a sort of wise "I get it" look, she smiled back and then rolled her eyes dismissively.

Matt looked worn out. He reached languidly for my hand and clutched it with his before resting his head back and closing his eyes. I reached for my drink from the tray table and sucked it down in three large gulps. It was delicious and the alcohol took effect almost immediately. I leaned against Matt's shoulder again and fell asleep.

"I FORGOT TO ask, how are we getting to your mom's?"

Matt reached for my purple suitcase off the luggage carousel. "She's coming to get us."

When we reached the curb outside of LAX, a maroon minivan pulled up. "That's her."

Matt slid the large door open and threw his arms out to his sides. "Mama!"

She beamed with happiness. "Matthias, I've missed you! Get in here, you two."

"Mom, this is Grace," Matt said. I stood by, nervously as he loaded the luggage into the back.

"I've heard so much about you, Grace. It's nice to meet you. I'm Aletha." She reached out and took my hand in hers. She had a subtle Greek accent and was small-boned, with exaggerated but beautiful features and the same perfect nose as Matt. Her dark hair was streaked through with gray, and she wore a long, thin scarf wrapped around her neck so many times that it looked like a high-necked sweater.

"Nice to meet you too, Aletha."

Matt got into the front seat and I buckled up in the middle bench seat in the back. The third-row bench seat that was normally in minivans had been replaced with art supplies, including a large metal pottery wheel.

"Matthias, I just picked up that wheel in the back for pennies. I need you to set it up in The Louvre; it's too heavy for me."

"Of course, Mom."

She shot a glance his way and smiled radiantly. "No more Mama? Is my son too old to call me Mama?"

"Mama," Matt said in a squeaky baby voice.

"You silly boy." There was an ease between them. I wished my mother and I had that kind of relationship.

"So, Grace, Matthias tells me you're a musician?"

"Yes, I'm studying music."

"The cello, is it?"

"Yes, but I can play other instruments, too. I'm just best at the cello."

"Well, Matt's father has a beautiful grand piano at his house. You must play for them while you're there. It would be a shame for that instrument to live out its life as a piece of furniture."

"I agree," Matt chimed in.

"Maybe I will. I'll have to think of something to play that they'll like." I wasn't sure if I liked that idea, though. From what I knew of Matt's family, they sounded judgmental toward artists of any sort.

A short while later, we pulled into a long, narrow driveway next to a small but charming Craftsman bungalow, with green wooden shingles and maroon-painted double-hung windows.

The front yard looked like an English garden of wild, waist-high plants but it was manicured enough so it appeared more enchanting than overgrown. The air was crisp but it was nowhere near as freezing as New York.

"This place is so neat," I said, stepping onto the path.

"Now that my boys are big, I have a lot of time on my hands to putter around in the garden." Aletha unlocked the front door, flanked by bronze mica sconces. "Come on, Grace, I'll show you to your room. Matthias, please get the wheel, honey." We stepped into the house as Matt ran back to the minivan.

I didn't know what to expect. Was she going to give me the third degree or state the house rules? I felt terribly out of place and nervous. I stumbled into the guest room behind her, and she immediately opened the window to let in some fresh air—the same thing Matt did upon entering a room. They were so similar in their graceful movements, their easy temperaments. It made me wonder what traits Matt had gotten from his father, if any.

She came toward me and clutched my arms. My stomach dropped.

She smiled warmly, "No need to be nervous. I wanted a moment to tell you that Matthias seems so happy lately, and I imagine that has something to do with you."

"Oh?" I tried to be cool.

"Well, I just want to say welcome to my home."

I set down my suitcase and noticed that she had put Matt's bag in the corner. "Thank you so much for having me, Aletha. I feel really lucky that Matt was able to bring me out here for the holidays." I pointed to the double bed, covered in a floral quilt. "Is this where I'll be sleeping?"

"Yes, I think you two will be comfortable here. Matthias loves this bed."

I swallowed. *You two.* My eyeballs felt dry and pasty, as if I hadn't blinked in a while. Maybe I hadn't. Aletha laughed and then pulled me in for a hug. "Oh, Grace," she said, "Sweet Grace. I wasn't born yesterday."

She left the room with me standing there, stunned. I plopped onto the bed, exhausted.

LATER THAT EVENING, after a long nap, Matt and I sat at the oak dining table while Aletha served us steaming bowls of hot, fragrant chicken soup.

"Have you spoken to Alexander?" she asked Matt after she brought the bowls to the table.

"No."

She looked up from her soup and squinted over square spectacles balanced on the end of her nose. She looked incensed, but I didn't know her well enough to tell for sure.

"I haven't, Mom. Alex and I didn't have a great talk the last time I saw him."

She put her fork down, glanced at me, then back to Matt. "You're brothers. You two were inseparable as boys. What's happened to this family?" Her voice cracked.

Matt looked affronted before his expression softened. "I'll talk to him, Mom." He reached his hand out to her. She took it and kissed the back of it, then let him go. "It's just that I can't help but feel that people like Alex are holding us back as a species. He wears pink shorts and polo shirts, and he actually refers to himself as an Adonis." Matt grinned.

I choked on a piece of chicken and couldn't help but fall into a fit of laughter. Even Aletha couldn't hold back. Tears rolled down her cheeks as she let loose boisterous guffaws, laughing so hard she couldn't even take a breath. She managed to squeak out, "Hey! He's my son."

The mood instantly lightened. "It's not your fault," Matt said, still chuckling as we all caught our breaths.

"Oh, boy, Matthias. That's the one thing you get from your father."

"What's that?" My interest suddenly piqued.

She smiled warmly. "He and his father are so lighthearted. They can't be serious about anything for more than two minutes without turning it into a joke."

"He's not like that anymore," Matt interrupted.

Aletha's shoulders bounced with silent laughter. "Well, at least your father *used* to be that way."

We finished our soup in the glow of pleasant conversation, then Matt stood from the table. "Mom, Thank you. This was delicious. Grace, you want to shower while I help my mom clean up?"

"Yes, okay. I can help, too."

"Don't be silly, Grace. We've got this." Aletha walked over and patted her son on the shoulder.

Before I left the dining room, a wooden hutch full of photos caught my attention. Matt followed my gaze. There were various childhood pictures of Matt and Alex, as well as a slew of art projects, beaded lampshades, old cameras, handmade pottery pieces, and several black-and-white photos of a much younger Aletha, laughing joyously. "I took those when I was a kid," Matt said.

"They're amazing." I stood to get a closer look and Matt followed. "She was like your first muse."

I turned and looked up into his dark, squinting eyes. Everything froze for a moment. He looked at my mouth, slightly parted. He ran his fingertips down my cheek and the callused pads of his thumbs felt divine against my skin. I shivered.

"You're my first muse, Grace."

The music Orvin had taught me how to hear was back. The sounds rushed through my ears as Matt bent and kissed me tenderly on the lips.

MATT'S SIDE OF the bed was cold and empty when I woke up the next morning. I shuffled into the dining room to find Aletha sitting alone at the table, sipping coffee and intermittingly spooning globs of oatmeal from a wide bowl.

"Good morning, dear."

"Good morning, Aletha. Did Matt leave?"

"Yes, he's out running errands. He didn't want to wake you. Oatmeal?"

"Just coffee for me, thanks."

"Have a seat." When she stood, I noticed she was wearing a paint-spackled apron and garden shoes. She noticed me scanning her attire.

"I was in the Louvre. That's my art studio in back, more popularly known as a garage. I call it that because, hell, I want my artwork in the Louvre, and this is about as close as I'll get. I can take you there after breakfast." She went into the kitchen as I took a seat. I mindlessly began tracing a vein in the wood with my finger while I watched Matt's mom search a high cabinet for a mug. Aletha seemed like someone whose soul was so at peace, like life was no a longer a mystery to her.

"I'm nervous to meet Matt's dad and his family," I admitted, without thinking if she would take offense by my referring to them as his family.

Her movements stopped just for a second as she peered into the cabinet, balancing gracefully on her tippy toes. It was long enough for me to tell that my comment had jarred her.

"You'll be fine," she said, without looking over at me. When she returned to the dining room, she handed me a hand-thrown pottery mug full of black, thickly aromatic coffee. She was smiling. "Matt's dad, Charles, was a lot like Matthias once."

"Once?"

She pointed to the center of the table where a silver tray held a tiny metal pitcher of cream.

"Black is fine for me," I answered her unspoken question.

She sat down on the other side of the table, leaned back in her chair, and removed the glasses from the end of her nose, setting them beside the empty oatmeal bowl. Seconds of silence passed before she continued. "Sometimes money changes people. As for Matt's brother, Alexander, don't worry about him. Monica is the one you'll have to keep an eye on, especially when she's around Matthias. She's the conniving one. Alexander is just . . . well, I think Matt described him pretty well last night. Harmless but not exactly benevolent. I think that's the nicest way to put it."

I opened my eyes wide, shocked by her candor.

"I just tell it like it is, Grace. Monica always had a thing for Matt. It's just that her thing for money was stronger. I think Alexander knows that, and it's driven a wedge between him and his brother. They were always different but they were close before she came along."

Desperate to change the subject, I nodded and sipped my coffee while my stomach did somersaults. "I'd like to get something for Matt." I paused and she waited. "I don't have much money. Do you have any ideas of what he might like?"

She looked up from her coffee and smiled. "Yes, I'm glad you asked. I think I know the perfect thing. Come on out to my studio."

I followed Aletha out to the garage, which looked as old as the house but wasn't maintained as well on the outside, its beige, battered shingles in need of repair. She ushered me inside and closed the door quickly, giggling like we were conspiring schoolgirls. There were racks everywhere with drying pottery, sculptures, and an easel with a half-finished landscape painting. The walls were lined with large shelving systems that went all the way up to the ceiling and were filled to the very edge with brushes in tins, metal tools, and glass jars. The new potter's wheel sat in the corner. The only gleaming, untouched surface was the large, round metal top of the wheel. From the back of the door, Aletha grabbed a smock and handed it to me. "How about you make something for Matthias?"

"Sure, but what? I'm not very good at this." I picked up a metal coffee cylinder filled with tiny silver tools. "What are these for?"

"Leather tooling."

"Oh! Matt needs a belt. He's been wearing two shoelaces tied together."

"Perfect," she said. She walked to a long metal cabinet and pulled out a solid leather strip with four round holes punched through one end. "All you'll need is a buckle. We can go thrift-store shopping for that."

I was falling more and more in love with her by the second.

Taking a tiny hammer and a few tools from the coffee tin, I held them up. "So do I just tap these into the leather?"

"First, we must wet the leather a bit so it'll be pliable enough. That way the design will set and last longer, maybe forever." She went to the farmhouse sink and returned a moment later with a wet rag. She saturated the leather using the small towel and then took a step back. "Have at it, honey."

"What kind of design should I do?"

"That's up to you."

I studied the tools with different shapes on the end. There was a circle made of three squiggly lines. I grabbed it, along with a tiny solid circle, and pressed the larger circle into the leather with ease, leaving a permanent indentation. Then I took the smaller circle and tapped it into the center of the design I had already made.

She stood over me. "Wow, that looks just like an eye, doesn't it?"

"Yeah, I guess it does."

"Let's girlify it then. May I?" I nodded and she picked up a tool with a narrow teardrop shape at the end and made three divots above the eye design and three below. Then she tapped in a second eye and repeated the process. She took a half-moon-shaped tool and pressed it, striking it quickly several times in a row on the top and bottom edges, creating a border. Before I knew it, two inches of the belt was designed, abstract enough to resemble a paisley print or women's eyes looking out from a pattern of tribal swirls.

"That is so impressive," I said.

"Now you have the design. 'Eyes on Matt,' I assume, if we had to name it." She laughed.

"'*My* Eyes on Matt,'" I corrected, and she chuckled even harder.

"He'll love it. Just repeat the design over and over until you're at the end of the belt." She scooted a tall wooden stool behind me, so I sat down and got to work.

14. Did You Have Doubts?

GRACE

Hours later, I finished the belt just as I heard the rumbling of a motorcycle pulling into the driveway. Aletha had gone into the house to make tea. I hung the belt inside the cabinet, closed it, and went to the door of the shed just as Matt opened it. He pushed me back inside and kissed me hard. I wrapped my arms around him and let him lift my legs around his waist. He slammed the door and pushed me against it.

"Don't say no to me," he said near my ear.

"Matt, your mom."

"Take this off." He set me down and removed the smock. "Actually, take all of this off." He reached for my T-shirt but I stopped him. "She won't come in here," he said breathlessly.

"What, why?"

He let his hands fall to his sides. "Because she knows we're in here. Now, where were we?" He looked up to the ceiling and tapped his chin, then pointed his index finger at me. "Oh yes, we were undressing you."

"Wait, maybe she thinks we have a tiny bit of respect."

"Maybe she thinks we're young and in love," he countered quickly.

Silence, as if the air were sucked out of the room and we were left in a vacuum, wordless, our eyes glued to each other. Matt's expression remained impassive.

I arched my eyebrows.

He gave a quick shrug. "What?"

"Are we?"

"Young? Yes, relatively."

"No . . . are we . . ."

"What do you think, Grace?" And then his mouth was on mine, except there was no urgency behind his kiss anymore. The kiss went on and on, like we were trying to melt into each other, romantic and sweet.

Finally, I pulled away. "You have a motorcycle?" I asked, dreamily.

He answered by nodding into my neck and kissing me right below the ear.

"Wanna take me for a ride?"

"You have no idea."

"You know, we never really talked about the other night."

"Do we need to talk about it?" His tone was suddenly stiff.

A sudden wave of paranoia slammed me back a couple of feet, out of Matt's embrace. He was avoiding the topic. Why? I wondered if there was something he didn't want to tell me. *Was I not good enough? How could I be?* I thought. He was like a god, dripping with an intoxicating blend of sweetness and sex. I couldn't take my eyes off him most of the time. On top of it all, he was kind, smart, strong, and artistic.

Really, universe? That's plenty. That's just fucking plenty! You cannot make one person this delicious. It's not fair.

Matthias was the kind of guy girls dreamed about marrying. The kind of guy whose last name you would doodle after your first name in wispy cursive letters across the cover of your Trapper Keeper. *Graceland Shore. Graceland and Matthias Shore. Mr. and Mrs. Shore.* Images of your family photos would zip through your mind in blurry streams, like stars moving at warp speed. You, standing there, glowing and pregnant for the twelfth time, with all of your beautiful little Adonis and Aphrodite children clinging to your legs as you and your husband gaze into each other's eyes. You'd shout it out to the world, "This. Man. Is. Mine!" And you'd always give him lots of blowjobs. I hadn't even done that yet, but I planned to. Anyway, the point is, you'd do anything for him.

And then, like a mythological creature, he would annihilate your heart with mere indifference.

Do we really need to talk about it?

Ouch.

He squinted at me, pleading, searching. Or was he playing with me? My stomach spasmed with anxiety.

"Okay, Grace, what the hell is going on?"

I couldn't hold it in. "Was I terrible in bed?"

"What? What's wrong with you? Are you kidding me?"

"Well, are you going to answer my question?"

He stood up straighter, "Do I really need to point out that I basically just told you I'm in love with you? I thought you got it. Fucking Christ, Grace. I have a raging hard-on and I'm trying desperately to defile you against the wall of a disgusting shed in my mother's backyard. I thought actions speak louder than words?" We glared at each other and then he lowered his voice. "The other night was easily the most enjoyable night of my life, I swear to you. I doubt anyone else could ever top it. You are so uniquely beautiful and sexy, and you moved so perfectly that I haven't stopped thinking about it since." He looked down at his pants and laughed. "Which has made life on airplanes and in Aletha's house extremely awkward."

Heart slayed. He owned me.

He grabbed my hand. "Come on, silly girl. I want to take you over to my dad's for lunch, and it's already getting late."

"Really?" I looked at my watch. I didn't realize Matt wanted to see his dad on such short notice. "Oh shit." I ran through the door of Aletha's house like a whirling dervish, spinning in frantic circles. "I don't know what to wear," I moaned.

Matt trailed behind me and sat back on the guest bed, watching me, hands propped behind his head, a satisfied, smug grin on his face. "Just pick something. You look great in everything . . . and nothing."

"Oh my god, oh my god, oh my god." Clothes went flying out of my suitcase and across the room. "I have nothing!"

"This," Matt said, picking up an item of clothing from the floor. "Wear this." It was *the* dress, the one with the black little flowers and a cut out in the back. "With tights and your boots. You look amazing in it."

Grabbing it from him, I scanned the wrinkled material. "Throw it to me," came a voice from the doorway. Aletha held her hands out. I almost started to cry when I looked up to see her warm smile. When I was at my home, I was expected to iron not only my own clothes but my dad's and my siblings', too. My mother always said it was about doing my part. Even when I was home from college on holidays, I would spend hours doing chores and ironing. I despised ironing. The mere sight of an ironing board made me angry. Aletha's small gesture reminded me how much I yearned for a nurturing mother—one who didn't let my father's drinking rule our lives. One who sounded excited, who wanted to know me when I called. One who wasn't spread so thin.

"Thank you, Aletha."

"My pleasure, sweetie." I think she meant it. Like ironing my dress actually made her happy.

Within twenty minutes, I found myself fidgeting in the passenger seat of Aletha's van while Matt blared the Sex Pistols and banged on the steering wheel to the beat, weaving in and out of traffic, totally oblivious to my nervousness.

"Hey!" I yelled over the music.

He turned it down and glanced at me. "Don't freak out, Grace. They're a bunch of pretentious assholes. Just play a song for them. They'll all be totally impressed. Monica will be jealous. Alexander will be a douche. My dad and his wife will be cordial but smug. They'll all talk about how some famous chef cooked our meal and then my dad will remind you how much he paid for the wine."

"I feel bad for showing up empty-handed."

"My mom gave me a bottle of Prosecco to bring."

"What's that?"

"It's sparkling wine, like champagne."

I breathed a sigh of relief. "Perfect."

When we pulled into the driveway of what I would modestly call a mansion, my eyes bulged out of my head. The house was decorated in white Christmas lights and there was a grand Christmas tree in the center of the circular driveway, covered in large, extravagant bows and huge ornamental glass balls.

"My stepmom loves this shit but she doesn't do any of it herself. She just hires people."

I spotted the wine behind his seat and grabbed it. We both shuffled toward the door apprehensively. Matt pressed the doorbell; I thought it was strange that he couldn't just walk into the house he grew up in.

A plump woman in her midsixties, wearing an apron I thought only people in movies wore, answered the door. She was Alice from *Brady Bunch*, but not cheery.

"Matthias," she said. Her accent was thick and obviously German.

He leaned in and kissed her cheek. "Naina, this is Grace."

"Nice to meet you." She shook my hand firmly and turned. We followed her through an entry and down a long hall.

Who is that? I mouthed.

"Housekeeper," he whispered, and then leaned in toward my ear. "She's mean." My eyes grew wide.

Naina turned around and stopped midstride. "I can hear you, boy."

Matt grinned. "Naina has been here since I was twelve. She helped me with all my homework, taught me a bunch of German swear words, and would always sneak me tons of sugary snacks."

Naina stomped her foot and put her hands on her wide hips. "Matthias," she scolded, but it only lasted a second before her cheeks turned pink and she started laughing.

"Come here, you." The rotund woman practically lifted Matt off his feet in a bear hug. "I've missed you, Matthias. It hasn't been the same around here without you." They pulled away from each other.

Matt pointed a thumb at his chest. "I'm her favorite."

"Come on now, enough of that," Naina replied as she turned and continued down the hall. She blew off the remark, but I knew it was true.

It was two days before Christmas and I was about to meet Matt's dad, his brother, his stepmother, and his vindictive ex-girlfriend/soon-to-be sister-in-law. I was happy to have something to carry into the room; it felt like a shield against whatever was waiting for us in the grand living room. Matt yanked the bottle of Prosecco out of my hands—so much for my shield—and entered the room ahead of me, holding his arms out wide, his chest up, bottle dangling from his right hand. "Merry Christmas, family. I'm here!"

I saw Matt's dad and stepmother standing near a floor-to-ceiling window that looked out onto a huge backyard and sparkling pool. His father was wearing a dark suit and tie. His stepmother wore a beige pencil skirt, white blouse, and a glowing set of pearls. She was the polar opposite of Aletha, with her blonde hair, cut into a flawless bob, and her taut, medically altered skin.

His dad had the distinguished looks of a man who spent a lot time in front of the mirror, but his smile was genuine, like Matt's. From the couch rose a figure, who I knew without a doubt was Alexander. He was in a stark white suit, pink dress shirt, and no tie. The three top buttons were open, revealing his tan, hairless chest. His hair was lighter than Matt's and plastic looking from gel.

He reached Matt in three strides. "Matt's here and late as usual," he said, cheerily. Taking the bottle from Matt's hand, he examined it. "And look, everyone, he's brought us a bottle of poor man's champagne. Whaddya say? Maybe we can roast the pig with it."

Was he for real? My god.

My gut clenched and my heart dropped at the thought of Aletha giving Matthias the bottle and Matt knowing how they would receive it, but not having the heart to tell her . . . or me. It must have been why he took it from me at the last second.

Ignoring his brother, he stepped out of the way and took my arm. "Everyone, this is Grace."

I waved awkwardly and then his stepmother approached. "Hello, darling. I'm Regina."

While I shook her hand, Matt's father walked up to Matt and hugged him wordlessly, then he turned his attention to me. "Hello, Grace, lovely to meet you. I've heard about you and your music."

I swallowed, wondering what he had heard. "Thank you, sir. Nice to meet you."

"Please, call me Charles."

The urge to say, *How 'bout Charlie?* struck me, and I laughed nervously. "Okay, Charles."

Alexander stood back until I saw a black-haired women enter the room from the other side. She was beautiful, in a girl-next-door kind of way. Long, sleek hair with bouncing curls at the ends. Big brown eyes, surprisingly warm. I smiled as she approached but then noticed her Joker grin, big and fake, with a hint of mischief. Her movements were feline as she slinked toward us. "Matthias." Her voice was haughty.

"Hi, Monica. This is Grace."

Her creepy, closed-mouth smile was back as she slowly looked down to my boots, then back up to my face. I stuck my hand out to shake hers but it dangled there, helplessly. Finally, she took it. "Nice to meet you. You look like his type."

"Uhhh . . ."

Monica looked back to Matt. "Does she speak?"

"Kids, let's take this into the dining room," Charles interrupted. I was grateful.

The six of us sat around a large, shining black table laid with silver serving pieces and crystal champagne flutes. Matt and I sat across from Alexander and Monica while Regina and Charles capped each end of the table. Naina moved quickly and gracefully in and out of the room, setting dishes on the table.

Charles announced that the food was prepared by Chef Michael Mason. I leaned over and whispered to Matt, "Who's he?"

"Who cares?" Matt said out loud, but no one acknowledged him.

Regina and Monica were having a conversation about some designer who was working on Monica's wedding dress, while Charles droned on to Alexander about the firm's latest contract negotiations. They basically ignored us for the better part of the meal, and I should have been thankful. By the time dessert came around, and Monica and Alexander had had a few flutes of champagne, they turned their undivided attentions on us.

"So, you play the cello?" Alexander asked.

"Yes."

"Oh." Monica's voice was filled with knowing. "*You're* the cello player?"

"Yes," I said again. I saw worry etched on Matt's face. He was staring hard at Monica, trying to read her tone.

Her saccharine smile and fake laugh sent a cold shiver through me. She looked at Alexander but pointed to me. "This is the one?" Her eyes darted to Matt's dad. "The one you bailed out, right, Charles?"

"Excuse me? Um . . . bailed out? I don't know what you mean," I said, barely getting the words out above a whisper. *Who was this meek, stupid girl I had become around these people?*

"Nothing. This isn't lunchtime conversation, Monica." There was an edge to Matt's tone.

I pushed my chair back from the table. "Restroom?" I asked to anyone who would rescue me.

"Down the hall, second door to the right," Regina said.

When I stood, I swayed, dizzy from the champagne. Matt got up but I quickly moved past him down the hall. I could hear his footsteps behind me. I went into the bathroom and tried to close the door but Matt's big steel-toed boot was jammed in the opening. "Wait. Let me in."

"No," I barked.

"Grace, I'm serious. Let me in . . . please."

My eyes were watering and I was looking down when I finally let go of the door and let him in. He lifted my chin. His eyes were burning, like rum on fire. "Listen to me. I borrowed some money from my dad to help you get your cello back. I didn't go into detail with him because I knew he wouldn't fucking understand your circumstance. They don't even deserve to know. You're good and kind and pure, and you don't need these people to tell you that. Let them think the worst. Let Monica unleash her judge-y bullshit. Let Alexander think we used the money for your fifth abortion. Let them all go to hell. I don't care, and you shouldn't either. They will never be satisfied in life because, no matter how much they have, they will always want more. Right now they want to strip some dignity from us because we have something they don't."

I sniffled. "What's that?"

"This." He bent down and kissed me softly, slowly.

When he broke away he moved across the bathroom, opened the cabinet below the sink, and reached as far back as he could. "Got it! Naina never fails." It was a bottle of tequila. He unscrewed the top and took a swig. "I have to drive, but you're welcome to get blasted. It'll numb the pain of being around my family, trust me."

After three large gulps, I could feel the heat spreading over my face. I turned instantly pink-cheeked when I drank tequila. "I'm ready."

He messed up my hair. "There we go. Now you look perfectly just-fucked. Let's make them squirm."

The group was in the living room standing near the gleaming grand piano when we returned. Monica look startled when she saw us. Alexander looked jealous, and Charles and Regina looked curious, as I fanned myself.

"Took you long enough," Alexander said.

Passing Alexander from behind, I murmured, "Yes. Matt takes his time." As I sat down at the piano bench, I made one last dramatic fanning gesture before placing my hands on the keys. "Can I play you all something?"

"That would be wonderful, Grace," said Charles.

The tequila was blasting through my veins, working loose all the stressed-out muscles in my body. I began playing, first slowly, allowing the song to build. The music started swirling over and over, higher and higher, bringing every emotion to the surface like a spiritual experience. I felt like shouting, "Can I get an amen?!" I closed my eyes and played for five minutes without missing a single note.

When I was finished, there was silence. I nervously waited to open my eyes until I heard the sound of clapping. I looked to Charles first, who was beaming. "That was fantastic, Grace. Who was that, Bach?"

"Pink Floyd. 'Comfortably Numb.'" I smiled.

"Well, it was beautiful at any rate," Regina said.

"Thank you." I stood and noticed that Monica was standing at Matt's side, staring at him. He was unaware because his eyes were on me and he was grinning, a full, cheesy, million-megawatt grin full of pride.

As I walked toward him, he held his fingers up to his face like he was snapping the shutter of an imaginary camera and mouthed, "You're so fucking beautiful."

Monica saw the whole thing, but the best part was that Matt didn't care whether she saw it or not. I'm not sure she even existed in his mind anymore. Just as I reached him, Alexander smacked Matt hard on the back. "She's really talented, bro."

Matt's eyes went wide. He was shocked, clearly. Maybe it was the reminder of an old brotherly love they once shared, or maybe it was because Alexander was looking at me as a prize.

"Yeah, she is," he said, still staring at me. "We have to go now." Matt took my hand and pulled me toward the door then wrapped his arm around my shoulder. "Thanks Dad, Regina. Lunch was great. We have to get back with Mom's van now." Leaning over, he kissed my ear and whispered, "I want you all to myself."

We turned back just before walking out the door. Matt gave a big "Merry Christmas!" and we were gone, leaving behind a room full of gawking faces.

"What was that all about?" I asked as we pulled out of the driveway.

"That was me telling them you're mine."

I couldn't stop smiling.

The Sex Pistols came back on. Matt turned it up and began doing his best Sid Vicious imitation, chanting something about holidays in the sun. I smiled and stared out the passenger window, watching the traffic on the other side of the highway blur into streams of red.

WE SPENT THE next three days at his mom's, exploring the streets on Matt's motorcycle. At a thrift store, I found a cool, square belt buckle made of black pewter with a gray owl in the center. I made Matt wait outside while I paid for it.

When I got out the door, he was in the parking lot, straddling his motorcycle, looking sexy as ever. His arms were crossed over his chest and he was wearing that cocky Matt smirk, his eyes squinting against the sun. A gust of wind blew my hair back as I came walking toward him. He held up the invisible camera and took a shot.

"Gracie, I hope you got me that owl belt buckle."

I punched his arm. "You jerk. Why'd you have to ruin it?"

"Kiss me."

"You ruined my surprise," I whined.

"KISS. ME."

On Christmas morning, we all sat around Aletha's tree and exchanged our mostly homemade gifts. Aletha had thrown four beautiful mugs on her new pottery wheel and gave them to both of us.

"I had them glazed. Two have your initials and two have Grace's on the bottom," Aletha explained as Matt pulled them out of a box.

"Huh," Matt said. "These are great, Mom. Thank you."

He handed her a large wrapped frame. "It's from both of us." I squeezed his hand gratefully. He knew I hadn't been able to buy her anything.

She unwrapped it and stared. I didn't know what she was looking at so I got up to stand behind her. When I finally saw what was framed, I swallowed and felt tears fill my eyes. It was a matted collage of us. You couldn't see our faces in any of the photos but they were all of Matt and me, just our legs, arms, hands, hair, mostly on each other, or embracing, or lying across one another lazily. Some were blown out by the light so you could only see our silhouettes. It was a breathtaking collection, and it truly showcased Matt's talent so beautifully.

"Matthias," Aletha started, already breathless. "Son, these photos are so incredibly stunning. And Grace, you are such a naturally beautiful subject. I will cherish this always."

A tear fell from my cheek and landed on Aletha's shoulder as she hugged me. She looked up at me in surprise. I shook my head, embarrassed, and looked away.

"You hadn't seen this, Grace?" she asked.

"No," I said, my voice strained. "It's amazing, Matt."

"Glad you like it, 'cause I got you the same thing." He laughed. "It's waiting for you in your room when you get back. I snuck it in there right before we left."

I plopped onto his lap and kissed him quickly. He hugged me close. "I love it. Thank you."

When I gave him the belt, he examined it. "Gracie's eyes," he said, and I nodded.

"I told you he would get it," Aletha added.

ONCE WE GOT back to New York in early January, we fell into a regular routine. We'd explore the city, go to our classes, study together in the dorms, or are at least try to study. We couldn't keep our hands off each other. On the nights Matt worked at the PhotoHut, I'd practice music with Tati.

About a month later, Matt asked me to meet him in the lounge, with only the hint that he was going to take me somewhere special.

"This is the other part of your Christmas present I was waiting to give you," he told me, his eyes twinkling as he grabbed my hand and led me out of the dorm.

All bundled up in coats and scarves, we walked to Arlene's Grocery, a small venue where local bands played. "Don't look at the signs," he urged.

We made our way through the crowd to the stage. Matt forged ahead, pushing people to the side, but I couldn't see anything beyond people's backs. When I finally looked up, I was staring right into Jeff Buckley's eyes as he tuned his guitar.

Holy. Shit.

We watched the entire set, right there at the front of the

crowd, swaying back and forth, three feet from my favorite musician of all time. At one point, I thought I caught a smile from Jeff but then he looked away and started rambling about his nicotine patch. I looked back at Matt and mouthed, "OH. MY. GOD." I knew I was in the presence of greatness.

Jeff disappeared after the show, but I didn't bother looking for him. A year earlier, I might have waited around like a groupie so I could get a handshake or tell him what a devoted fan I was, but that night I just wanted to get back to the dorm with Matt. I was inspired. I wanted to play music.

Walking home, I said absently, "He didn't play 'Hallelujah.' That's too bad."

"He's probably sick of playing it," Matt replied as he swung our hands back and forth.

"Yeah, you're right. Thank you, by the way. That was amazing."

"Anything for you."

"Don't go getting mushy on me, Matthias."

He laughed. "Now who's the one who can't be serious?"

15. Gracie . . .

MATT

After the holidays, Grace and I spent as much time as we could together—mostly naked. It felt like we were trying to condense a whole relationship into a few short months before I left for South America. We must have told each other a million times that what we had was casual, but it didn't feel that way. Grace avoided all conversations about what she was going to do when I left for the summer. She'd constantly reminded me that we were young, which sometimes felt like she was minimizing our relationship. I think she was trying to protect her heart. Maybe I was, too.

We hung out with Tati and Brandon a lot and went to seedy music venues on the Lower East Side and in Brooklyn every Friday. On Sundays, we'd lounge around, playing games or studying together at Senior House. But as the winter ended and we headed into early spring, we all got busy preparing for the end of college and the next phase of our lives. If I hadn't lived right next door to Grace, I don't know how we would've seen each other.

Finally, on the first warm day of April, Grace, determined to get the four of us together, gave us strict orders to meet up outside of the Old Hat at ten in the morning. The Old Hat was a grimy dive bar we'd go to after nicer bars closed for the night, so it was an unusual place to start the day.

I rubbed my hands together and clapped once. "All right, lady, what's this all about?"

"Whiskey," she deadpanned.

Brandon chuckled.

"It's ten a.m., Grace," Tati said with her hand on her hip, clearly not amused.

Grace grabbed my hand and pulled me toward the door. "Isn't that a beautiful thing, you guys? We have all day. C'mon, we're young. Let's take advantage of it."

The bartender at the Old Hat greeted us. Grace held up four fingers. "Four whiskeys, please."

"Oh, geez," I heard Tati mumble.

"What are we doing, Gracie? For real." I was totally confused.

The four of us sat in a row at the bar. "Everyone has been so busy lately and Matt's leaving soon. I just want to spend some time with you guys, getting drunk and having fun and not studying. I have the whole day planned for us."

Tati held up her shot. "You've convinced me. I'm game."

"Bottoms up," Brandon said.

After we drank our whiskeys, Grace turned to us. "All right, let's hit it."

"Where to now?" I said.

Her eyes lit up. "The dark room." She handed me a roll of film. "We need to develop that."

"Please tell me it's not naked pictures of you guys," Brandon said.

"No, they probably have enough of those," Tati added.

"It's not," Grace said. "It's a clue."

"What are we gonna do while you guys develop that?" Tati asked.

"You're coming with us," Grace said. "Matt can show you guys how to make a print."

I smirked. "Yeah, it'll be fun."

We walked to the photo lab on campus, soaking in the warm spring air along the way. There were a series of small rooms where students could develop film negatives and then a bigger room filled with red light, enlargers, and developing pans for students to make prints. I set up some negatives in enlargers from a roll of film I had left in the room, so Tati and Brandon could make prints. They were shots of me and Grace making stupid faces at the camera; it was kind of a throwaway project, but at least Brandon and Tati could amuse themselves while Grace and I developed the roll.

We walked down the hall and I pulled Grace into one of the smaller rooms and closed the door. "Thanks for planning today. This is fun." I kissed her against the door and hitched her leg up around my waist, running my hand up her thigh and pushing her dress higher.

"I thought you told me people don't do this in here."

"I don't know what other people do, and I don't really care."

She whimpered but pulled out of my embrace. "We need to develop that film, Romeo."

"Killjoy," I muttered. "Fine, I'll get it started, but I'm gonna get some after."

"I'll be at your disposal then, but get that roll going first."

"All right, I have to turn the red light off to develop it so it's going to be completely dark in here for about twelve minutes."

She wrinkled her nose. "What's that smell?"

"It's developer." The chemical smells were overwhelmingly pungent inside the eight-by-eight room, which was warm and humid. There was a stainless steel sink and counter on one side, along with a tall, narrow vat where film negatives were dropped into developing solution. On top of the counter was a large timer with glow-in-the-dark hands. On the other side was a wooden bench.

I bent and flicked the radio on below the sink. Music came through a speaker overhead—some kind of smooth jazz from the university's station. "I can't change it, but it's something." I looked back at Grace sitting on the bench. "You ready? I'm going to turn off the red light now."

"I'm ready."

I hit the switch. Photo labs are so black and warm that you feel instantly sleepy. Grace yawned audibly from the other side of the room. All my other senses went into overdrive. I popped the film open and blindly attached it to a clip. Feeling my way over to the sink, I managed to drop it expertly into the vat without making a sound.

"You okay, baby?" I asked.

"Yeah," she said drowsily.

"Give me one more minute." I set the timer and then a mental image of Grace riding me flew through my head.

"Get naked."

She laughed. "Are you serious?"

"I can do a lot in twelve minutes," I said as I felt my way over to her.

I gripped her arm first and then we were kissing. There was no need for any other senses; it was all touch after that. I kissed her from her ear to the base of her neck and then pulled her dress over her head. She unbuckled my belt and yanked at my jeans. I turned her around. From behind, I kissed her shoulder and smoothed a hand down her back, over her butt, and then my fingers were there, inside of her. She didn't make a sound.

"You okay?" I asked.

"Don't stop," she panted.

And then I was sliding inside of her. Our breaths were hard but we muffled them as best as we could. I moved in and out, slowly at first, then harder and more urgently. She pushed back against me, matching my movements. There was no sound other than tiny mewling sounds and heavy breathing. When I felt her tighten around me, I lost it. The cold surge shot through me like all my nerves were breaking apart. I pulled her toward me and buried my face in her neck. In one motion, I pulled out, collapsed onto the bench, and lifted her onto my lap.

We were kissing slow, sleepy kisses when *buzzzzzz*! The timer went off. I stood and flipped on the red light. Grace stood beside me, stunned. I wrapped my arms around her and kissed the top of her head. "That was amazing. Are you okay?" Synapses must have still been misfiring in her brain because she just nodded.

I went to the sink and pulled about four feet of negative out of the vat and dropped it into a container full of water that acted as a stop bath. We quickly got dressed and left the room with the film.

After the negatives dried, I scanned them and found that most were black until the very end. There were three photos, each with a single word on a piece of paper. *Piano. PBR. Peanuts.*

I looked up at Grace. "Three Peas?" I asked, referring to a little dive bar near our dorm, which had a piano open mic night on Fridays. I often hassled Grace to play and sing for me there, but she never would.

"You got it. Let's get Tati and Brandon. This is so fun!" she squealed, and then yanked me down the hall toward our friends.

Outside, Tati produced a flask of whiskey from her purse. "You don't mess around," I said.

"I thought Grace was gonna drag us to a bunch of museums. I had to be prepared. Want some?"

I took a swig and then Grace yanked it from my hands. "I'm the one who's gonna need it. Let's go."

By the time we got to Three Peas, we were all sufficiently buzzed. It was empty except for a female bartender I didn't recognize. Grace leaned over the bar. "I'm doing this little game for my boyfriend and my friends, and I was wondering if I could do a supershort song up there?" She pointed to the stage.

"Oh my god, she's gonna do it," Tati said.

The bartender looked up and smiled. "Knock yourself out. No one's here. You want somethin' to drink?"

"Sure. Four PBRs."

The bartender served our beers, and we all watched Grace down hers in three large gulps. "Oh boy," I said.

Just as she made her way to the piano, I heard the jingling of bells as the door opened. I turned around and watched a few suits on their lunch break enter and head for the open stools. There were seven of them. Grace's audience had grown exponentially in a second.

She scooted the piano bench closer to the piano, which made a screeching sound across the wooden planks of the stage floor. "Sorry." She mumbled into the microphone, which was set way too loud. The suits and the bartender turned their attention toward her. She looked thoroughly nervous. I smiled at her and her face softened a bit. She leaned back and turned a dial on the sound system. "Better?" I nodded.

Tati yelled, "You got this, girl!"

"Okay, here's a song I wrote, but it's also your next clue, so pay attention, you guys." Her nervous laugh echoed through the silent bar.

"Grace writes songs?" Brandon asked.

Tati and I both shushed him at the same time.

Grace played a long rhythmic introduction that sounded like typical jazz bar fare and then picked up the pace until a melody emerged. She could play any instrument so effortlessly; it was mesmerizing. Still, when she started to sing, we were all holding our breath. No one had heard her really sing, but like everything else, she was a revelation.

Run to the place where your royals play,
Your friends gather and we hide away.
In the open but unseen,
How reckless those moments we have are,
How precious.

Why don't we run to the place where the children dance,
Generals stand,
And we can wade to our knees in the summer . . .

When she was finished, we all stood up and clapped. "Bravo!" Tati yelled. The businessmen all clapped and shouted, "Great job!"

"Dude, that was pretty good. I didn't even know she could play the piano," Brandon said.

"She's amazing," I said quietly as I watched her step down from the stage. Tati nudged me in the arm and winked.

The bartender called Grace over. "You're a million times better then most of the people who come in here on open mic night." I pulled her into my arms, beaming down at her. She was looking up at me, smiling. Her face was beet red. I kissed her on the nose. "Washington Square Park?"

She laughed. "Was it that obvious?"

"Kind of. You suck at clues, but this is still fun. Shots before we go?"

The bartender poured us a round of whiskey shots, and then we bought hot dogs from a cart on our way to the park. We were severely drunk, and it was only one o'clock in the afternoon. I was afraid if we didn't eat a lot more than hot dogs, I'd have to carry Grace back to the dorms by the time this was all over.

"I'm having fun. I'm glad you arranged this," I told her. The truth was that Grace and I could have fun folding laundry, and Brandon and Tati were always up for whatever we had planned. It was just easy with the four of us.

Once we were in Washington Square Park, we sat together under our usual tree. Brandon lit a joint and we all took turns passing it around. I laid my head in Grace's lap. "I can't think of a better way to spend a Wednesday." I yawned.

"You know, Graceland used to do this for her brother and sisters back home." Tati said.

"You did?" I looked up at her and smiled.

"Yeah, just to pass the time." Grace said absently. "But, actually, this case is a little different." She paused and drew in a deep breath. "I wanted to gather you all together and tell you that I got into grad school. I get to stay at NYU!" She threw up her arms in celebration.

"Oh my god!" I stood and picked her up, spinning her around. "I'm so happy for you!"

I noticed that Tati was quiet and Brandon seemed clueless. Grace noticed, too.

When I put her down, she turned to them. "Aren't you guys happy for me?"

Tati shrugged. "I guess. Yeah, Grace I'm happy for you." She stood up and grabbed her bag. "Listen, Brandon has a paper to write and I was going to meet with Pornsake about the summer thing."

Something flitted across Grace's expression. "So you're officially going?"

"Well, you got into grad school. Why does that bother you?" Tati asked wryly.

"It doesn't. We don't even play the same instrument. What do I care?"

"Seems like you care a little. Not sure why, though. You're the one who turned him down."

"I didn't exactly turn him down."

"He bought you an eleven-hundred-dollar bow, Grace."

"So?"

I scowled at Tati. "She's going to grad school. That's why she's not going to Europe with Pornsake."

"No, she's waiting around for you, Matt. For when you come back to New York."

"Tatiana!" Brandon scolded her.

"What? It's true."

"I'm going to grad school because I want an advanced degree. You can gallivant all over Europe with Pornsake for the next year and a half. I don't care."

Grace turned and stormed off toward the chess tables.

I turned to Tati, furious that she had ruined Grace's big announcement and our afternoon. "I didn't pressure Grace to stay, if that's what you think."

"You guys can't be away from each other for a whole year, even though this traveling orchestra would be an insane opportunity and experience for her."

I looked at Brandon and then back to Tati. "You think you two can be away from each other for that long?"

"We're solid, Matt. Brandon and I can spend five minutes away from each other and not go crazy, unlike you guys."

"If you guys are so solid, why don't you marry him then?"

"Oh, grow up, Matt. What are you, five?"

"I'd marry Grace in a heartbeat. That's how solid we are." I looked back to see Grace halfway across the park, playing chess with a short, gray-haired man.

Tati smirked and then stuck her hand out. "I smell a challenge."

"What are you talking about, Tati?" Brandon said, suddenly shaking loose from his high.

"Oh, shut it, Brandon." She looked back at me. "You don't think we'd do it?"

I laughed. "I don't know, Tati, Brandon doesn't seem all that keen on the idea."

She turned back to Brandon, who stood wide-eyed behind her. "You'd marry me, wouldn't you? I mean, the things we've done . . ." She arched her eyebrows in a knowing way.

"I . . . I guess."

Turning back around, she said, "See, Matt. You're the one who's all talk."

I stuck my hand out. "I bet we do it before you guys do."

"It's on." She glared at me.

"What are we even betting on?"

"Loser buys the married couple a night out," she said.

We shook on it. "I'm in," I said, although I would have done it for nothing.

16. I Should Have Told You

MATT

I left Brandon and Tati near the tree and headed for Grace with a new mission in mind. Sitting on a bench near the fountain, I smoked a cigarette and waited for her to finish playing chess. I blew smoke rings into the air while I thought about how I would get her to marry me.

I need to get her drunker.

Grace came walking toward me with a smile. It looked like all the tension was gone and I was relieved.

"Who was that?" I asked.

"Orvin. The man who made my bow."

"Oh. The one Pornsake bought for you?" I scrunched up my nose.

"Would you stop that?"

"What did the old man give you?"

"The number for a guy in a band who plays down at that place on Allen Street. They're looking for a cellist and I could probably make a few bucks. Did Tati and Brandon leave?"

"Yeah."

Grace looked disappointed, as if she hoped this thing with Tati would blow over by the time her chess match was over. "All right, let's go."

"Wait, you haven't seen me double dutch yet, have you?" In my drunk brain, this was how I was going to win her over and get her to marry me. It was a brilliant plan.

"What? You don't double dutch."

"I do, too. See those girls over there? I met them two days ago. I showed 'em up."

"I don't believe you."

"You don't need to. I'm gonna prove it."

We walked toward the girls, and the one who was jumping stepped out when she spotted me. With her hand on her hip, she said, "Oh yeah, Matty, Matty Double Dutch is here."

I looked over at Grace, "See?"

Her eyes were as big as sand dollars. I began stretching, touching my toes, and bending to the side. Grace doubled over laughing.

"You're not gonna . . . ?" she started.

"Oh yes, I am. Watch me."

I got ready. The two girls starting turning the ropes and I did a goddamned flawless cartwheel into the center and started jumping. It was a risky move. I had only pulled it off once before but I knew it was time for the big guns. I did everything the girls sang out: *"Matty, Matty, turn around. Matty, Matty touch the ground. Matty, Matty, show your shoe."*

I hopped on one foot.

"Matty, Matty, that will do. Matty Matty, go upstairs."

I jumped higher as the ropes got faster. Grace was in hysterics by now.

"Matty, Matty, say your prayers. Matty, Matty, turn out the light. Matty, Matty, say good night."

They stopped singing and the ropes swung faster and faster until finally those little brats got me and I tripped up. Grace was laughing so hard, I think she stopped breathing; she looked like a tomato.

The girls clapped along with a small crowd that had collected. I puffed my chest out, huffed on my fingernails, and rubbed them against my shirt. "Not bad, huh?"

"You're full of surprises," Grace said, catching her breath.

"And I will be . . . forever."

"Where did you learn how to do that?"

"I was a camp counselor last summer."

"Ha! Saint Matthias."

"Actually, I got fired."

"Why?"

"You don't want to know," I said.

"Actually, I do, especially because you were fired from a job while working with kids. That's a red flag right there."

"It was all Clara Rumberger's fault. She was another counselor. Her mom, Jane, was the director."

"So, what happened? You got caught messing around with Clara?"

"Not exactly. Jane was the one who kind of had a thing for me."

"The mom?" Her expression froze.

I nodded, growing more embarrassed by the second.

"What'd you do, Matt?"

"Clara sort of caught me and her mom, um . . . well, in a delicate situation in the camp kitchen after lights-out."

"Oh. My. God. You pig." She punched me in the arm. "I can't believe you were hot after a cougar. So, why'd you get fired?"

"Well, apparently Clara threatened to tell her dad, Jane's husband, unless I was fired."

"She was married?"

I held up my hands in a defensive gesture. "She told me they were getting a divorce."

"Man, Tati would have a field day with you."

"Which reminds me. What was the deal with you guys earlier?" We headed back to the tree as we talked.

"I don't know. She's mad because she thinks I'm giving something up for you."

I grabbed her hand and swung her around. She looked up at me and then looked away quickly. "Look at me, Grace. Are you giving something up for me?"

"No." She didn't hesitate.

"I would never want you to feel that way. You said yourself that we're young, that we should do what we're meant to do."

"What's that?" she whispered.

"I'm not sure, but I know I'm taking the internship, and you should go with Pornsake, if you think you should. You could always go to grad school later."

"Dan wants to travel for a year and a half, Matt. He has a tour planned. He's been saving and preparing for a long time."

"Okay . . ."

"That means you and I wouldn't see each other for that long."

The thought made me physically ill. "But if it's what you think you should do after we graduate, then do it."

She blinked up at me and then shook her head and

looked down. "That's it? That's how you feel? 'Just go ahead, Grace, leave for over a year, and good luck'?"

My heart was pounding out of my chest. "Is your scavenger hunt over?"

"Change the subject much?"

"Let's get drinks and talk," I offered.

"Yes, Matt, because we always make such great decisions when we're drunk."

"Just come on," I said. "I have an idea."

We found a pub and spent the rest of the afternoon there. But instead of talking, we drank away the questions that surrounded our futures . . . that surrounded us. Grace picked ten songs on the jukebox and insisted on staying until each one played. By the time the last one came on, we were well and properly sauced.

"Are you drunk?" I slurred.

"Are you, MatthiUSSSS?"

"I nee' take you somewhere, 'kay, Gracie?" I pulled her along as we stumbled out onto the street and down to the subway. We were laughing hysterically as we tried to keep our balance without touching the subway poles. The other riders were not amused. We got off downtown and walked a few blocks. "Look," I said, pointing to City Hall, "we ssshould totally get fuckin' married righ' now, Grace! Thass the only thing that'll make this ALL better." I grabbed her shoulders and looked her right in the eyes, which were alight with happiness—or maybe it was drunkenness. "Wanna?"

"Thass a grea' ideeea, Matt."

I don't know how but we managed to fill out all the nec-essary paperwork and fork over the fifty bucks. The justice of the peace, an irritated, short, red-haired woman told us,

"You need a witness, and I've only got fourteen minutes left on the clock. You'd better hurry."

"Wait," I said, "Hold on." I came back a few minutes later with a homeless man who said his name was Gary Busey. I had to pay him ten bucks.

The ceremony was over in about a minute. I think I said, "I do," as did Grace, and then we kissed sloppily.

Gary Busey cleared his throat behind us. "Come on you two, get a room." We hugged him and then ran into the bathroom and washed Gary's overwhelming salami smell off our hands. When I came out, Grace was waiting in the hall. I held my hand out. "Mrs. Shore, may I have this dance?"

"Yes, husband, I would be honored."

We danced around like fools for a few minutes and then stumbled out of the building, laughing. After we took the subway to the East Village, I gave Grace a piggyback ride eight blocks to Senior House, where we passed out, eating tortilla chips in the lounge.

DARIA SHOOK MY shoulder. "Matt? What are you two doing down here?"

I looked up at her and squinted. My head was pounding and the small desk lamp on the end table in the lounge was like a powerful Vita-Ray blasting my skull. "Oh shit," I said, holding one hand against my head and the other against my stomach. I had achieved the mother of all hangovers.

I turned to see Grace passed out beside me on the grungy couch. "Grace." I shook her and she groaned and made a pained sound, whimpering like an injured animal.

Daria helped us get up, and we headed to our rooms.

I worshipped at the porcelain altar of a vengeful god all morning before passing out again.

Later, I went to Grace's dorm and found the door cracked. "You okay?" I asked as I walked in.

"Yeah, come in," she said. I found her lying on the floor, her face pressed to the germ-y carpet. Her pallor had a greenish tint to it.

Swaying in the doorway, I dry heaved and then braced myself against her desk. "Are you sure you're okay?"

"Ouch," she said, sounding like E.T. She reached her index finger out toward me and said, "Eliot, phone home."

Chuckling weakly, I pressed my hand to my forehead and buckled over. "Shit, don't make me laugh, my head is killing me." I moved across the room and sat on the edge of the bed, my head drooping between my legs. "We got so messed up yesterday."

"We got fucking married, Matt." She opened her bloodshot eyes wide for emphasis.

"I know." Although a part of me hadn't been totally sure until now.

I looked across the room at myself in the mirror. My hair was sticking up in every direction, and there was a mysterious stain across my white T-shirt.

"Holy. Shit," she said.

"What?"

"What are we gonna do? Was that even really official?"

I pointed to her finger, where I had placed a ring made out of a gum wrapper. I held up my own matching gum-wrapper ring. "I mean . . ."

"Wait. Did you say 'nanu-nanu' when you put this ring on my finger?" she asked. I gave her a guilty smile and nodded. "Oh my god, I can't believe you did this for a bet, Matt! What is wrong with you?"

"Wait, what? How did you know?"

"Tati came by this morning and proceeded to roll around on the floor, laughing her ass off, while I puked my guts out. She said she'd been bluffing and couldn't believe you went through with it. All news to me, thank you very much."

"That bitch," I whispered. "She still owes us a night out."

"You're an asshole."

"Hold on a second. You stood there, right next to me, with Gary Busey as our witness, and said I do. I didn't force you to do anything."

She sat up and held her head. "I was fucking wasted, Matt."

"Grace, wait, let's calm down and go lie on your bed."

"No. No way. We need to figure how to get this thing annulled. Like, today."

"We can get it annulled tomorrow. Let's just take a shower and go back to sleep, okay?" She sat there, rubbing her head for a few seconds. "Or, and this is just a thought . . . maybe we don't have to get it annulled?"

She looked up, shocked. "What? Have you lost your damn mind?"

Her tone was like a knife to the heart. She wouldn't even entertain the idea. Granted, it wasn't exactly an ideal way to get married, but she acted like the idea of being married to me repulsed her.

"You want everything from me, Grace, and then you act like this? Like being married to me is the worst thing in the world? Why don't you just go to Europe with Pornsake? What difference does it make? We're so young, and we should get to do everything we want to do. Isn't that what you always say?"

"You know what? I *should* get to do everything I want to do. Tati's right; maybe I'm turning down a great opportunity just to stay here and wait for you. Maybe I will go with Pornsake after all." As the words left her mouth, I felt both of us tense up. I waited for her to turn to me, to apologize, to take it all back. But she turned away. She wouldn't even look at me. "Leave me alone. I can't deal with you right now."

I stood up from the bed, fuming. "Don't worry. You won't have to deal with me ever again." I stormed out of her room and slammed the door. I didn't know what had happened, but in the span of a minute, I felt like my whole fucking life was over.

I waited a day, hoping she would come to me and apologize.

Nothing.

I waited another day, resisting the urge to apologize myself.

On the third day, I slipped the annulment paperwork under Grace's door, if only to get her to talk to me. I heard her crying that night through the wall and then she played the Bach suite on her cello for three hours straight. I fell asleep with my ear to the wall.

Still nothing. Not a single word exchanged between us.

Days turned into a week. A week turned into weeks. We didn't talk. I didn't even see her. I felt like shit. When I'd hear her door open or close, it took everything in me not to run out into the hall and grab her and say, *What the fuck are we doing to each other?*

17. We Belong Together

GRACE

We hadn't talked for weeks, and all the while I was brutally aware of time passing. Matt was going to leave for South America in six days.

I had lost so much weight since our fight, and I felt weak and sick all the time. It was impossible to concentrate on anything, or even think about having a social life.

Tati apologized profusely for being at least partly responsible for that afternoon that ended everything between me and Matt. "It's probably for the best. You didn't want to pull a Jacki Reed anyway, did you?"

Jacki Reed was a girl I went to high school with, and I used to tell her story to my friends like a cautionary tale. Jacki Reed used to brag at the lunch tables about her college boyfriend off in Nevada somewhere. For a long time, none of the other senior girls at my high school even believed the dude existed. Jacki always acted like they were so evolved because they were in a long-distance relationship—like that meant he liked her more. She actually referred to it as an LDR. I told her that you can't make up acronyms for everything; people won't know what you're talking about. When we graduated, she enrolled in a shitty junior college in Nevada just to be near him, even though she got accepted to Yale. He dumped her two months later. Now she lives back home and works at the Dairy Queen. We all thought she was the biggest moron.

Poor foolish girl was probably just in love.

It wasn't Tati's fault, or the Jacki Reed story. Matt and I fell apart because the walls were closing in on us. Him serving the annulment papers to me proved to me that he wasn't all-in like he said he was. He probably realized what I had realized: we were on separate paths.

Graduation was approaching so I spent a lot of time in my room, filling out forms for grants and trying to hide from everyone. Matt tried to stop me in the hall once, but I ignored him. I regretted it later when I saw that he had left a sandwich for me outside my door. I cried the entire time I ate it.

There was a stack of mail on my desk that I had been ignoring for a week because I knew what one particular piece contained. It was in a regular envelope, addressed to me by my mother. There's nothing cheery about a standard, white envelope. I picked it up and stared at it. The front return address was blurry, like someone had spilled water on it. I realized, after reading the letter, that it could have been her tears.

Finally, one morning, I decided to open it.

Dear Graceland,

I'm so sorry that I couldn't tell you this in person but there is just not enough money in the bank to pay for a

*flight home for you this summer. Your brother needed
a new backpack for school and we hadn't bought your
sisters any new school clothes this year. Everything is
falling apart. How can I say these words to you? Your
father's drinking has gotten to be too much for me. We
are getting a divorce and he is going to live with your
uncle. Your brother and sisters and I are going to move
into Grandma's until we can get on our feet.*

*I know your father loves you and we are so proud
of you. We don't want you to take any of this on as
your burden. Right now we just can't help out, and I
don't think we will be able to afford to come for your
graduation. Please understand. You've always been so
independent, and we didn't think you would want us
there anyway. You've always been able to make ends meet
on your own, Grace, and we are proud of you for that. We
love you. When you can afford it, come home and visit
and we will make a bed for you on Grandma's couch.*

*I must tell you we had to sell the piano and some of
your things that I don't think you wanted anyway to help
pay for your sister's tooth. We love you. Keep doing a
good job.*

Love, Mom

To say I was hysterical would be an understatement.
I could not stop crying. *How could they?* I thought. How
could they just abandon me because of their own mistakes?
I didn't even have a car or money to live on, and my mother
was using my sister's tooth as an excuse again when I had
given her half of my student loan for it. Where had that
money even gone? It was all too depressing to think about.

The second envelope was a notice from the Student Financial Services office stating that I still owed eight hundred dollars for housing. Sitting in the corner of my room as the tears ran steadily down my cheeks, I thought about all the things I could do. I could do some cello gigs, but that would be a minimal amount of money.

With my knees propped up and my head dropped down between them, I sobbed. I could sell my cello. I could go home and live on my grandma's couch and get a job at the Dairy Queen. I could give up.

And then I heard Matt mumble, "Baby?" as he pushed my door open. I hadn't heard his voice in three weeks.

"I'm fine, Matt."

He came over to me. "What happened?"

Without looking up, I held the two tear-soaked pieces of mail toward him. He read them quietly, then sat down next to me.

"I can help you."

"No."

He brushed his thumb over my cheek, capturing the tears. "I have money to cover this."

"No, Matt. You're going to ask your dad and I don't want him bailing me out again."

"It's not my father's money. I sold a photo. I was going to tell you but you wouldn't fucking talk to me."

"I thought we were broken up." I stood, walked over to my desk, and grabbed the paperwork I had received confirming our annulment. I tossed it to him. "And you divorced me."

Matt quickly made a paper airplane out of it and sailed it out of my open dorm window. "I hereby declare you my ex-wife. So what? Who cares. It means nothing."

I stared at him.

"It's not gonna be that easy, is it?" he said.

"I need time."

"We don't have much."

I sat on the windowsill, looking out at the lone tree in the courtyard, swaying back and forth. "That's my problem. Time." I turned to him. "Which photo did you sell?"

"The one of you. The first day we met. The one where you're picking the button off the floor. Mr. Nelson chose it for the university gallery and it sold the first day. I jokingly put a thousand dollars on the price tag, thinking no one would buy it. It's as much your money as it is mine. I want you to have it." His look was sincere and sweet. We were talking and it felt good.

"It's not mine."

"Well, as my ex-wife . . ." He started laughing. "We might have been married at the time the photograph sold. Who would know?"

I couldn't help but laugh, too. "We were married for a couple of days. And anyway, it would be fifty-fifty."

"Okay, fine. I will take the other five hundred and then give it back to you for all the modeling work you've done for me."

"I wish I could really laugh about this, but I'm just so angry with my parents right now. I can't believe they act like I wouldn't want them here for my graduation," I said.

"It's their way of making themselves feel less guilty."

"They're gonna fuck me up with this pressure."

"No." He was suddenly serious. "No, they're not. As soon as you stop thinking that way and you see how amazing you are, all that resentment you have for them will turn into gratitude. You'll be like, 'I'm glad my parents didn't give a shit because it made me fuckin' awesome.'"

Letting his words sink in, I sat there quietly for several moments. I knew what he meant. "Yeah, I guess. Someday I'll be like, 'Thanks, Mom and Dad. You fuckers.'"

"Exactly!" Matt said, triumphantly.

"Thanks, Matt."

"Anytime," he said, standing up and walking toward the door. "Hey, will you stay here for a bit? I need to run and get something."

"Okay."

He returned a short while later with donut holes, orange juice, a tiny practice amp, and an electric guitar that I recognized as one of Brandon's. I was lying on my bed so I turned on my side, propping my elbow under my head, and watched Matt move around the room. He put three rainbow-sprinkled donut holes on a plate and handed it to me, along with the mini bottle of orange juice. He didn't say a word; he just gave me a small smile. It was early but already hot and stuffy in the room.

He kicked off his shoes and pulled his Smiths T-shirt over his head then threw it at me. "You can wear it if you want."

"Matt . . ."

"What, you like wearing my shirts."

That was true. I stripped down to my bra and underwear and then pulled Matt's T-shirt on. That Matt smell made me feel all warm and tingly.

"See? Better," he said. I nodded.

He wore only his black jeans and the belt I had made for him, with his wallet chain swaying back and forth as he moved around the room.

Squatting near the amp, he plugged it into the wall and looked up at me. Tears were filling my eyes again. "You okay?"

I nodded. I wasn't crying about the letter or the money or the photo; I was crying because the thought of Matt leaving, even just for a few months, killed me. He would be leaving in a week. He'd be a world away, and I would be left behind, crying over being too young to give it all up or to ask him to give it all up. Crying that I hadn't met him later, when getting married would have made sense and neither one of us would have freaked out.

My face was throbbing and puffy with tears as I watched him sit on a wooden stool and position the green-and-white Telecaster on his thigh. He strummed it once and looked up for approval. It wasn't loud; it was a perfect, clean sound. I had never seen him play an instrument or even attempt to, but something became very clear to me in that moment. Matt had been practicing . . . for me.

"Before I start, I just want you to know that I'm sorry."

"I'm sorry, too," I said, instantly.

"Can we please go back to the way things were?"

"But what about . . ."

"Grace, can we please enjoy the time we have with each other?"

"Yes." I burst into tears.

His fingers plucked one note and I knew he was playing "Hallelujah." I cried even more.

He sang the words softly and flawlessly. I marveled at him, so young and beautiful, sitting shirtless and barefoot, with undeterred focus. When he was finished, he strummed one last time and looked up at me. At that point I was a blubbering fool. His smile was a pitying, sad kind of smile, reserved only for when a person knows there's nothing that can be said to make things right. He was leaving. And I couldn't stop him.

In a shaky voice, I told him how beautiful his playing was and I asked how he learned the song. He told me that Brandon would sometimes hang out at the PhotoHut, so he had asked if Brandon would teach it to him. He'd practiced it over and over for me since the Jeff Buckley concert so I'd finally get to hear it live.

18. We Were in Love

GRACE

The last weeks of the semester passed by, and with them came more pressure from Tati and Dan to join the orchestra. I always said no.

They were set to leave for their first stop in France in early August, so at least I had Tati for part of the summer. Matt would be leaving in the beginning of June, right after graduation.

One day, while eating sandwiches near the fountain in Washington Square Park, Tati said to me, "If Matt stays in South America longer than the summer, you should join the tour."

"First of all, he's not gonna stay down there longer than three months. And second, I'm going to grad school and *that's* the reason I'm not joining the tour. You know that."

"How are you gonna pay for it?"

"I'm staying at Senior House for the summer for cheap while I get some paying gigs."

"Dan said we're going to be making good money. You could always save up and go to grad school later."

"No, I can't. I can't just leave and go cruising around Europe with you guys for a year and a half. Why do you always bring this up?"

"Calm down, Grace. Shit, you always get bent out of shape over this. You can mess up your life for a guy all you want to," she mumbled.

I couldn't take it anymore. I got up and walked away.

She came running after me so I gave her a little piece of my mind. "You think I'm bent out of shape? Because I don't want to run away and join Dan's circus? May I remind you that you couldn't stand him before? And since when do you call him Dan?"

"I'm sorry Matt is leaving and that you're going to be miserable."

"That's not it at all." Though that was totally it.

"Dan really cares for you. For all of us. He bought that picture Matt took because he knew you guys needed the money."

"What?" I stared at her in shock, my emotions spinning out of control. "Why do you want to hurt me when you know I'm already hurting so badly?"

"I don't. I just want you to do the right thing for you, not for you and Matt. It sounds like he's doing what's right for him."

We were standing at the entrance to the subway. "I gotta go, Tati." I ran down the stairs and took the next train that arrived, riding around for hours to clear my head.

By late afternoon I was sitting in front of Orvin's closed shop, wishing I could talk to him, when Dan passed by.

"Grace, Orvin's is closed on Sundays," Dan said.

"Yeah, I realize that."

He was staring down at me with his kind smile. "Can I sit?"

"Sure."

"Something you want to talk about?"

"No."

"Have you been practicing?"

"Of course." The last thing I needed was Dan with his professor hat on. I turned and looked at him pointedly. "Why'd you buy that photo?"

He didn't miss a beat. "Because I liked it."

"That had to have been the highest price paid for a piece of student artwork. Ever. In the history of college artwork."

"Honestly, Grace, you know I'm a straight shooter. It's a beautiful photograph and I think Matt's work will be worth something someday."

"You didn't buy it because you knew we needed the money?"

"Not at all." *Little white lies.* "Will you tell me what's bothering you?"

I shook my head and looked down to his lap, where he was holding a few folded sheets of paper. "Is that new music?"

"No, actually, this is the paperwork to get my last name changed. Believe it or not, I could handle it as a professor, but as a composer and conductor, I need something new."

"So you're changing your name? Just like that?"

"Yeah, I even ran the idea by my father, thinking he would be offended, but he told he was happy to have the name end with him. I'm making a small adjustment from Pornsake to Porter."

"Daniel Porter. That has a nice ring to it."

"Why thank you, Graceland."

Hot wind blasted my face from a passing bus. I felt a tinge of nausea and closed my eyes.

"You okay, Grace?"

"I feel like I'm gonna throw up." And then, just like that, I was heaving the pastrami on rye I'd had in the park with Tati into a nearby trash can.

Dan was rubbing my back and repeating nice things to me. "Get it all out . . . that's it."

I stood up straight. "Jesus, that was gross." I wiped my mouth. "I better get home, I feel like crap."

"It'll be okay, Grace. Whatever you're going through, you'll figure it out," he called out to me as I headed toward my dorm.

"Thanks, Professor." I held up my hand as I walked away.

"It's Dan!"

AS THE DAYS careened past me in a rush, I tried to memorize every moment with Matt. When I wasn't with him, I wished I was. One day, he brought a betta fish to my room after class. "I bought him to keep you company while I'm gone. His name is Jeff Buckley."

I laughed and then leaned up and kissed him. "Thank you, you're sweet." But, really, I only wanted Matt to keep me company.

I spent graduation day with Matt and his dad and stepmom. After the ceremony we had dinner and went back to Matt's dorm, where he and I stayed for the next few days. He wouldn't let me out of his sight.

On June fourth, the day before Matt left, while he was at the doctor getting necessary inoculations for his trip, I stopped into my favorite café in the East Village for a coffee. I was sitting at the bar, looking out the front window, when I overheard the café owner's daughter, who worked as a waitress there, mumbling about an "utter tragedy." She was crying to her father as he held her. An older, hippie-looking woman came over and wiped down the wooden bar top. "Did you hear?"

I shook my head.

"They found his body."

I didn't know what she was talking about.

She sighed heavily. "Poor guy, used to hang out around here all the time."

"Who?"

"Buckley."

I put my hand over my heart. "*Jeff* Buckley?"

"The very same. Handsome kid. So talented, gone too soon."

Her eyes crinkled as she shook her head mournfully.

"What happened?" I could barely speak.

She stopped cleaning and stared out the window in a daze. Her voice was low and wobbly, like she was on the verge of tears. "Drowned in the Mississippi with his damn boots on. He'd been missing, and they just found his body on the shore. Used to see him walk by here all the time."

I melted into sobs, feeling such sadness for someone I didn't even know but had felt intensely connected to for so long. It was the first time I really thought about how fleeting it all is. *Was this life?* I wondered. You can spend hours upon hours engaged in meaningless, arbitrary bullshit, and then die while taking a dip in the river, your bloated body washing up onshore like discarded trash, only to be buried and forgotten?

The first time someone young and vibrant dies—someone you look up to, someone you relate to—it blows you back, right off your feet. *Oh, fuck, we're all gonna die, nobody knows when, nobody knows how,* you think. And in that moment, you realize how little control you have over your own destiny. From the time you're born, you have no control; you can't choose your parents, and, unless you're suicidal, you can't choose your death. The only thing you can do is choose the person you love, be kind to others, and make your brutally short stint on earth as pleasant as possible.

I left the café in a blur of tears, too sick to finish my coffee. The waitress wouldn't let me pay, probably because she didn't realize how much the news would affect me. "It's on me, hon." I nodded gratefully and ran all the way back to Senior House. When I saw Matt standing outside the building, I slammed right into his chest and dissolved.

"Grace, what is it?"

I rubbed my tears and snot all over his shirt and broke the news through sobs. "Jeff . . . Buckley's . . . dead."

"Oh, baby, it's okay." He rubbed my back and swayed with me. "Shh, don't worry, we can get you another fish."

I pulled away and looked up at him. "No. The *real* Jeff Buckley."

His face turned ashen. "Oh shit. How?"

"Drowned a few days ago. They found his body today."

"That's terrible." He held me to his chest, and I could hear his heart beating fast.

"I know, I can't believe it," I said through tears.

But the truth was, I wasn't sad for Jeff Buckley as much as I was sad for Matt and for me. For us. For the short time we had left together.

If I asked, would you stay?

He knew my thoughts somehow. He bent and kissed me once on each cheek, then my forehead, then my chin, then my lips. "I'm going to miss you."

"I'm going to miss you, too," I said through my tears.

"Grace, will you do something with me?"

"Anything." *Ask me to go with you. Tell me you'll stay. Tell me you'll marry me. For real this time.*

"Let's go right now and get tattoos."

"Okay," I said, a little stunned. Not exactly what I was expecting, but I would do anything he asked in that moment.

We each got three words in wispy script. Mine went across the back of my neck, just at the base, and Matt's went across his chest, right over his heart. We each chose the words for the other, writing them down on a piece of paper and handing them to the two tattoo artists. We didn't know what they would be until the ink was pierced into our skin. It was like our version of a blood oath.

While we were getting tattooed, we stole glances at each other and smiled. I wondered what he was thinking. All the times he told me that he cared for me still wasn't enough. It was never enough when I knew he was leaving the next day.

My tattoo was done first, and I used a mirror to read what Matt had chosen. The type was small and looked cute and feminine, and I loved it before I even read it. I looked closely and saw the words: *Green-eyed lovebird.*

"It's perfect!" I squealed. Matt watched me, smiling happily, trying not to look down at his own tattoo.

When his was done, he stared into a handheld mirror with curious eyes. "'just the ash.' Is this Leonard Cohen?"

"Yep. You know it?"

"What's the whole quote again?"

I swallowed hard and tried not to cry, but my entire body was betraying me. The tattoo artists walked away and gave us a moment. Matt stood from the chair and wrapped his arms around me carefully, tucking me against his chest on the opposite side of his bandaged tattoo.

"'Poetry is just the evidence of life. If your life is burning well, poetry is just the ash.'"

He buried his face in my hair. "My life is burning well."

Yes, but for how long?

Even though it was still healing, I must have kissed the words over his chest a hundred times that night. He'd kiss the back of my neck and tell me how much he was going to miss his green-eyed lovebird, and then I would call him a cheese ball and we would laugh and then I would cry.

The next morning, Tati left to borrow her dad's Chrysler to take Matt to the airport. Meanwhile, Matt rushed around trying to pack everything that he wasn't taking with him so he could ship it back to L.A.

"Why are you sending all your stuff back? You can just leave it in my room." I was lying on my stomach across his bed, watching him scurry around frantically.

"Because I don't want you to have to deal with any of my shit."

"I want to deal with your shit."

He stopped and looked at me. "It's better this way."

"But you're coming back?"

"Yeah, but I hope to have a job by then so I can live in a real apartment. I'm not coming back to New York to live in Senior House."

"Senior House is for undergrads. I'll be in a new dorm by the time you're back," I mumbled into the pillow.

"All the more reason. I don't want you to have to move my stuff when I can easily ship it to L.A. and get it later." He was frustrated.

"You're only going to be gone for a few months, Matt. It's a lot of hassle."

"Right, but you never know."

This was not a good time for phrases like "you never know."

"Come here," I said. I rolled onto my back and held my arms open to him. I was wearing his favorite dress. He glanced over his shoulder and his eyes turned soft. Stalking toward me, he smiled his sweet, sexy smile. As he bent to kiss me, I stopped him right before his lips touched mine and whispered, "Would you stay if I asked you to?"

He jerked back and crossed his arms over his chest, cocking his head to the side. "Would you ask me to?" Frustration could be read in every line on his face.

Lying there beneath him, I felt more vulnerable than I ever had before. I wanted to ask him to stay, but how could I be so selfish? If I asked him, would he love me less, if he even loved me at all? I couldn't take his dream away to make mine better. I wouldn't do it. I wouldn't destroy what we had created.

"Answer me. Would you fucking ask me to turn this down?"

I didn't want him to, but I just needed to know if he would. "Would you stay if I asked you to?"

His jaw clenched. He was breathing heavily. Through gritted teeth, he seethed, "Yes, but I'd hate you for it. So ask me. Go ahead." It felt like he was taunting me. I began to cry. "Ask me to fucking stay here and work at the PhotoHut while you go to grad school. Do it."

I shook my head but couldn't form the words.

He bent over and gripped my face hard, glaring into my eyes. "Fucking Christ, Grace, this isn't good-bye. This is 'see you later.' Tell me you can handle that, please. Say that you can handle that."

I was hyperventilating now. He was angry but his expression revealed love beneath the ferocity.

"We made no promises to each other," I whispered. "I'm sorry I brought it up. We'll just see how things go, okay? This is just a 'see you later.'"

He nodded. "That's right."

You told me I was yours and you were mine.

Sniffling, I said, "Make love to me?" And then he did, sweet and tender and so full of emotion that I cried as he held me for a long time after, though it wasn't nearly long enough.

A few hours later, we drove to JFK. Tati stayed in the car while I walked Matt to his gate at the airport.

"I'll try to call you as soon as I can."

"Okay. Where will you be?"

"Northern Bolivia at first." He had a duffel bag slung over his shoulder but set it down and stared at his shoes. "Grace, I don't know how remote it's going to be down there. You might not hear from me for a while, but I'll write to you and we can figure out how to call each other." He squinted into my eyes as we memorized each other's face. "Grace, Pornsake bought the photo."

I blinked. "I know. Why did you wait to tell me until now?"

"I just thought you should know. He's a good guy."

"How nice of you. And how nice of him," I said, sarcastically.

"I didn't want you to find out that I knew and didn't tell you."

"Okay." I understood. Matt was trying not to leave loose ends.

An airline worker announced final boarding over the speaker. "It's time." He opened his arms and I rushed into them with such force, like I was trying to jump inside of him so he could take me along, a stowaway inside his heart. He squeezed me hard and for a long time. "I'll see you, Grace."

We let go of each other and stepped apart. "I'll see you later, Matt."

He smiled and walked away. Just before he reached the Jetway, he turned back, pulled something out of his pocket, and held it up. "I stole this, just so you know!"

It was a practice tape, a recording of me playing the cello. He laughed and then he was gone.

The love of my life was gone.

19. What Happened to Us?

GRACE

The day after Matt left, I auditioned for a grunge band as a cellist at a little venue off Allen Street in the East Village. Their music was like Nirvana, with haunting runs and loud, screaming choruses. I imagined that we would end up on VH1's *Unplugged*, and I'd have an awesome career as a rock cellist, guesting for all the who's-who bands in New York. I felt like I was finally following my dreams.

I kept to myself, played well, practiced a lot, and collected my money at the end of the week. For three nights, I made a hundred and twenty dollars. Things were promising, and I was excited to tell Matt about it.

A week and a half after he left, he called for the first time. I was practicing in my room when Daria knocked on my door and yelled, "Grace! Matt's on the phone for you in the lounge."

I ran down the stairs, wearing nothing but one of Matt's

T-shirts and an old tattered pair of underwear. I didn't care—I was so fucking excited.

"Hello!" I said, out of breath.

"Fuck, this phone call is costing me, like, seventy bucks."

My excitement died a little at his greeting. "Oh, I'm sorry."

"Never mind. Oh my god, I have so much to tell you."

"Tell me."

"*National Geographic* is launching a television channel in September. There's going to be tons of new job openings, and I've already totally impressed Elizabeth."

"Who's Elizabeth?"

"She's the lead photographer on this project. She's supercool and she personally picked me for the internship after she saw my portfolio. I didn't even know."

I wanted to ask him how old she was and if she was pretty. "I'm so happy for you, Matt."

He yelled, "I'll be right there!" to someone in the background. "Hey, Gracie, I had to take a bus three hours to get to this phone. There's nothing down here so I don't know when I'll be able to call you again."

"Okay, no worries."

"I gotta go. The next bus is leaving soon, and they're holding it for me. Hey, I miss you." The last part sounded like such an afterthought that it made my stomachache.

"I miss you, too. See ya."

"Bye." He hung up.

It's not good-bye. It's not good-bye. Never say good-bye.

Staring at my bare feet, I thought about how he didn't ask me what I was up to. I never even got a chance to tell him about the band gigs.

Tati stood there, leaning against the doorjamb of the front door with her arms crossed over her chest. "Where are your pants?"

"That was Matt."

"I figured. Are you gonna get dressed today? I've come to pick you up for lunch. You can tell me all about it then."

"Yeah."

"Come on." She motioned with her head toward the door.

"Okay," I said. "Sandwiches?"

"Anything's better than ramen."

Tati and I met for lunch every Wednesday for the next month. Sometime in early July, she asked if I had talked to Matt, and I told her no.

"How come he hasn't called?"

"I might have missed him. I don't know, he's in the middle of nowhere. It's hard to coordinate these things. I'm sure he's fine."

When I got home that day, one of the summer RAs had taped an envelope to my door with a note that said, *Way to go, Matt!* I had told her all about Matt's internship since she was a photography major at Tisch, plus I was always checking in with her to find out if Matt had called.

I opened it up to find an article from a photography magazine. The cover was a photograph of Matt taking a picture of a woman taking a photograph of herself in a mirror. The headline said, "The Beauty Behind the Camera."

I swallowed hard and tried to fight the nausea as I read all about the young, beautiful Elizabeth Hunt, who was making a huge name for herself at *National Geographic*. And then, at the very end, I read three sentences that changed the course of my life forever.

Hunt points out that her partnership with Matthias Shore, a promising young talent who recently emerged from New York University's Tisch School of the Arts, has proven to be a fruitful union. Their next assignment includes a six-month expedition off the coast of Australia, exploring the Great Barrier Reef and the great white shark's breaching behavior while hunting. "Matt and I are thrilled about this opportunity and excited to take our partnership to the next level," Hunt said.

We were so young, and life was already offering so many twists and turns. But did I have to accept what I had just read without arguing my case?

No way.

I immediately called Aletha in a daze. "Hello, Aletha, it's Grace."

"So good to hear from you, dear. How are you? Everything okay?"

"Fine," I said with little emotion. "I wondered if you had heard from Matt?"

"Oh yes, sweetie, I just talked to him yesterday."

I was gutted. Why hadn't he called me? I was practically sleeping by the phone in the lounge. "You did? What did he say?"

"Oh, we're all so proud of Matt. He's really making a name for himself in such a short time."

"Yes, I've heard," I said, somewhat icily.

"Nothing can slow down Matt's career, and his father is so proud of him. You know what that means to Matt."

"Oh, wonderful." My voice was shrinking by the second. "Did he mention me by any chance?"

"He said if anyone asks, to let them know that he's okay." *Anyone?*

"Well . . . I guess if you hear from him in the next couple of days, will you ask him to call me?"

"Yes, of course, Grace. He's been calling every week, so I'll let him know."

Oh, he has, has he?

I hung up with Aletha and ran back to my room, barely able to comprehend all the new information I had just learned. Elizabeth Hunt . . . Australia for six months . . . Weekly phone calls with his mom . . .

Three more days went by, with still no word from Matt. I dragged myself out of bed, too tired to cry and too sad to eat. I went to the lounge and called Tati.

"Hello?"

"It's Grace."

"Hey, how are you?"

"Can you come over?"

"I'll be there in a bit." She could hear the pain in my voice.

She came thundering into my room fifteen minutes later. I held the article about Matt and Elizabeth out to her. She read it to herself. All she did was shake her head and offer me a cigarette.

"I'm okay, Tati."

"Don't overreact, Grace," she said.

"I'm not overreacting." By then I had stopped crying. "Just let Dan know I'm in. I'm going on tour with you guys."

Tati grinned back at me. "Good. You won't regret it."

THIRD MOVEMENT:
NOW, FIFTEEN YEARS LATER

20. You Remembered . . .

GRACE

The present is our own. The right-this-second, the here-and-now, this moment before the next, is ours for the taking. It's the only free gift the universe has to offer. The past doesn't belong to us anymore, and the future is just a fantasy, never guaranteed. But the present is ours to own. The only way we can realize that fantasy is if we embrace the now.

I had been closed off for a long time, and I hadn't allowed myself to imagine the future because I was still stuck in the past. Though it was impossible, I had tried to re-create what Matt and I once had. I wanted nothing else; he was all I could imagine.

But Orvin once told me that time is the currency of life. And I had lost so much of it. It was that idea of lost time that finally made me realize I needed to move on, that I would never have what I once had with Matt. I had to mourn our relationship and move on.

At least, that's what I told myself.

Two months ago I was walking around in a thick fog of regret. I was going through the motions but wasn't feeling anything. I'd stare at my new wrinkles in the mirror and wonder where they came from. I wasted more time, repeating the same thing day in and day out, barely present in my own life. I wasn't looking to break out of the cycle in search of anything meaningful.

Until I saw Matt in the subway station.

Everything changed. I could see in color again, every image vivid and crisp.

Over the last fifteen years, the pain of what had happened to us waxed and waned. Many times I tried to force myself to stop thinking about him, but there were too many reminders. I thought, if I ever saw him again, he'd look right through me, like I was a ghost from his past. That's how he made me feel that summer after college: someone who no longer existed.

But when I saw him in the station, his eyes locked on mine. He recognized me instantly, and all I could see in his face was pure wonder. It was like he was seeing the sunset over the ocean for the first time. As my train disappeared into the tunnel, his expression turned to desperation, and that's when I knew there was a missing piece to our story. What was behind his desperation? What had happened to him in the last fifteen years that would send him running down the platform, his hand outstretched, his eyes full of longing?

I needed to find the answer. I had an idea of where I could find Matt, but I was too scared to look.

"Ms. Porter?"

"Yes, Eli?" I stared into the big blue eyes of one of my senior trombone players as I cleaned up sheet music from a table. We were in the band room at the high school where I taught.

"Do you know what Craigslist is?"

I smiled. "Of course. I'm not that old, Eli."

He blushed. "I know you're not." He seemed nervous. "I'm asking because I saw your tattoo the other day when you put your hair up." He swallowed.

"Go on," I said, totally curious.

"'Green-eyed Lovebird.' That's what it says, right?"

I nodded.

"Did someone used to call you that?"

"Yes, someone I used to know." My pulse quickened at the thought. *Where is he going with this?*

He fished a folded rectangle of paper out of his pocket. "So remember when we did that band tournament and there was that girl from Southwest High who played the tuba?"

"Sure." I had no idea what he was talking about.

"Well, I kind of thought we had a connection but neither of us acted on it. Anyway, I was looking to see if she posted a message for me in the Missed Connections section of Craigslist when I saw this."

He unfolded the paper and handed it to me.

To the Green-Eyed Lovebird:

We met fifteen years ago, almost to the day, when I moved my stuff into the NYU dorm room next to yours at Senior House.

You called us fast friends. I like to think it was more.

We lived on nothing but the excitement of finding ourselves through music (you were obsessed with Jeff Buckley), photography (I couldn't stop taking pictures of you), hanging out in Washington Square Park, and all the weird things we did to make money. I learned more about myself that year than any other.

Yet, somehow, it all fell apart. We lost touch the summer after graduation, when I went to South America to work for National Geographic. When I came back, you were gone. A part of me still wonders if I pushed you too hard after the wedding . . .

I didn't see you again until a month ago. It was a Wednesday. You were rocking back on your heels, balancing on that thick yellow line that runs along the subway platform, waiting for the F train. I didn't know it was you until it was too late, and then you were gone. Again. You said my name; I saw it on your lips. I tried to will the train to stop, just so I could say hello.

After seeing you, all of the youthful feelings and memories came flooding back to me, and now I've spent the better part of a month wondering what your life is like. I might be totally out of my mind, but would you like to get a drink with me and catch up on the last decade and a half?

M
(212)-555-3004

My mouth was open in shock as I reread it to myself three times.

"Ms. Porter, is this letter for you? Do you know this M person?"

"Yes," I said, my voice shaking. Tears began to fill my eyes. I reached out and hugged him. "Thank you."

"That's pretty cool. I didn't think those posts ever worked. Good thing you have that tattoo. Are you gonna call the dude?"

"I think so. Listen, Eli, I really appreciate what you've done, but I need to head out. Can I take this?" I held up the paper.

"Of course. It's yours."

I gave him a grateful, teary smile, grabbed my things, and hurried to the steps at the front of the school to call Tati.

She answered right away. "Hello?"

"Hey, are you busy?"

"I'm at the salon," she said. Soon after we graduated from college, Tati got dumped by Brandon. She immediately ran out, cut her hair very short, and dyed it jet black. She'd been wearing it that way for fifteen years, I think as a reminder of some kind. She hadn't been in a committed relationship since Brandon, except for the one she had with her hairdresser.

"Can I meet you there?"

"Sure. What's up? Why do you sound so weird?"

"I don't." I was breathing hard.

"Okay, come on over."

Remember speed-walking? It was a short-lived exercise fad in the eighties. It's a really goofy way of walking so fast that your hips jut from side to side. It's actually an Olympic event still.

I speed-walked six blocks to the salon so fast, I could've won a gold medal.

I exploded through the door and found Tati in the first chair, wearing one of those black salon capes. Her hair was coated in purplish-black dye and covered in a cellophane cap while her hairdresser gave her a shoulder massage.

"I'm processing," Tati said, pointing to her head.

"Hi," I said to her hairdresser, "I can do that."

The girl smiled and walked away. I stood behind Tati and started rubbing her shoulders.

"Ooh, easy, your cello hands are too rough," she whined.

"Oh, shut it. I have to talk to you."

"Talk then."

"He wants to meet with me."

"What are you talking about?" I had told Tati about seeing Matt on the subway, but that had been two months ago.

"Read this." I handed her the piece of paper.

A moment later she was sniffling.

"Are you crying?" I asked from behind her.

"I must be hormonal. This is just so sad. Why does he sound so oblivious in this post?"

"I don't know."

"You have to call him. Grace. You need to go home right now and call him."

"What do I say?"

"Just feel him out and see what his deal is. I think this sounds like the old Matt, thoughtful and deep."

"I know, right?"

She popped out of the chair, looked at me, and pointed toward the door. "Go, Now."

21. I Looked for You Inside of Everyone Else

MATT

One Tuesday, a few weeks after I posted the letter for Grace to Craigslist, I was walking to my building from the subway when my eight-year-old nephew called, wanting to know if I'd sponsor his jog-a-thon. I adored the kid and said I totally would, but just as I was about to hang up with him, his mother got on the line.

"Matthias, it's Monica."

"Hey. How's Alexander?"

"Great. Working like a dog and outshining all the other partners, as usual. You know Alexander."

"Sure do," I said, not unbitterly. "And you? How's life in Beverly Hills?"

"Cut the shit, Matthias."

"What's up, Monica?"

"Elizabeth called me and said she and Brad are having a baby." My sister-in-law could win an award for figurative ball size.

"Yeah, I'm aware. I get the privilege of working with those assholes every day."

"She was my sister for eight years, Matthias. Don't you think I have the right to know?"

I laughed. "You guys weren't exactly pals, so calling her your 'sister' is ridiculous. And she *left* me, remember?"

"You're an ass. She wouldn't have left you if you weren't so hung up on Grace."

"Grace had nothing to do with my marriage or divorce."

"Yeah right. Elizabeth said you never got rid of your photos of her."

"I never get rid of any photos I take. Why would I? I'm a photographer. Grace was the subject of a lot of my early work. Elizabeth knows that better than anyone. Also, why are we even having this conversation?"

"I just wanted to make sure she gets a gift from us."

"The postal service can help you with that. She still lives in our old apartment. You know, the one I gave up so she could play house and make babies with her boyfriend."

"Husband," she corrected.

"Bye, Monica. Tell Alexander I said hi."

I hung up, took a deep breath, and wondered again, for the tenth time that week, what the fuck had happened to my life.

When I got to work, I found Scott getting coffee in the break room.

"You get any responses from that post?" he asked.

"Nope, just a few really sweet ladies who offered to be my green-eyed lovebird."

"Dude, what's your problem? Take advantage of the situation. She'll probably never see it, but that doesn't mean she's the only green-eyed lovebird out there." He batted his eyelashes at me.

"That's the thing. On my way here, I was thinking about my life."

"Uh-oh."

"No, listen. My first girlfriend, Monica, and I had this stupid relationship that was all about being fake and trying to impress each other and everyone else."

"You were young. So what?"

"It was the same thing with Elizabeth, at least in the beginning. My relationship with Monica set the precedent for my marriage with Elizabeth. When things got real, neither of us could handle it. It wasn't like that with Grace. Ever. It was always real with her."

"There are other Graces out there."

"There aren't, man. I'm telling you. I just met her at the wrong time. Fifteen years have gone by and I still think about her. I was married to another woman, a beautiful, smart woman, but sometimes I would think about Grace and wonder what it would have been like if we'd stayed together. I'd be making love to my wife and thinking about Grace. How fucked up is that?"

"'Making love'? That's really sweet, Matt." He grinned, on the brink of laughter.

"Don't patronize me."

"I'm just saying it's time to start nailing chicks. You're long overdue. No more making love for you. Doctor's orders."

He slapped me on the shoulder and walked out.

Later in the week, Elizabeth stopped by my cubicle. I was leaning back in my chair, playing Angry Birds.

"Matt?"

I looked up to find her wearing a flowing maternity dress, looking like Mother Earth herself, caressing her baby bump. Elizabeth was pretty in a natural, granola kind of way. Plain features, plain brown hair, nice skin, and a sun-kissed glow all year long. It was her personality and her easy betrayal of our marriage that made her ugly.

"What's up?"

"Don't you have, like, a thousand photos to edit?"

I returned my focus to the screaming birds. "Done. Submitted."

Out of the corner of my eye, I could see her put her hand on her hip like a stern parent. Her patience was dwindling. I didn't care.

"You couldn't pass them by me first?"

My eyes shot up to her and then back down to my phone. "Well, that's a fine-lookin' high horse you're on, Lizzy." I *never* called her that. "You think you're my boss now?"

"Matt. I can barely tolerate this strife between us."

"Strife?!" I chuckled as I leaned back in my chair. My phone buzzed in my hand. Incoming call from a local Manhattan number I didn't recognize. I held my finger up to Elizabeth, shushing her before I pressed talk. "Hello?"

"Matt?"

Oh God.

Her voice, her voice, her voice, her voice.

Elizabeth was still glaring at me. She threw her hands up and said, "Can you just call this person back? I'm trying to talk to you."

"Hold on, Grace," I said.

"Grace?" Elizabeth's mouth fell open.

I covered the receiver. "Get the fuck out of here!"

She put her hand on her other hip. "I'm not leaving."

I uncovered the receiver. "Grace?"

God, I wanted to fucking cry.

"Yeah, I'm here."

"Can you give me two minutes? I promise I'll call you right back." I thought I was going to throw up.

"If it's a bad time . . ."

"No, no, I'll call you right back."

"Okay," she said, uncertainly.

We hung up. "So, you're seeing Grace?" Something about her tone smacked of satisfaction, and her eyes said, *Of course you are.*

I sucked in a deep breath through my nose. "No, I'm not seeing her. That was the first time I've talked to her in fifteen years, and you just ruined it."

"This is your job, Matt. This is a workplace."

"Is that what you said to Brad before you fucked him in the copy room?" I shot back, flatly. I felt like someone had stabbed me in the chest and I was bleeding out. I felt weaker and weaker by the second. "I don't feel good. Can you leave me alone please?" My eyes started to water.

She flushed. "I . . . Matt . . ."

"Whatever you're about to say, I don't care, Elizabeth. Not at all. Not even one iota." I shrugged.

She turned and walked away.

I went to my recent calls and hit send on Grace's number.

"Hello?"

"I'm so sorry about that."

"That's okay."

I took a deep breath. "God, it's good to hear your voice, Grace."

"Yeah?"

"How have you been?"

"I've been okay. It's been . . . a long time, Matt."

"Yeah. It has, hasn't it?" She sounded a little apprehensive. I was, too. "So what do you do now? Where do you live? Are you married?"

"I'm not married." My stomach unclenched. *Thank God.* "I live in a brownstone on West Broadway in SoHo."

"You're kidding. I live on Wooster."

"Oh, wow. That's very close. Are you still working for the magazine?"

She knew I worked for the magazine? "Yeah, but I do more for the TV channel now. I'm not traveling as much. How about you? Still playing the cello?" A memory of Grace playing the cello in our dorm room, wearing nothing but her flowery underwear, drifted into my head. The light from the window had silhouetted her so I had pressed the shutter on my camera and snapped away as she played. I still had those pictures somewhere. I remembered that I had set the camera down, gone up to her, and traced the indentations above her cute little ass. She had gotten tripped up on the music and started giggling. I wondered now if I'd ever hear that giggle again.

"Uh-huh. Not professionally, I teach high school music classes now."

"That sounds great." I cleared my throat awkwardly. I wanted to tell her that she sounded different, doleful, un-Grace-like, but I kept those thoughts to myself.

Several moments of uncomfortable silence passed by. "So you saw the post, I take it."

"Yes, that was really sweet . . ." She hesitated and took a deep breath. "When I saw you, I didn't know what to think."

"Yeah, um . . . the post was a shot in the dark, I guess."

"You've had a great career. I've followed you a little."

"Have you?" My throat hurt, my head began throbbing, and I was suddenly very nervous. *Why had she followed my career?*

"Is Elizabeth . . ."

"Pregnant?" I blurted out. *Why did I say that? And how does she even know about Elizabeth?* I wanted to fill her in on everything, but all the wrong words were coming out of my mouth.

"Matt." Another long, uncomfortable pause. "I feel really confused about seeing you, and the post and . . ."

"Elizabeth isn't—" I started to say, but she interrupted.

"It was nice talking to you. I think I'd better go."

"Coffee? Do you want to get a coffee sometime?"

"Um, I'm not sure."

"Okay." Another awkward silence. "You'll call me if you change your mind?"

"Sure."

"Grace, you're okay, right? I mean, you're well? I need to know."

"I'm well," she whispered and then hung up.

Fuck!

Elizabeth chose that moment to come back with a stack of photos. She had the worst possible timing. "Can you review these and have them on my desk by tomorrow morning?"

"Yeah, fine, leave them." I didn't look up. My heart was hammering in my chest and I was about to cry. I felt

Elizabeth's hand on my shoulder. She squeezed, the way a football couch might do. "You okay?"

"Yep."

"It's hard for you to see me like this, isn't it?"

What? I was so taken aback, I almost laughed. Elizabeth had a way of making everything about her. "You think it's hard for me to see you pregnant? No, I'm happy for you."

"I guess that makes sense since you never wanted children." Her tone was inscrutable.

I always wanted children, just not with you.

I took her hand in mine and did what needed to be done. "Elizabeth, I'm sorry I wasn't a better husband to you. I'm happy for you and Brad. I wish you both many years of marital and familial bliss. For the sake of all that is good, including our workplace sanity, let's never, ever talk about our crappy marriage again. Please?" My eyes were pleading.

She nodded in agreement. "I'm sorry, too, Matt. I went about everything the wrong the way."

I released her hand. She smiled warmly, sympathetically, almost piteously. It was better to let her think I was lonely and pining for her than to fuel the fiery resentment she had always had toward me because I never got over Grace. Her suspicions were right, but I would never admit the truth to her.

Brad had been my friend since I'd first started at *National Geographic* as an intern. I had met him around the same time I met Elizabeth. He'd always had a thing for her and she'd always had a thing for me. I'd almost felt like an asshole for marrying her, so when she cheated on me with him, I wasn't shocked. In fact, I'd had a strange urge to high-five him. Isn't that terrible?

Elizabeth went back to her office and I headed to Brad's office. It was time to be the bigger man, or at least the equally flawed, human man. I had blown the phone call with Grace, but it had shaken me loose; I didn't want to stay in this rut of self-pity and hatred forever.

Standing in the doorway of Brad's office, I cleared my throat.

He looked up at me from the other side of his desk. "Heyyyy, man." He always stretched the "hey" out, stoner-like.

"Brad, I just came by to say congratulations on the pregnancy. Well done, my friend. We all know I couldn't have done it better myself."

"Matt—" He tried to stop me.

"I'm kidding, Brad. I'm happy for you guys. I swear."

"Yeah?" He quirked an eyebrow.

I nodded. "Yeah."

"How 'bout a drink after work. Just the two of us?"

Well, I'm sure you fucked my wife on every available surface of the apartment I used to own, and now she's pregnant with your child, so . . .

I clapped my hands together. "What the hell. Why not?"

We went to a hoity-toity cocktail lounge on the Upper West Side near my old apartment, which he and Elizabeth now shared. I fucking hated that bar, but it was familiar territory for both of us.

My scotch was served in a martini glass with an ice cube. There were so many things wrong with the drink but I downed it anyway. "Are cigars in order yet?"

"No, that's after the baby's born. You're not really into kids, are you?"

"No, I hate them. I just want an excuse to smoke a nice Cuban," I lied, for fun. What else is there in life?

"Well, the time will come. By the way, your sister in-law called. She's sending us the antique bassinet."

"What?"

"Yeah, she thought it should go to us. She thinks of Elizabeth as a sister."

The bassinet was a family heirloom; it was meant to be kept within the family. "Monica is not the damned keeper of the bassinet."

Brad picked up on my hostility and tried to change the subject. "Are you dating anyone these days?"

"No, just fucking," I lied again, for amusement. "Finally got rid of that old ball and chain, you know?" I was finding it hard to stick to my goal of being the bigger man here.

"That's great for you," Brad said, uncomfortably.

"Another scotch please!" I called out.

"You know, sometimes Lizzy gets pissed at me for the smallest things. Like the toilet seat—she's mad if I leave it up, but she's mad if I leave it down." He looked at me and shook his head. "She says my aim isn't good enough."

I actually felt sorry for him. "Listen, you're gonna have to learn to piss sitting down. It's part of being married. It's actually kind of relaxing, like a little break."

"Really?"

"Totally."

My second scotch came. I drank it faster than the first.

"You know, I forgot to tell you that Lizzy found another box of your pictures and some rolls of undeveloped film. She said she wanted you to come by and pick them up since we're . . . you know . . . trying to prepare the spare room."

Jesus. "Okay."

He checked his phone. "Shit, we have Lamaze class soon. I gotta go, man. Want to come up to the apartment and grab that box?"

"Sure, let's go."

We walked the few blocks to the apartment, hardly speaking along the way. Once we got to the building, I shuffled behind him into the lobby. The two scotches, combined with the weirdness of being in my old building, suddenly hit me. "You know what, Brad? I'm just gonna wait here for you to bring the box down."

"Are you sure?"

"Yeah, I'll wait." I smiled weakly and took a seat near the elevator. A few minutes later, he returned with a dark gray plastic tote.

"Thought you said it was a box?"

"Uh, yeah, it was, but Lizzy took everything out of the box and put it in here for more efficient storage."

"More efficient storage?"

He could barely make eye contact with me. "Yep."

I was sure Elizabeth had gone through the entire box and thrown half of it away. I wasn't surprised. "Thanks, Brad."

"See ya, buddy." He slapped me on the back as I turned to walk away.

Once I got back to my loft, I sat on my old leather couch, turned on U2's "With or Without You," kicked my feet up on the plastic tote, and closed my eyes. I imagined that I had built a life, not just a career. I imagined that my walls were covered with pictures of my family, not animals from the fucking Serengeti. Taking a deep breath, I leaned forward and opened the tote.

It was everything from that time, preserved in black-and-white photographs. Grace and me in Washington Square Park. At Tisch. In our dorm. In the lounge. Grace playing the cello. Grace naked on my bed, taking a photo of me, the camera masking her face. I ran my finger over it. *Let me see your face*, I remember saying. Grace and me in Los Angeles, playing Scrabble at my mom's house. My mom teaching Grace how to throw pottery in the Louvre. Grace sleeping on my chest as I looked up into the camera.

Slowly, I took each photo out of the tote. The last photo I pulled out was taken on the day I left for South America. It was what they call a "selfie" now. Grace and I were lying in bed, looking up into the lens as I held the camera over us and clicked the shutter.

We looked so happy, so content, so in love.

What happened to us?

At the bottom of the bag, I found a cassette tape and an undeveloped roll of film. I removed it from the canister and held it up to the light. It was in color, something I rarely used back then; it wasn't until I started working for *National Geographic* that I used color on a regular basis.

I got up, set the roll on the counter, popped the cassette into an old tape player, and drank until I passed out, listening to Grace and her friend, Tatiana, playing a violin-and-cello duet of "Eleanor Rigby." They played it over and over, and each time, at the end, I could hear Grace giggling and Tatiana shushing her.

I fell asleep with a smile on my face, even though I felt like one of those lonely people they talk about in the song.

THERE WERE STILL a few film-processing stores around downtown. The PhotoHut was long gone, but I found a camera store on my way to work the next morning and dropped off the mysterious roll of film.

When I arrived at the office, I spotted Elizabeth in the office kitchen, near the coffeepot. "I thought you're not supposed have caffeine when you're pregnant?" I said.

"I'm allowed to have a cup," she shot back as I brushed past her. I smirked and walked toward my cube. I could feel her walking behind me, her ballet flats shuffling against the carpet, kicking up electrical currents. She had a habit of dragging her feet.

I flipped on my computer and turned to see her standing behind me, waiting to acknowledge her. Her hair was sticking up, floating off her shoulders from the static electricity. I couldn't help but laugh.

"What?"

"Your hair." I pointed, like a five-year-old.

She scowled and wrapped her hair in a bun, grabbing a pencil off my desk to hold it in place.

"Thanks for getting a drink with Brad and picking up the tote last night."

"Thanks for organizing my personal shit for me. Did you toss anything from the original box?"

"No, I could barely look inside of it. It was like a shrine to Grace."

"Why were you so determined that I get all that stuff back, then?"

She shrugged. "I don't know. I feel bad, I guess."

"What exactly do you feel bad about?" I leaned back in my chair.

"Just . . . you know. How . . . I don't know."

"Tell me," I urged with a smug grin. I couldn't help but take pleasure as she struggled for words. She was clearly still envious of Grace.

"Just the way you put her on a pedestal and talked about her, like she was the one who got away."

I leaned forward. "You're not telling me everything—you're doing that weird eyebrow thing that you do whenever you lie."

"What weird eyebrow thing?"

"You wiggle one eyebrow, all crazylike. I don't know how you do it. It's like a creepy twitch."

She self-consciously raised a hand to her brow. "It's nothing that you don't already know. I mean, we were so busy back then."

"What are you talking about?"

Elizabeth's eyes darted all over the room, like she was mapping out her exit strategy. She looked down at her overpriced shoes. "Grace called and left a message for you once, and . . . it was just . . ."

I stood. "What are you saying, Elizabeth?" I didn't realize I was shouting until the room went completely silent. I could feel our colleagues peering around the walls of their cubicles at us.

"Shhh, Matt!" She leaned in. "Let me explain. It was while we were in South Africa." She crossed her arms and lowered her voice. "You and I were already fucking. I didn't know why she was calling."

My mind raced to figure out the timeline. It would have been roughly two years after Grace and I last saw each other. After she disappeared.

"What did she say?" I asked, slowly.

"I don't remember. It was so long ago. She was in Europe or something. She wanted to talk to you and see how you were doing. She left her address."

Every nerve was on full alert. "What did you do, Elizabeth?"

"Nothing."

She was acting so weird. Shifty. Like she still wasn't telling me the whole truth.

"Just tell me what you did."

She winced. "I wrote her a letter."

"You didn't . . ."

"I was in love with you, Matt. I wrote to her, but I was kind. I said that you had moved on, that she was part of your past, but that I wished her the best."

My eyes were burning with fury. "What else did you do? For the love of God, Elizabeth, I'm about to make a headline out of us, and I'm not a violent man. You know that."

She started crying. "I was in love with you," she repeated.

I was stunned. I always thought Grace ran off. She hadn't left me so much as a note—no address, no phone number. I had been devastated, always believing that she had been the one who left me.

"If you were in love with me, why didn't you give me the choice?"

Brad walked up behind her and wrapped his arms around her. "What's going on? What are you saying to her? She's pregnant, man; what's wrong with you?"

My chest was heaving. "Leave. Both of you."

Elizabeth turned into Brad's arms and started to cry against his chest. Brad glared at me and led her away, shaking his head, like I was the one who had done something awful.

Ever since I'd seen Grace on the subway, I'd been replaying everything that happened to us fifteen years ago, how the last conversation we'd had seemed so typical, just six week before I was supposed to fly home, back into her arms, back into the routine we'd set for ourselves during that year of heaven.

After work, I picked up the roll of film I had dropped off earlier. It was a Friday, and I had nothing better to do than go to my mostly empty loft and digest the news that Grace had tried to get in touch with me years ago. I sat on the couch near the big floor-to-ceiling windows overlooking the street.

Next to me, on the end table, was one small lamp; in my lap, the developed photos. The first three were blurry, but the fourth caught me off guard. It was a picture of me and Grace in our pajamas, standing in front of the blurry traffic lines. Our faces were slightly out of focus, but I could see that we were looking right at each other. *That night we went to that diner in Brooklyn.*

Every other photo was of Grace: in the lounge, in the park, sleeping in my bed, dancing in my dorm. All of her, captured in color.

I laid out each photo on my coffee table and stared at them as I thought back, reliving all the memories with her. *Did I tell her I loved her? Did I know I loved her? What happened?*

It was eight thirty and I hadn't eaten all day. I was sick, disgusted by what Elizabeth had done. It all started to make sense—the way Grace had acted, so guarded on the phone. She had tried to reach out to me.

I hopped onto my computer and did a reverse phone number search. I found the name G. Porter on West Broadway. *She was married?* Even though I had been married, too, the realization stung. I Googled "Grace Porter musician nyc" and found a link to the high school where she taught music. I clicked through several more links and found out her department was having a special performance that night at the high school gymnasium, but it had started an hour before.

Without even looking in the mirror, I was out the front door. I just couldn't leave things at an awkward phone call.

Once I arrived at the school, I took the stairs two at a time down to the gymnasium. I could hear the sound of applause, and I prayed I wasn't too late. There was no one manning the double doors, so I slipped through and stood in the back, my eyes scanning the room for Grace, but all I saw were four chairs arranged at the far end of the gymnasium—three occupied, one empty. The crowd quieted as a man approached a podium set up off to the side of the incomplete quartet.

"Ms. Porter has something very special she would like to share with you all." My timing was perfect, if not fifteen years too late. "This is indeed a treat, and a rare performance, so let's put our hands together for her talented quartet."

Grace approached the podium, and I couldn't catch my breath. What I had loved about her all those years ago was still there: her unique mannerisms; how unaware she was of her beauty; her hair, still long and blonde, draped over one shoulder; her lips, a full, natural pink. Even at this distance, I could see her spectacular green eyes. She was dressed from head to toe in black—a high-necked sweater and pants, so striking against her light skin and hair.

She tapped the microphone and smiled as the thumping sound echoed off the walls. "Sorry about that." Then a giggle. *Jesus, how I missed that sound.* "Thank you for coming out tonight. I don't usually perform with the students, but we have something very special to share with you. Our first and second chair violinists, Lydia and Cara, and our first chair violist, Kelsey, will be performing with the New York Philharmonic next weekend." The crowd erupted in cheers and whistles. Grace looked back at the three girls, who smiled at her, poised with their instruments. "This is a very proud moment for me, so tonight I would like to join them in a performance of 'Viva La Vida' by Coldplay. I hope you enjoy."

Still my modern girl.

Grace walked to the farthest chair on the right and placed the cello between her legs. With her head down, she began the count. She had always played for herself, and as I watched her now, I could see that nothing had changed. I didn't have to see her eyes to know they were closed, the way they always were when she played near the window in our old dorm.

I watched, enraptured, my eyes never leaving Grace as the song filled the gymnasium. At the end, right before the last pass of the bow, she looked up at the ceiling and smiled. The crowd went wild, the place shaking with thunderous applause.

I waited through the rest of the performances, starving, tired, and wondering if it was all in vain. The crowd cleared out a little after ten thirty, and I waited, my eyes still trained on her. Finally, she made her way toward the double doors, where I had stood the entire time. When I made eye contact with her, I could tell she had known I was there all along. She walked toward me with purpose.

"Hi." Her voice was light and friendly, thank God.

"Hi. That was a great performance."

"Yeah, those girls . . . lots of talent there."

"No you, you're so . . . you play so"—I swallowed—"beautifully." I was a bumbling fool.

She smiled but her eyes were appraising me. "Thank you."

"I know it's late, but . . . would you like to get a drink?" She started to answer but I cut her off. " I know that phone call was awkward. I just want to talk to you in person. To"—I waved my hand around—"clear the air."

"'Clear the air'?" She was testing the words.

"Well, catch up. And yeah, clear the air, I guess."

"It's been fifteen years, Matt." She laughed. "I don't know if 'clearing the air' is possible."

"Grace, listen, I think some things might've happened that I didn't fully understand at the time, and—"

"There's a little dive around the corner. I can't stay out late though. I have something in the morning."

I smiled at her gratefully. "Okay, no problem. Just one drink."

God, I was desperate.

"Let's head out, then. This way."

We walked side by side down the dark street. "You look really fantastic, Grace. I thought so as soon as I saw you the other day on the subway."

"Wasn't that so weird? It was like the universe was teasing us; we saw each other just a second too late." I hadn't thought of it that way. I loved her mind. "I mean, apparently we live a few blocks from each other but we've never run into each other. It's kind of strange."

"Actually, I just moved into that apartment when I came back to New York last year."

"Where were you before that?"

"I moved to the Upper West Side five years ago, but then I left for L.A. for a little while. After my divorce from Elizabeth was finalized, I came back to New York. That was about a year ago. I'm renting the loft on Wooster now."

I watched Grace's reaction carefully, but all she said was, "I see."

Inside the dark bar, Grace selected a small table, hung her bag over the back of a chair, and pointed to the jukebox in the corner. "I'm gonna pick out a song. It's too quiet in here for a bar." Her mood seemed lighter. I thought about how she couldn't handle being indoors without music. She was fine outside, listening to nature, but when she was inside, she always had to have music on.

"Can I order you a drink?"

"A glass of red wine would be great."

I had to constantly remind myself not to reminisce in my head and to just be in the moment. There was a lot to say, after all. When I returned with our drinks, she was sitting, elbows propped on the table, her chin resting on top of her clasped hands. "You look great too, Matt. I wanted to say that earlier. You haven't aged much at all."

"Thanks."

"I like the long hair, and this . . ." She brushed my beard with her fingertips. I closed my eyes for a second too long. "So, you were in L.A.?"

I tried to control my breathing, to stop myself from

breaking down and crying. I was totally overwhelmed in her presence.

A sad song came on with a droning male voice. "Who is this?" I asked as I took a sip of my beer.

"It's The National. But, Matt, you said you wanted to talk, so let's talk. You went to L.A. after your divorce: did you stay with your mom? How's she doing? I think about her from time to time."

"I went before I got divorced, actually. To take care of my mom. She passed away while I was there."

Grace's eyes filled with tears. "Oh, Matt. I'm so sorry. She was such a wonderful woman."

My throat tightened. "It was ovarian cancer. Elizabeth thought Alexander should've stepped up, but he was too busy trying to make partner at the firm. My mother was dying and her sons were fighting over who should take care of her. So stupid." I looked away. "My marriage was already on the rocks. Elizabeth was desperately trying to get pregnant, but I was thousands of miles away, across the country. I think, on some level, she thought I was trying to avoid her. I just thought she was being selfish. We were both angry and hurting, I guess."

She nodded. "What happened after that?"

"While I was in L.A., watching my mother wither away, Elizabeth started having an affair with my friend and our co-worker Brad, a producer at *National Geographic*. Eight years of marriage—poof." I made an exploding motion with my hands.

"Eight years? I thought . . ." She hesitated.

"What?"

"Never mind. I'm really sorry, Matt. I don't know what to say."

"You can tell me this: why did you leave?"

"Leave when?"

"Why didn't you leave a note or a message when you went off to Europe? You just left."

She looked confused. "What do you mean? I waited. You never called me."

"No, I couldn't. I couldn't make any more calls. The only person I talked to was my mom because I could call her collect. I was out of cash. We got stuck in a village with a broken vehicle and hundreds of miles of rain forest around us. I just figured you'd understand."

She looked shattered. "What about that article in that photography magazine? It basically said you had a job with *National Geographic* and you were going to Australia after South America."

"Back in '97?"

"Yeah." She threw back her entire glass of wine. "There was a photo of you taking her picture and it said you were going to Australia with her for six months."

"I've never even read this article you're talking about, so I'm not sure what you mean. Elizabeth asked me to go to Australia, but I turned her down. I came back here to be with you after my internship was over, but you were gone."

"No." She shook her head. "I thought you were going to Australia. That's why I ended up joining Dan's orchestra."

I was shaking my head now, too. "No, I didn't go to Australia. I came back at the end of August. I tried to call you before I left, but I couldn't get through. I went straight to Senior House, thinking you'd still be there. When I couldn't find you, I thought maybe you had moved to grad student housing, so I went to check with the registrar. He told me you had deferred your grad school admission. On my way back to Senior House, I saw Daria and she said you had joined Pornsake's orchestra."

Grace started crying, full, quiet sobs into her hands. "Grace, I'm so sorry." I grabbed napkins from the dispenser on our table and handed them to her. "I thought *you* were the one who left *me*. I didn't know how to reach you. I didn't even accept the job at *National Geographic* until I found out you were gone."

She let out a laugh through her tears. "Holy shit. All this time . . ."

"I know. I tried looking for you a few times, but I could never find you online. I didn't know until tonight that your last name was Porter."

Grace was hysterical now. "I married Pornsake, Matt. He changed his last name to Porter."

My heart was murdered. "Oh."

"Not right away. I waited almost five years. He's dead now. You know that, right?"

"No. How would I know that?"

"I wrote to you."

"You did?" *Elizabeth*. Turned out she still hadn't told me the whole truth. It was like I had fallen into some alternate universe, where Grace loved me and I was the one who had left. All these years I had spent depressed over losing her, yet all this time she had been trying to find me.

I reached across the table and took her hands in mine. And she let me. "I'm so sorry about Dan. He was very kind. How did he die?"

"Enlarged heart. He died with a damn smile on his face," she said, proudly.

"Did you love him?" I knew I had no right, but I was dying to know.

"He was good to me." She looked up at the ceiling. "I loved him in my own way."

"Yeah?" I was getting choked up again.

Her eyes met mine. "Yeah. But not the way I loved you."

"Grace . . ."

"What the fuck happened, Matt?"

"I don't know anymore. I thought I knew. Elizabeth just told me she sent you a letter?"

"I got one letter from you, maybe in '99 or 2000. The rest of my calls and letters went unanswered."

"Elizabeth wrote that letter, not me. I swear to God, Grace, I never would have ignored your calls."

"Well." Her voice got very quiet, shrinking in on itself. "It's too late now, isn't it?"

"Why? Why does it have to be too late?"

"I would say fifteen years is pretty late. So much has happened to us and . . ."

I squeezed her hands. "Let's get a piece of pie or pancakes or something, like we used to."

"Are you insane?"

"Yes," I deadpanned. "We need to get out of this place."

"I don't know . . ." She withdrew her hands from mine.

I looked at my watch. "Breakfast for dinner?"

She ran a hand across her face and sat up straight, putting some distance between us. I couldn't tell if she was contemplating the idea or trying to think of a nice way to say no. I searched her eyes and she smiled. "Okay. I'll go with you, on one condition."

"What's that, Gracie?" She laughed at the nickname

and then her eyes started welling up again. "Please don't cry," I said.

"We have to forget for a little while who we are to each other. No talking about the past. That's my condition."

"Deal." I left a fistful of bills on the table, grabbed her hand, and pulled her toward the door. But just before we left, I turned to her. "Wait. Let's do a shot first. We're young, the city is ours, you don't have to wake up early tomorrow to teach, and I don't have an asshole for a wife."

"Sure. Why not?" Her cheeks turned pink. She suddenly seemed happier, younger. And though I had promised her we wouldn't talk about the past, I couldn't help but feel like we had traveled back to the best time of our lives.

We each had a tequila shot, left the bar, and found a little twenty-four-hour diner. "I think I want pie," I said as we stared into the refrigerator case.

"Me too. You wanna share a piece?"

"Let's share two pieces," I said, practically daring her.

"You're talkin' dirty now. I like it. Let's do a slice of chocolate cream and . . ."

"A slice of peanut butter?"

"That's so perfect. I'm gonna eat the crap out of that pie."

God, I loved her. "Same here," I said.

We ordered and then sat in a green vinyl–upholstered booth. She traced the sparkles in the retro tabletop with her finger. "So, how are Alexander, your dad, and Regina?"

"Great. My dad will never retire. He and my brother are partners at the same firm. Alexander and Monica have two kids and a big house in Beverly Hills. Regina is the same, except her face is tighter."

Grace laughed but then her smile faded. "I'm sad to hear about your mom. I really liked her. I felt like we were kindred spirits."

I thought back to the days before I lost my mom. She asked me what happened with Grace, and I told her it just didn't work out. I was confused as to why my mother was bringing Grace's name up after so many years had passed. She had no idea Elizabeth and I were having marital problems, but it was like she wanted me to know she still thought of Grace. I think she must have felt that they were kindred spirits, too. Elizabeth was never close to Mom, even after knowing her for a decade. One visit, and Grace was in my mom's heart forever.

"Yes. She went peacefully. My dad actually came to see her before she died. It was heartbreaking because, after all they went through . . . she still loved him. That's why she never remarried. I think, once everything was stripped away and he saw her near the end of her life, he loved her, too. At least, that's what he said to her. If he didn't mean it, at least my mom died believing it. I came to respect him more after that."

"I can understand that." She said it as if she spoke from experience.

I took a deep breath. "Let's talk about something happier."

"I followed your career for a while and saw that you won the Pulitzer. What an amazing accomplishment, Matt. Congratulations."

"Thank you. It was unexpected and hard to appreciate because, I think, at the time, I was in a really dark place."

"That was before your mother got sick though, right?"

"Yeah. She got to see me accept the award. She and my dad were really proud."

Grace was so interested, so compassionate. I thought I had made up all those things about her in my mind. How fitting her name was. How real, beautiful, and genuine she was in the flesh. All those times I had stared at her photos and wished I could hold her, touch her, or just see her in person, in color, here she was, just like I remembered.

The slices of pie sat untouched between us. I stabbed a piece and held the fork up to Grace's lips. "Pie makes everything better."

She took the bite, and I couldn't take my eyes off her mouth. I licked my lips, thinking about how she tasted — what it had been like to kiss her.

"That's soooo good."

"I know we aren't supposed to talk about the past, but I'm dying to know what you did after we graduated. How was the orchestra?"

"It was wonderful, actually. We traveled for a couple of years. Tatiana did, too. When we came home to New York, Dan got his old job back at NYU, and I got my master's in music theory in an online program. I taught at the college level for a few years, and now I direct the orchestra and band at the high school."

"That's fantastic, Grace. How is Tatiana?"

"She's good. Still single and feisty. She's with the New York Philharmonic so she travels a lot. She's a very dedicated musician."

"What happened to Brandon?"

She chuckled. "He was just one of many for Tati."

"I should have guessed. So you never wanted to go down

the same path as Tati? I might be biased, but I always thought you were a stronger musician than her."

"I did, but . . ." She started fidgeting. "I, uh, never had the discipline she had. She was always better."

"I don't think so at all."

"To the trained ear, Tatiana has more talent." She smiled. "Last bite?" She held a fork full of peanut butter pie up to my mouth.

I grabbed her wrist, leaned in, and took the bite. The instant intimacy between us felt too familiar.

"I'm so sorry, but I have to get back. This has been so nice. It was good to see you again, looking so well and healthy," she said.

"Let me walk you home."

"It's not necessary." She moved to the edge of the booth to stand.

"It's late, and I would feel better if you'd let me walk you." She hesitated. "Okay. You can walk me to my street."

On the walk over, she twisted her hair up into a bun, exposing her tattoo. *Green-eyed Lovebird.* I couldn't resist reaching out and running my fingers across the back of her neck. *So it really happened.* She flinched. "What are you doing?"

"I just wanted to touch it, to see if it was still there."

She laughed. "Tattoos are pretty permanent."

"I just wondered if you had it lasered off in anger."

"I was more heartbroken than angry."

Ouch.

I took her hands in mine. "I'm sorry. You don't know how sorry I am."

"I know. I am too. You still have yours, I assume?"

I stretched the neck of my black T-shirt, pulling it down to reveal the tattoo over my heart. "Yep, still there."

She ran her fingers over it and whispered, "Just the ash."

Her head dropped to the ground. I lifted her chin to look at me and her eyes were full of tears. "We were victims of bad timing. But here we are again."

She smiled weakly. "I have to go." Before I could stop her, she turned and rushed quickly down the street. I waited until I saw her walk up the steps of a brownstone, and then I headed home, pissed at the world, wanting to murder Elizabeth for screwing up my life in more ways than one.

As soon as I got home, I called my brother. It was only nine o'clock on the West Coast. Monica answered. "Hello?"

"Is Alexander there?"

"Hello to you too, Matthias. Alexander's not here. He's filing a big motion tomorrow so he's still at the office."

"Monica, you said you and Elizabeth were like sisters, right?"

"Well, we were family for eight years."

"Uh-huh, sure. Did you know that Grace tried to contact me, and each time, Elizabeth found a way to keep that information from me?" My voice was harsh, accusatory. "Did you help her with these little deceptions, by any chance?"

"Stop."

"No. You gave her the fucking family bassinet. You talked to her all the time. You told me yourself that she said things to you about how I was hung up on Grace. You didn't like Grace from the beginning, and I knew that. You were both so jealous of her."

"I'm going to hang up in two seconds if you don't stop."

I was breathing heavily, my pulse racing. There was nothing left inside of me but pure anger and adrenaline.

"I don't know what you're talking about. I was never jealous of Grace. She was in your life for five minutes, and now you accuse me of this? Elizabeth never said anything to me except that you had a bunch of pictures of Grace that you refused to get rid of."

"Elizabeth is the main reason I haven't talked to Grace in fifteen years. Elizabeth is probably the reason I'm not married to Grace at this very moment."

She sighed heavily. "Matt, you're being melodramatic."

"I don't even know why I'm telling you all of this."

She was quiet for a moment. "I think you're telling me because we're family." Her words surprised me. "You should get some sleep, Matt. You sound torn up. I'm sorry if what you said is true. I never saw Elizabeth as a conniver."

"Me neither. But she did it."

"I'll let Alexander know and have him call you, okay?"

"Okay. Thanks, Monica. Goodnight."

I was still staring out the window at two in the morning. My head was foggy, so I decided to take a walk. Before I knew it, I was drifting toward Grace's street. It was totally quiet as I stood staring up at four brownstones. I didn't know which one was hers—they were completely identical.

"Grace!" I called out. I could have phoned her and said, "Gracie! Grace, please, I need to talk to you!" but if you're going to insist on talking to someone at two in the morning, you might as well pay them a visit. "Grace, please!"

A man across the street opened a window and yelled, "Get out of here or I'm gonna call the police."

"Do it!" I yelled back.

"He's fine, Charlie!" It was Grace's voice. I turned back to see her standing in the doorway of one of the brownstones. I ran up the five steps to the door, my chest heaving. I was inches away from her face as she looked up at me. She was wearing a pink flannel pajama set with Christmas trees on it. It was May. I smiled.

"What are you doing here?" she asked.

I took her hands in mine and stared down at them between us. "I wanted to kiss you earlier but I was too chicken." I leaned in and kissed her slowly, tenderly. Her lips were soft but her movements were eager. She kissed the way she always kissed, with passion. She threw her arms around my neck, pressing our bodies together as we deepened the kiss. She moved her hands to my sides, then to my waist, and under my T-shirt. Her fingers traced the designs on my belt.

She pulled away and whispered near my ear. "You still have this?"

"You were always with me, Grace. I never found a way to let you go."

She dropped her head to rest on my shoulder. "What are we going to do?"

"Date?"

She laughed. "You want to date me?"

I'd marry you right now if you'd let me.

"Yeah, I want to date you. You're my favorite ex-wife." She lifted her head and I searched her eyes. I was relieved to find amusement in them.

"I'm free on Tuesday after class."

"Want to meet in front of Senior House around three?"

She laughed again but her tears shone in the moonlight.

I had made Grace cry too much for one night. "Yeah. I'll see you there."

I leaned in and kissed her on the cheek. "Sorry I woke you up. Go back to sleep, young lady." I kissed her nose, turned, and jogged down the steps. "Tuesday at three," I called back. "I'll see you."

"Keep it down," Charlie shouted from the window.

"Go to bed, Charlie!" Grace yelled.

22. Why Not Now?

MATT

My entire weekend was devoted to buying things for my apartment and making it feel lived in, just in case Grace came over.

When I woke up Monday morning, I could already feel the anger boiling over in me as I prepared to see Elizabeth at work. I went for a run to blow off some steam, took a shower, and headed to the office. I saw Scott in the hallway as I headed to my cubicle.

"Hey, can I talk to you?" I asked.

"What's up, man?"

"Can we go into your office?"

"Sure."

We sat across from each other at his desk. "I can't be in this office anymore. Can I work from home?"

Scott leaned back in his hair. "Bro, you've hit me with a lot of requests in the last couple of years."

"I know, and I'm sorry, but I can't handle this office bullshit."

"You and Elizabeth made the decision to leave the field and settle down here." He arched his eyebrows, as if to say, *Remember?*

"Scott, I'm going to be frank with you. It's not about working in an office. I think it would be in everyone's best interest that I not work in the same building as her."

"Really? I thought you handled the divorce surprisingly well. And it's been over a year already. Are you really that hung up on her?"

"New information has surfaced. I can't work with that psychopath anymore." I smiled, which probably made me look like the psychopath.

"Come on, Matt, let's be reasonable."

"I'll go freelance, Scott. I did it before, and I won a goddamn Pulitzer."

Scott narrowed his eyes. "Don't fucking threaten me, Matt."

"I'm not threatening you, and I'm not going to go into detail about what she did. Suffice it to say, she ruined my life and I can't work with her anymore, okay? And I don't think it's unreasonable for me to not want to work with my pregnant ex-wife and her new husband. I put in a fucking request months ago and I'm still here. It's either her or me."

He signed heavily. "We want you on our team, but you know Elizabeth's not going anywhere. She's pregnant; she'd sue our asses off if we tried to get rid of her."

I threw my hands up. "I don't care, man. I'll walk."

Scott swiveled around in his seat while I stared him down. He ran his hand over his shiny bald head and then crossed his arms over his chest and leaned back. "Okay, you can work from home. We never do this, by the way—I need you to know that you're getting special treatment here. But it's only until we get you going on something else. You'll need an assistant to be your proxy at the production meetings if you really can't stand to drag your ass back into this building. Maybe Kitty?" He grinned.

I stood up and clapped once. "That's a great fucking plan, Scott. I love you." I walked over, grabbed his face, and kissed him on the cheek. "I'm outta here. Oh, and I'll find my own assistant," I called over my shoulder as I left his office.

Moments later, I was cheerfully strutting down the hall with all my belongings in a cardboard box when I ran into Elizabeth. *Just remember, Matt: if you kill her, you'll go to jail.*

"What are you doing with all your stuff?" She put her hand on her hip, blocking my path.

"Move."

"Why are you being so mean to me? I'm pregnant, you jerk."

"I'm aware, and so is every other person with their vision intact. And where I'm going is none of your business. Outta my way."

"Did you get fired?"

As desperate as I was not to engage her, I couldn't control myself. "I know about Grace's calls and letters and how you hid them from me. Thank you for that."

She rolled her eyes and looked to the ceiling. "Oh, for God's sake, I knew this would come up. Look, when you came back to New York in '97 and she was gone, you were a fucking mess, Matt. I had to pick up your sorry ass and carry you for years. You think you'd have this job if it weren't for me? You were an incipient alcoholic, fumbling around like a loser. I saved you from destroying yourself. And she wasn't here for you."

I laughed. "Incipient alcoholic? Is that the narrative you created for yourself to justify your deception? That's such bullshit. You and I never would have gotten married if I knew she was trying to get in touch with me."

"Do you know how pathetic that makes you sound?"

"You always have to get your way, no matter what the cost. You wanted me, so you did what you had to do. You wanted a baby, and I wasn't around to give one to you, so you went out and found the next willing participant, even at the expense of our marriage. You're the pathetic one, Elizabeth. Not me."

She was tongue-tied. "I thought . . . I thought you loved me." This was a typical fighting tactic for Elizabeth. She could do a 180 from angry and accusatory to self-pitying in one second flat.

"I loved the person I thought you were, but I realize now she never existed. I have to go." I tried to move past her but she blocked my way again.

"Wait, Matt."

"Please move out of the way."

"Why was she still pursuing you after she knew we were married? I mean, it was public knowledge. Don't you think there's something wrong with that?"

"Can you blame her for wanting closure? For wanting to know what happened between us? She was torn up inside, Elizabeth. Just like me." Pausing, I looked down at her growing belly. "For the sake of that poor human being growing inside of you, I hope you learn something from this. Despite your every effort, we didn't work out. We're not together. It was all for nothing." She started crying, but it didn't phase me. "Please, Elizabeth, get out of my way."

I had hit the crest of my anger, and now everything seemed totally ridiculous. I was beyond yelling and screaming now; it was all a fucking joke, but the joke was on me. I could either take it and move on or I could give this life-sucking person another second she didn't deserve.

I brushed past her. "See you never."

It was spring in New York, and I was free to pursue what I wanted.

The sun was shining down between the skyscrapers as I made my way to the subway, clutching a medium-sized box filled with career mementos. I was smiling on the train as I tried to recall every detail of my kiss with Grace the Friday before. How soft her hair felt between my fingers, how she always, even fifteen years later, kept her eyes closed seconds after the kiss was over, like she was savoring it.

I couldn't let anyone, or anything, get in my way again.

ON TUESDAY, I went for a run in the morning and counted down the minutes until three p.m., when I was supposed to meet Grace. I arrived way too early and sat on the steps of Senior House until she came striding up, right on time. She seemed revived since I'd last seen her, and she had a Grace-like bounce in her step. She was wearing a flowery skirt with tights and a sweater. It was a slightly more grown-up version of her college style. Glancing down at myself, I realized my style hadn't changed much either: jeans, T-shirts, and Chucks. Had that much time really passed? If it had, there was little physical evidence beyond a few wrinkles on our faces.

I stood up and shoved my hands into my pockets.

"Have you eaten?" she asked.

"I'm starving." I lied. I wanted to do whatever she wanted to do. "What do you feel like?"

"How about a hot dog and a walk in the park?" I smiled. Nothing had ever sounded better. Granted, she could have said, "How about a gondola ride through the Venice canals?" or "How about we sit in Death Valley with no water?" and it all would have sounded equally good to me, as long as she was there.

"Sounds good."

We walked shoulder to shoulder as we exchanged small talk. I told her about my job, skimming lightly over the confrontation with Elizabeth.

"How are your parents?" I asked her.

"The same, except my dad is sober now and my mom is remarried. My brother and sisters have all grown up and moved away. I'm closest with my youngest sister. She lives in Philadelphia and I see her often. I thought about moving back to Arizona after Dan died, but I love New York so much. I have friends here and I could never sell the brownstone."

I felt an ache in my heart. I wished I had been the one to buy her the brownstone.

We ate our hot dogs on the fountain steps in Washington Square Park and watched two toddlers splash around in the water. One tiny blonde girl, about three years old, was laughing hysterically. I mean, really belly-laughing for, like, five minutes straight as her little brother splashed her.

"That kid is adorable."

"Yep. Got any pot?" she asked, casually.

"Abrupt subject change, no?" I squinted at her for a moment. "Wait, are you serious?"

"Why not?" She reached up and wiped mustard from my lip with her index finger, then stuck it in her mouth.

Jesus Christ, woman.

"I can get us some pot," I said in a daze.

"Maybe next time." She shrugged goofily, a flash of Grace from the past.

"Aren't you worried one of your students will see you?"

"I was thinking we could go back to your place."

"Uh, sure. We can." I nodded vigorously, like an over-eager schoolboy. "Yeah, not a problem."

"Look!" She pointed to a young guy giving his girlfriend a piggyback ride, running in circles as she screamed joyously.

Grace smiled up at me and then her eyes filled with tears. *Fuck, don't cry, Grace. Please. I'll die.*

"I can still do that. I'm not that old," I told her.

She started laughing as tears ran down her face. "Well, Old Man Shore, I'd let you try, but I'm wearing a skirt."

"You were saying something about going back to my place?" I tried to pull off an innocent look.

"Yeah, if you want. I'd like to see your place."

"You would?"

"Of course. I want to see where you live; I'm not offering to sleep with you."

"Pfft. I know. . . . I wasn't thinking that." Though I was totally thinking that.

The subway was crowded during rush hour. Grace stood with her back to my front and leaned against me. I wondered if her eyes were closed. I bent and whispered near her ear, "We could have taken a cab or walked. I forget that we're grown-ups now."

"I like taking the subway with you."

I pulled her closer against my body. It felt like all the years I'd lost with her never existed.

When we got to my building, the elevator opened to my loft on the fourth floor and Grace stepped out in front of me. She immediately looked up to the exposed-beam ceiling. I flipped on the lights. "This is gorgeous, Matt."

"I like it."

There was still a little bit of light left in the sky, casting a nice glow throughout the room. Grace walked to windows. "You can probably see the top of my house from here."

"No, you can't." She turned and smiled. "Can I get you a glass of wine?" I asked.

"That would be great."

She walked around my sparse loft as I went into the kitchen. The bedroom, kitchen, and living room flowed into each other within a large, high-ceilinged, open space, separated only by a few beams. As I poured the wine, I watched her run her hand across my white comforter.

"Your place is really nice. I like the rustic feel. Usually people go for modern in a space like this."

"Call me old-fashioned."

"I don't think you're old-fashioned." She was standing near the wall, staring up at the picture that had won me so many awards.

"Passé?" I asked as I handed her the glass.

"Timeless," she answered with a grin. I wished instantly that she was speaking of us. Weren't we though? Timeless? Nothing could change what we'd had all those years before, even if the idea of what might've been lingered between us.

"Oh, well, thank you. That's a nice sentiment."

She pointed up to the picture. "But that . . . that's powerful. Children and guns . . ." She shook her head. "How tragic. Were you scared when you took that?"

"No, not scared. Sometimes the camera feels like a shield. In the beginning, when I was on location like that, I took a lot of risks."

"Do you think you'll win another Pulitzer?"

"It's kind of a once-in-a-lifetime thing, but I do want to go back into the field."

"I bet some of the best photos are happy accidents."

"Such is life." I stepped toward her and tucked her hair behind her ear. "I want to kiss you."

She took a quick sip of her wine. "Um . . . do you ever go to any shows around here?"

I chuckled. "You're an amazing subject changer."

"I don't think I can say no to you much longer, and I really want . . ." She swallowed and looked around.

"What, Grace?"

"I really want a do-over." The conversation was making her nervous; her chest was heaving in and out.

"What do you mean?"

"You were my best friend." She choked back tears and looked away.

"Please don't cry."

When her eyes met mine again, they were intense, blazing. "I'm trying to tell you something, Matt."

I took her in my arms and held her against my chest. She wanted to take it slow, the way we had done before—all of those amazing moments in our dorm just being together, dancing, singing, playing music, taking pictures. That's the problem with adults. There's no taking your time because you think, even at the relatively young age of thirty-six, that your days are numbered. You think you know everyone inside and out, heart and soul, after talking to them for five minutes.

Pushing back her shoulders, I searched her face. "I have an idea. Stay here, get comfortable, take off your shoes." I pointed to the shelves of vinyl. "Pick a record. I'll be right back."

I left the loft, took the elevator, ran across the street, and hustled up three flights of stairs in one minute. Rick Smith was the only stoner I knew in a five-mile radius. I pounded on his door.

He answered wearing sweats, a rainbow-colored sweat-band, and no shirt. He had an extremely toned body for being a fortysomething writer who only left his house to walk his cat, Jackie Chan. "Matt, my man, what's up?" He was out of breath.

"Sorry, Rick, did I catch you at a bad time?"

"No, no, I was just doin' Tae Bo."

"Oh, Tae Bo. Is that still around?"

"Well, it's not like it could disappear; it's an exercise, bro. Come on in." He held the door wide open. I had never been in his apartment, only to the door; I had returned Jackie Chan once after he got out.

It was like I had traveled back in time, and I kind of liked it. Everything in his apartment was old but in perfect condition. The Toshiba TV in the corner was paused on Billy Blanks in midmotion. Rick was exercising to a seriously old Tae Bo video. "Is that a VHS?"

"Oh yeah, my VCR works like a dream. Why get rid of it, you know?"

"Yeah." I expected his apartment to seem like that of a hoarder, but it was totally the opposite.

He walked to the kitchen and grabbed a water bottle out of the refrigerator. "Welcome to my humble abode. Can I offer you some water, or perhaps a wheatgrass shot? I have an emulsifier, too, if you'd like me to whip you up a nice, fresh juice."

"Oh, thank you, Rick. You are too kind." He was a health nut. I thought idly that I probably should have read one of his books before I came over and asked him for pot.

"To what do I owe this visit?"

"Yeah, so um, I don't exactly know how to say this, but . . . I have an old friend over and we . . ."

"You guys need some reefer?"

"Yes!" I pointed at him like he had won *The Price Is Right*. No one used the term *reefer* anymore, but whatever.

"Why'd you think I'd have any? You think I'm a stoner or something? You think I'm some kind of drug dealer?" His face was blank.

"Oh shit." I would have sworn on a Bible that every time I saw him his eyes were bulging and bloodshot, and he reeked of pot.

"Ha! I'm kidding, bro. I'll totally spot you." He chuckled and then slapped me on the shoulder as he passed by me. "One sec."

He came back holding a prescription canister with no label. I could see the buds inside. Lifting it up to my face, he said, "Listen and listen closely. This is King Kush. It's medicinal marijuana. I got it from the first medical marijuana dispensary on the East Coast. I rented a car and drove all the way to fucking Maine to get this shit. Do not pass go, do not fuck around, do you understand me?" His beady eyes were shooting lasers at me.

"Rick, I don't know. You're starting to scare me."

"It superstrong. You'll love it and you'll thank me." He pulled a pack of papers from a drawer and held them out. "Need these?"

"Uh, yeah." I took the papers and the pot and shoved them into my pockets.

"Roll her thin, man, and smoke like half with your buddy at first before you do any more."

"What if my buddy is a five-foot-five, small-boned woman?"

"She'll be fine. Women love this shit."

Walking toward the door, I turned back. "Rick, I don't know how to thank you."

"Ah, no worries. Consider it payment for bringing Jackie Chan back that day."

Back in my apartment, Grace was sitting on the couch with her tights-clad feet propped up on the coffee table. She had put Coltrane on the record player and her eyes were closed, head resting back against the couch, looking like she was at home. *God, I love her.*

"Guess what?" I held up the pot.

She looked over at me. "We're gonna get stoned and dance?"

"Preferably naked."

"Don't press your luck."

I knelt by the table and rolled a very imperfect joint. Grace was giggling the entire time. "Don't laugh at me."

"Here, let me do it." She took a new paper and rolled a nice, skinny, perfectly tight one.

"Gracie, why are you so good at that?"

"Tati and I do this every once in a while. Well, more like every first Sunday of the month."

"You're kidding? Leave it to Tatiana to delegate specific time for weed smoking."

"Yep, some things never change." She lit it and took a puff. Holding the smoke in, she said in a tiny voice, "Who would want them to?"

We smoked and things got a little hazy. I put on Stevie Wonder's "Superstition" and Grace got up and started dancing around. She flipped her hair all over as I watched in awe, bobbing my head, wondering how the fuck I ever let her get away.

"Dance with me, Matt."

I got up and we danced around until the song was over, and then "You Are the Sunshine of My Life" came on. We froze, staring at each other, until Grace buckled over, cracking up. "This is such a cheesy song."

"Graceland Marie Starr, this is a great song. It's a classic." I took a hold of her and spun her around, then brought her to my chest and made a few exaggerated dance moves.

"It's Porter."

"Huh?" I pretended not to hear her. "The music must be too loud, what did you say?"

She shook her head and let me spin her around until we were dizzy and exhausted.

An hour later, we found ourselves sitting on my kitchen floor, eating grapes and cheese. She was leaning her back against the refrigerator with her legs out straight in front of her, and I was sitting the same way against the cabinets across from her.

She lobbed a grape up into the air and I caught it in my mouth.

"I have an idea. . ." she said.

"Tell me."

"Let's play a game. Do you have a blindfold?" I wiggled my eyebrows at her. "It's not what you think."

I pulled a long, red dishtowel out of the drawer and tossed it to her. She leaned forward on her knees and proceeded to tie it around my head.

"I'm getting scared, Grace."

"We're gonna play, 'Guess what I just put in your mouth.'"

"Sweet Jesus. That sounds like a game I'll like."

"Don't get too excited."

Too late.

I heard her tinkering around in the kitchen, and then a few minutes later she was sitting next to me again. "Okay, open up." I felt a cold spoon hit my tongue. Something slid off it and hit the back of my throat. It was confusing and disgusting and the texture gave me the chills. "Gross, what is this?"

"You have to guess; that's the whole point of the game."

"Grape jelly and soy sauce?"

She lifted the blindfold to reveal her ecstatic face. "It's true! I thought that would be impossible."

I shook my head. "This isn't as fun as I thought it would be."

"Wait, I have more."

"No."

"Just one more?" she whined.

"Fine." I pulled the blindfold back down.

She scampered away and came back a moment later. "Open up, Matty."

Her finger was in my mouth, and if that wasn't sweet enough on its own, it was coated in Nutella. "Nutella à la Grace?"

She undid the blindfold, her face beaming.

"My turn," I said. I tied the towel-blindfold around her eyes, stood up, and pretended to gather things from various drawers. I sat back down. "Ready?"

"Yep!" She opened her mouth and I kissed her, starting at her bottom lip and then moving to her neck and back to her mouth until our tongues were twisting and our hands were lost in each other's hair.

We made out on my kitchen floor and then, suddenly, Grace cut it short.

"Walk me home?"

I pulled back, searching her face. "Of course. You know you're welcome to stay if you'd like to. No funny business, I promise."

"I have to get home."

"Okay." I held my hand out and helped her to her feet. She went to her purse, checked her phone, and then popped a mint into her mouth.

"Are you dating anyone?"

"I thought I was dating you?" she said.

"Right. We are dating. Very slowly."

"Are you pressuring me, Matthias? You were more patient as a twenty-one-year-old. What happened?" There was amusement in her tone.

I laughed. "Well, I didn't know what I was missing then. Now I do."

We left my loft and I walked her home. When we got to the stoop of her brownstone, I turned to her. "Want to get dinner Friday?"

"I'd love to." She leaned up and kissed me for a long time. "I had fun tonight."

"Me too. It was the best PG experience I've had in a long time."

"The explicit language, provocative dancing, finger sucking, and drug use are surely worth a PG-13 rating," she said, before leaning up and pecking me on the cheek one last time.

"Night, Gracie."

"Night, Matty."

I walked home, got into bed, and fell asleep with a smile on my face.

ON FRIDAY, I made a reservation at a little Japanese place within walking distance of both of us. When I got to her brownstone to pick her up, she was waiting for me on her stoop, wearing a leather jacket and a dress that reminded me of the one she used to wear in college that drove me crazy.

"You look great."

"You do, too." She linked her arm in mine as we walked, and we talked about our week. We ate sushi, drank a lot of sake, and I fed her from my plate. After dinner, we ended up at a bar that had a band playing gospel and blues rock. There were periods that night when we said nothing to each other and just moved to the music and then there were times when we were laughing hysterically and yelling over the music.

By eleven, we were totally tipsy. When I kissed her

outside the bar, she broke away first and pulled me down the street. "Where are we going now?"

She turned, grabbed my face hard, and kissed me again. "My bed, Matt. That's where we're going."

My heart thumped wildly at the thought. "Good idea."

I followed her up the steps to her front door, trying desperately to keep my cool and not look overly eager. When we entered her apartment, I had to squint through the darkness. I turned around and watched her silhouette, lit only from the streetlight coming through the window next to the front door. She threw her keys on the entry table, then her jacket. She kicked off her shoes, pulled her tights off, then lifted her dress from the hem, over her head, and threw that aside, too.

My jaw was on the floor.

I caught her as she jumped into my arms and straddled me, her hands diving into my hair, her sweet lips on my mouth. I walked backward down the dark hallway to a stairway and looked up. "No, my room is here. End of the hall to the left."

Pressing her against the wall, I kissed her from her mouth to her neck to her ear and back to her shoulder where I tried to catch my breath. When I set her down, she reached for my shirt and pulled it over my head, then took my hand and led me to her bedroom.

Standing near the bed, she tugged at my belt, fumbling with it.

"Slow down, Gracie."

"No one has ever said those words to me." She undid my belt and pulled my pants and boxers down as I kicked off my shoes. She was different from college Grace. I could see that now. She was more confident, more self-assured.

I took her face between my hands. Even in her dark room, with little more than the glow from the streetlights streaming through the window, I could see that her eyes were bright, brilliant, and full of wonder. "I want to slow down, otherwise this won't be fun for you," I said.

She nodded and we kissed again, but sweeter and slower this time. I ran my hand down her neck to the top of her breast and traced the line of her bra with my fingertip. I kissed a trail down her neck while my hands unclasped her bra in the back, letting it fall to the ground. She was more beautiful somehow now, though I didn't think that was possible. Her body was still so soft and smooth, but it was also womanly, strong, exquisite, the most beautiful thing I had ever seen. I had an urge to find a camera but an even stronger urge to touch her. "God," was all I could say as she leaned into me, finding my mouth again.

I pulled away. "Let me look at you." Dropping to my knees, I took her panties with me to the ground and kissed her stomach, her thighs, the space between her legs. There was no sound but my lips on her body and her soft breaths, getting faster and faster, more urgent, until she moaned from her chest.

"I want you, Matt." Her voice was strained.

My hands were moving of their own accord now. I sat on the edge of the bed and she climbed into my lap, wrapping her legs around my waist. She started to move against me, and I thought I was gonna lose it.

"Grace?"

"Shh, Matt." She ran her hand down my jawline. "I like this. It's sexy. You're sexier now, more defined . . . bigger." She giggled.

I wanted to be inside of her so bad. "I need to tell you something," I said.

"Okay." She kissed my neck more slowly but continued the subtle movements of her body.

"I've thought about doing this with you a lot over the last fifteen years. Is that weird?"

She leaned back and smiled. "If you're weird, then I'm weird, too."

"Yeah . . . but I like that about you." I grinned.

She thrust her hips against me and I moaned. "Make love to me," she said.

I plunged my face into her neck, kissing her feverishly, as I stood, her legs still wrapped around me. I lay her across the bed and stepped back to look at her. She sat up and pulled me down, her legs spread wide and her body warm, welcoming me. She guided me inside of her, and like any typical man, all thoughts were swept from my mind.

"You're beautiful," I whispered as I slowed my movements, trying to prevent any premature embarrassment. Two cautious thrusts and I was back in control, but Grace was falling apart around me.

"Just gooooo, Matt."

"You feel so good," I whispered against her ear. My lips met her neck just as her back arched and her head pressed hard against the bed. I felt her pulsing around me, and I was a goner, sliding into temporary death.

I collapsed on top of her, breathing hard. She reached down and took my hand in hers and held it between us like she needed to hang on to something. I rolled to my side. "I'm not going anywhere, Gracie."

"You promise?"

"I promise."

"No matter what happens?"

I pulled her to my chest and wrapped my arms around her. "What's going on with you?"

She buried her face in my chest. "I was never convinced that you moved on just like that. I had to accept it, but you weren't there to tell me if it was true or not. The letter was so unlike you, so indifferent. I couldn't believe you said those things, and for so long I didn't believe it. But then there came a point when I realized I wasn't living anymore. I had to give up on the idea of us being together in order to love Dan the way he deserved to be loved. But I never stopped thinking about you."

"I know, Grace. Me too. I'm so sorry. Elizabeth totally messed up my life. I just wish I had known sooner."

"But your life isn't the only one she messed with."

"I know, and I hate her for it."

"There's a ripple effect, Matt."

"I know, and I'm sorry." I kissed her forehead quietly. "But I don't want to dwell on the past anymore. We're here now, together. I just want to sleep with you in my arms, okay?"

She cuddled up to me even closer. "Okay."

Her breath evened out and her body relaxed. That was the last thing I remembered before I woke up in her bed, alone.

23. Who Did You Think I Was?

MATT

Grace's bedroom was bright with morning light, and I took in my surroundings for the first time. There was an antique dresser, a floral quilt, and Impressionistic paintings of the French countryside hanging on the walls—surprisingly generic décor for someone like Grace.

When I heard Grace tinkering in the kitchen, I slid out of bed, feeling invigorated. I put on my jeans and shoes and searched for my shirt, but I couldn't find it. The door was cracked open, and I peeked down the long hallway. At the other end of the hall was the kitchen. I could see Grace sitting at a small, round table, sipping coffee, wearing a robe and pink slippers, her hair in a topknot. She looked up as the door creaked. The smell of coffee was beckoning me, but as I stepped into the hallway, something caught my eye.

The walls were covered in pictures. On the right was a black-and-white photo of Grace and Tatiana on a balcony in Paris, with the Eiffel Tower in the background. It was the face I had known, plump with youth. I smiled and looked down the hall at Grace, who was watching me with a blank expression.

I saw another photo of Dan conducting, with Grace sitting in the orchestra, her bow poised over her cello.

Then I saw a photo of Dan and Grace sitting in a park, a baby on her lap. I stepped closer and stared at it, my mind racing. *They had a child? Had I even asked her if they had a child?*

There was another family photo of the three of them right next to it, but the little girl was older, maybe five, sitting on top of Dan's shoulders in Washington Square Park. And then another when the little girl was even older, maybe eight. I looked at Grace, whose eyes looked more weary than I had ever seen.

The little girl progressed in age as I walked toward the kitchen until I found myself at the end of the hallway, staring at a school photo of a teenager, maybe fifteen years old, with Grace's long blonde hair, Grace's lips, Grace's light skin. But it was her eyes that sent me reeling.

They weren't the spectacular green of Grace's eyes, or the dull blue of Dan's.

They were deep-set, so dark they looked black. . . .

They were *my* eyes.

I covered my mouth as a moan escaped from my chest. I heard sniffling and looked over at Grace to see tears running down her face. Her expression was still blank, as if she had learned to control it, even when she cried.

I blinked as tears fell from my own eyes. "What's her name?"

"Ash," Grace whispered. She dropped her head into her hands and sobbed.

Oh my god.

I put my hand over my heart. *The evidence of a life burning well.* "I missed everything, Gracie," I said, still in shock. "I missed everything."

She looked up. "I'm so sorry. I tried to tell you."

I stared at her for what felt like a wordless eternity. "Not hard enough."

She sobbed loudly. "Matt, please!"

"No . . . you can't. What the fuck? What is happening?"

"I wanted to tell you."

"Am I losing my mind?"

"No, listen," she pleaded.

I wasn't looking at her anymore. I couldn't look at her anymore. "No talking. Oh, Jesus, what is going on?" I had a daughter whose childhood I had totally missed.

I headed out the front door and walked home, shirtless and dazed. I kept repeating in my head, *I have a daughter, I have a daughter, I have a daughter.*

I spent the next six hours in my loft, drinking vodka straight from the bottle. I watched people walking up and down the street, fathers holding their children's hands, couples in love. The anger I felt toward Grace and Elizabeth was boiling over inside of me. I felt powerless, as if these two women had decided my entire adult life without me.

I called my brother but got his voice mail. "You're an uncle," I said, flatly. "Grace had a baby fifteen years ago, and I think Elizabeth kept this information from me. Now

I have a teenage daughter who I don't know AT ALL. I'm fucked. Talk to you later."

He didn't call back.

I hid in my apartment, mostly drunk, for the whole weekend.

On Monday morning, I kicked a pizza box across the floor and punched a hole in the wall. I decided that it felt really good, so I did it again, and then I spent a few hours trying to patch the holes. I thought about calling Kitty or one of those numbers on the back of the *Village Voice*, but instead I went to the liquor store and bought a pack of cigarettes. I hadn't smoked in more than a decade, but it was like riding a bike. Really, it was.

I chain-smoked on the bench outside my building until I got a call from Scott.

"Hello?"

"You're gonna wanna kiss me again."

"Probably not."

"Why so sad? You miss your fwiend?" He attempted a baby voice.

"No. What do you want?"

"I have good news."

"Talk."

"I got you something in Singapore."

I didn't hesitate for a second. "I'll take it. How long?"

"Wow, you really want to get the hell out of New York, don't you? Anyway, there *is* no 'how long'—it's a permanent job. You'd be working with production on our live series based out of Singapore, but you can keep shooting on the weekends. It's a great location."

"Great. When?" I never thought of myself as the type

who ran away from things, but I was utterly helpless and hopeless. I felt like a caged animal.

"In the fall."

"That far away?"

"Beggars can't be choosers."

"Fine, I'll take it." I hung up.

Grace tried calling me several times, but I never answered and she didn't leave a voice mail. Finally, at ten p.m. that night, she texted me.

> **GRACE:** Ash is a very strong-willed girl.
>
> **ME:** Okay.
>
> **GRACE:** I'm sorry to drop this on you. She told me to tell you that if you don't want to know her then you'll have to tell her to her face.
>
> **ME:** Grace, while you're at it, why don't you come here and cut my balls off or steal a kidney?
>
> **GRACE:** I'm in so much pain over this but Ash doesn't deserve any more heartache. She's your flesh and blood.

I didn't even know Ash, but suddenly the thought of causing her pain caused me pain. I knew I had to see her.

> **ME:** Fine I'll meet her. What time will she be home tomorrow?
>
> **GRACE:** Three thirty.
>
> **ME:** I don't want to see you.
>
> **GRACE:** That's fine.

When I got to Grace's building the next day, a taxi was just pulling up and I could see a teenage girl through the window. *Ash*. I wished I had five extra minutes to prepare what to say, to figure out how to tell this kid that life sucks and it's too late to go back and fix things, to just forget about me.

She stepped out of the cab and marched right up to me. "Hi," she said, holding her hand out. "I'm Ash." She was bold and confident. Not unlike her mother.

"Hi . . . Ash." I was still testing out the name on my tongue. My face was frozen in a look of both curiosity and dread.

She wasn't smiling but she wasn't glaring, either. Her expression was soft. "Just so you know, my mom told me everything, and I've seen pictures of you before."

"That's good."

"Do you want to get a coffee or something?" She arched her thin eyebrows. I was stunned by her friendliness. "Are you okay?" she asked.

Shouldn't I be asking her that? I had expected to run the conversation.

She was taller than Grace and wearing a shirt with the sides cut out; I could see her bra. I thought she couldn't really be my daughter, but somehow I knew that she was. How did I have a daughter her age? I felt old in an instant. This girl was a reminder of all the time Grace and I had lost.

"How old are you?" I asked, though I already knew.

"Fifteen."

"Fifteen going on twenty-five?"

"I had to grow up fast," she shot back. "Are you gonna start doing the dad thing right away, 'cause I'm cool with that, but I think we should have that coffee first."

"You're allowed to drink coffee?"

She laughed. I think she liked that I was concerned. "Yeah, I've been allowed to drink coffee since I was ten." A man walked past us and looked at me peculiarly. "Nothing to see, Charlie," Ash said. She leaned in, "Don't worry about him, he's just bored."

I nodded. *This is my kid. This is my daughter.* Reaching my index finger out, I poked her in the shoulder.

"I'm real," she said, smirking. "You have a child."

"Not really a child, though, are you?"

"Finally! The respect I deserve."

I laughed nervously. I couldn't believe how much I instantly liked her. She was funny and cute and so much like Grace when she was young. After a few awkward moments, she began walking up the steps.

"Ash, there's just a lot I have to absorb here."

"I'm not gonna be destroyed if you don't want anything to do with me."

I grabbed her arm and spun her around. I was just realizing that I did want something to do with her, but I didn't know how to say it.

"Look, I only learned of your existence less than a week ago." She looked down at my hand grasping her arm and then looked up into my eyes and squinted, searching for something. I recognized myself in her expression immediately. "Sorry," I said, looking at my hand like I had no control over it. "Let's get that coffee."

She huffed. "Okay, okay. Let me drop off my bag inside and tell Mom."

"Fine." I nodded, noticing how, instead of saying "my mom," she had said "Mom," the way a kid does when she references one parent to the other.

My mind wouldn't even let me attempt to make sense of how I felt. I watched the door until Ash came back out. She had wrapped her hair in a twisty bun on top of her head, the way her mother always did. Her face was scrunched up and she was scowling as she handed me my shirt. "Jesus Christ, she's a mess in there. Way to go."

"Your mom and I have some issues . . ."

"Grown-ups complicate things," she said before turning and heading down the street. "Come on."

I took my shirt and followed her like a puppy dog. She walked confidently, without looking back, as I trailed behind her. "Come on, it's just two blocks away. Are you gonna walk behind me the whole way?"

I sped up to walk beside her. "So, tell me more about you. Are you a musician, like your mom?"

"I can play the piano, but no. I prefer visual media; I guess I'm more like you."

"Yeah?" I could hear hope and pride in my voice.

"Yep. I hope it turns out to be a good thing." I didn't know what she meant by that. She continued walking. "I think I want to be a graphic designer."

"That's great. Do you do well in school?"

"School is a breeze for me. Kind of boring, actually, but I'm doing it. Not like I have a choice."

Who is this person?

She pointed toward a neighborhood café and we walked in. Ash ordered a latte and a scone, and I got my usual black coffee. There was a good-looking young man working the counter, and I caught Ash brazenly shooting him googly eyes.

I looked at her in shock. Teenage girls were a totally different species to me.

"What?" she asked.

"Uh, nothing."

We sat at a small, round table near the window and looked out. "It's a nice day. I love the spring."

"Are we gonna talk about the weather?" she asked directly but serenely. I couldn't get over how self-possessed she was.

"There's no manual for this, Ash."

"I know, and I'm trying to be sympathetic, but you're a grown man. . . ."

I chuckled. "You're right."

"Look, I know the story. Mom was very honest with me while I was growing up, and now we know you were totally in the dark about me this whole time."

I felt relieved. She was good at setting me at ease. "That's true, I was."

"No one blames you."

"I wasn't worried about that. But now that you mention it, what did you think of me before, when you thought I wanted nothing to do with you?"

"Well, my mom kept a book on you, sort of. It started out with a bunch of pictures and notes and things from when you two were in college, and then she would cut out articles about you and your work and add them in over time." The thought of Grace doing that choked me up. "And she took me to see some of your photos when they were on display for a workshop downtown, but she didn't really talk about your circumstances."

"Yeah, but what did *you* think?"

"Honestly, my mom always spoke pretty highly of you, but the story of your relationship was presented like a cautionary tale or something. A lesson for me to learn from. She didn't blame you, even before she discovered the truth, so I didn't think much of anything—just that you had a crazy career and kids weren't your thing."

I stared past her out the window. "I wanted kids. . . ."

"My mom didn't know, so you shouldn't blame her. She would always tell me how badly she wanted me. She told me that when people come together and . . . you know . . . do it"—her cheeks turned pink—"that they should always be on the same page about kids and the future and all that. I guess she thought you knew from the letters and that you didn't want to be a dad."

"It wasn't like that."

"I meant it when I say she never put you down. I'm smart enough to know it's because part of me is made from you; she'd be putting me down at the same time if she did that."

I was experiencing every feeling one could have at the same time, including love. I was feeling love for the sweet child sitting in front of me, defending me and defending her mom, equally, with such loyalty and insight. "You're very smart." My throat tightened. "You're like your mom in that way. Very perceptive and witty." I collected myself. "And your childhood . . . how was it?"

"It was pretty good. I mean, my dad totally loved me and my mom always did her best. I had everything I needed." She sipped her coffee.

"What's your last name?"

"Porter."

I felt a lump in my throat. "Of course."

"It was just easier that way. You're on my birth certificate, though."

"Am I?"

"Uh-huh. My dad tried to adopt me, like, five times. That's why, at the end of his life, Mom tried so hard to get in touch with you; you would've had to give up your parental rights in order for him to officially adopt me. It didn't matter because he was always my dad. That piece of paper would have meant more for him than for me."

"I'm so sorry, Ash. I didn't know. I can't tell you how sorry I am." She started to get a little misty-eyed but held it together. I was close to having a breakdown myself and felt conflicted about everything, including Dan. He was dead already so I couldn't kill him, but somewhere under the shock, I started to realize I should be grateful for him. After all, he raised my daughter into someone I would admire instantly.

Ash took a bite of her scone, smiled, and looked out the window as she chewed. It was like I was looking at Grace from a long time ago, but with my eye color and a tiny cleft in her chin, just like me, barely noticeable.

"Do you have any crooked toes?"

"Yeah, actually. My second toe is crooked. Thanks for that, by the way." We both laughed, but then we got quiet again.

"What was he like?"

"Who?"

"Your dad."

She looked me right in eyes, so brave, like her mom. "You're my dad now . . . if you want."

That was it. I started crying. I wasn't sobbing, but there were tears running down my face, and my throat was so tight that I thought I would stop breathing. I reached across the table, took her hands in mine, and closed my eyes. I realized that I wanted Ash in my life. The pain of missing her childhood was killing me. "Yes, I want to," I whispered.

She started crying, too. We both cried together, surrendering to the reality that we had to accept. No one could change the past or give us back the time we had lost, and there were no words to make everything better. We just had to accept the present for what it was.

We stood and hugged for a long time, and I was surprised that it didn't feel foreign to me; she didn't feel like a stranger.

There were a few stares from café patrons, but eventually everyone ignored us and went on with their conversations as I held my crying daughter. Gotta love that about New Yorkers. I felt bad for how things had worked out with Ash's childhood, but I was still intensely furious with Grace and Elizabeth.

On our way back to Grace and Ash's brownstone, she asked, "What's going to happen with you and Mom?"

"There's a complicated history there, Ash. I don't know what's going to happen."

"She loves you."

"I know."

Once we reached the brownstone, she pulled her phone from her pocket. "What's your phone number? I'll text you so you have mine. You can call me if you want to hang out."

I gave her my number. "You know, I don't just want to 'hang out.' I want to be a part of your life. It'll be weird at first, but I want this . . . if you do."

She grinned and socked me in the arm, "Alrighty, I'll see ya later then . . . um . . . what should I call you?"

"Call me anything you want."

She laughed. "Okay, see ya, George."

I shook my head. "Silly girl." I messed up her hair and then noticed Grace was watching us from the window. She looked terrible, and had obviously been crying nonstop. She was wearing a sad, small smile. I looked away.

"How about I call you Father for now . . . since you are my father."

"That's fine with me. Do you want to get breakfast tomorrow?" I didn't want to be away from her ever again.

"I can't, I'm going shopping with my friend."

"Okay, what about the next day?"

"School, and then I have chess club."

"Chess club?" I arched my eyebrows.

"Yeah, it's my goal in life to beat Mom. She's so good."

"Okay then." I was starting to wonder if there was really room for me to step into her life.

"Dinner on Tuesday?" she asked.

"Perfect," I said. "Wear your pajamas. I know a great place."

"You're weird."

"You are, too."

"Cool."

I walked home, hoping, sadly, that Grace would be able to stop crying.

I honestly didn't know what I was going to do except try to get to know Ash while I was in New York and be a dad, even though I knew nothing about what that entailed.

On Monday, I went to the library and read every parenting book I could get my hands on.

I texted Grace that night.

ME: I'm trying to wrap my head around all of it.
GRACE: I understand.
ME: I'm going to see Ash on Tuesday night for dinner.
GRACE: Okay.
ME: I want to see her regularly.
GRACE: Of course.
ME: Does she have a college fund?
GRACE: Yes.
ME: Can I give you some money?
GRACE: That's not necessary.
ME: I want to.
GRACE: Okay then. You can put it in her college fund. I'll get the account info for you.

A part of me wanted to say more, but I wasn't capable of talking to her about anything beyond the logistics of co-parenting.

The next day I was slammed with work stuff but I managed to get out and have lunch with Scott. When he started talking about Singapore, I told him about Ash. He didn't say anything; he was just shocked. He told me to take the rest of the week off. I didn't realize I really needed to until that moment.

When I returned to my building, I found Monica sitting on a bench near the elevator. She had the family bassinet balanced on her lap.

Her eyes were full of compassion, but her nostrils were flared and her jaw was set in a rigid line.

"Monica, don't say it."

"I was going to stab her in the eye with my heel." I looked

down at her five-inch stilettos. *Yep, those would get the job done.* "I'm so sorry, Matt. Alexander's in Tokyo, otherwise he'd be here. I came in his place."

"Thank you, Monica. I see you paid Elizabeth a little visit. You didn't actually hurt her, did you?"

"Of course not, but I did give her a piece of my mind. I wasn't gonna let her off that easy." She pointed her long index finger at me. "That woman took a shit inside the soul of this family."

"I know." I had already resigned myself to that reality, but I could tell Monica was still fighting it, or at least trying to figure out how to fix it. "It is what it is. I just have to try to be a part of my daughter's life from here on out." I nodded my head toward the door. "Take a walk with me?"

She hiked her large Gucci bag over her shoulder and picked up the bassinet. "Can we stop by Grace's?"

"You're going to give that to Grace?"

"Of course. As a gesture of apology for that wretched Elizabeth."

"I don't know if she's home, but we can go by there and see. Here, I'll carry it." I took the bassinet from her hands and looked at the ornate wooden legs and fading varnish and wondered what Ash would have looked like as a baby sleeping inside, peacefully.

As Monica's heels clacked down the sidewalk beside me, I laughed at the fantasy of her taking her shoes off and throwing them at Elizabeth. "What did you say to her?"

"Oh, I just told her that she was a thief and a liar. She stole something more precious from you than she could ever comprehend. Of course, she denied it and acted like she knew nothing. I told her I wouldn't believe anything she said. She is the worst kind of person, Matt. A self-deluded, self-involved bitch."

"Do you think maybe she didn't know?"

We got to the corner and waited for the stoplight to turn. Monica sighed and pulled an envelope out of her bag. "She knew something, but she didn't open the letters from Grace. She threw them away, all except for this one." She handed me a sealed envelope. "If she was getting a letter every year and going to such great lengths to hide it from you, she must have known Grace was trying to tell you something. I don't know if she really would've kept such a secret from you if she knew what it was, but denial through ignorance isn't an excuse."

I set down the bassinet, folded the envelope, and stuck it in my pocket. "You might be right."

"You're not gonna read it?"

We were approaching Grace's building. "I'll read it. Just not right now. This is it." I looked up to the front door of the brownstone and then held the bassinet out to her.

"Aren't you going to come with me?"

"No, Ash isn't home yet. She's still at school."

"You don't want to see Grace?"

"I can't, Monica. Just go, I'll wait here."

I turned around and watched an old woman walk her dog down the street, but I couldn't help but hear Grace answer the door. "Monica?"

"Hello, Grace. It's good to see you. It's been a long time."

"Yes it has. You look great. Life has been well for you?" Grace was still being sweet, even under the shittiest of circumstances.

"It has, but it got even better when I learned that I was

an aunt." Monica's voice didn't waver. She was determined to stay strong. "That's why I'm here, to deliver this to you. I know Ash is a big girl now, but I wanted you to have it until the next baby in the family is born, wherever or whenever that might happen."

"Thank you." Grace sounded choked up, but I still couldn't turn around.

There were a few moments of silence and then Monica said, "Here's my number. Please keep in touch. I know you tried, and I'm sorry about you and Matt and this whole big mess."

"I am, too."

"You're family now, Grace. Please know that."

"Okay."

A few seconds later, Monica was at my side. "Ready?"

"Yeah."

"Matt, why are you taking this out on her?"

"I missed my daughter's entire childhood, Monica."

"But that wasn't Grace's fault."

"I don't know. It's confusing and I can't think about that right now."

The truth was that I couldn't face her, knowing that she had spent the last fifteen years raising our child, mostly on her own. And for all of that time, she thought I was just a selfish asshole ignoring her letters and calls. *She had no faith in me.*

"I have to stop. My feet are killing me."

"Well, Jesus, it's those shoes. They're unnatural," I said.

She took them off and shoved them into her bag. "I know; stupid, isn't it? The things women do in the name of high fashion."

I put my arm around her shoulder. "You're all right, you know that? I'm glad my brother married you. Thanks for coming out."

She kissed me on cheek, "I love you. Now hail me a cab, would ya? I've got some shopping to do."

I flagged down a taxi and opened the door for her. She ducked her head and got in. "I'll be at the Waldorf Astoria if you need me."

Back at my loft I opened the envelope.

Dear Matt,

Our daughter is ten today. I said before that I wouldn't send any more letters, but I have an important reason this time. I'm very sad to tell you that Dan is sick. He's been having severe heart problems over the last year, and his condition is likely terminal. He so desperately wants to adopt Ash, and I'm writing to ask you if you would please consider signing over your parental rights, as you were named on her birth certificate. Ash is a wonderful child, witty and beautiful, with a great sense of humor. She is the joy of my life. I never blamed you for the choices I made a decade ago, but now I can change things for her and Dan by making it official with the adoption.

I know you're very busy, but would you please get in touch with us?

Regards,
Grace Porter
212-555-1156

The life she led, the tragedy, despair, and rejection, was all because of me. I could have blamed Elizabeth, but it wouldn't matter in the end because Elizabeth meant nothing to Grace. I knew that if you followed the trail of pain, it would lead to me, at least in Grace's mind, and my pain led to her.

Staring at my phone, a question popped into my head. I shot off a text immediately.

> **ME:** Why were you looking in the Missed Connections section?
> **GRACE:** I wasn't.
> **ME:** How did you get the note?
> **GRACE:** A student of mine recognized the title "Green-eyed Lovebird" when he was looking for his own missed connection and brought it to me.
> **ME:** So you didn't really want to find me? Was it just for Ash?

There was no response.

Two hours later, I was on their doorstep, wearing plaid pajama pants, slippers, and a coat. It was six p.m. and the sun was beginning to set. Ash came to the door wearing white flannel PJs with a green turtle pattern on it. She swung the door open wide and announced, "Hello, Father!"

"Hello, Daughter."

She pointed behind her with her thumb and lowered her voice. "Should I ask if she wants to come with us?"

I shook my head. Ash looked down for a second, as if figuring out what to do, and then yelled, "Bye, Mom! Love you, be back later."

"Love you. Be careful!" Grace yelled from the other room. "Ready?"

"Yep." She bounced out the door.

"We're going to a restaurant that serves breakfast any-time," I told her.

"Oh cool. I'm gonna get blueberry pancakes during the Renaissance," she deadpanned. I stared for a beat and then she started cracking up.

"You scared me for a second. I was concerned about your IQ."

"I got that joke from a TV show."

I laughed. "Now I'm really concerned about your IQ."

The place Grace and I used to go to was long gone, so I took Ash to a diner in our neighborhood.

"Mom told me you guys used to do this breakfast-for-dinner thing all the time in college."

"We did." I smiled at the memory but didn't want to dwell on the past. "How was school?"

"Good. Boring, except for ceramics."

"You like pottery?"

"I love it."

"My mom—your grandmother—loved it. She had a little art studio set up behind her house in California. She called it the Louvre." I chuckled at the memory.

"I know."

"Your mom pretty much covered everything, didn't she?"

"Why didn't you want her to come tonight?"

This daughter of mine didn't pull any punches. "Like I said before, things are complicated."

"You guys love each other, so why the hell aren't you together?"

"It's not that simple, Ash. I need time."

"Well, I think you're wasting it."

Why was the fifteen-year-old the smartest one in the room?

Because she doesn't have decades of bullshit clouding her judgment.

We ordered pancakes and milk shakes, and Ash told me about school and a boy she liked.

"Boys are pigs. You know that, right? Stay away from them."

She sipped her milk shake thoughtfully. "You don't need to do this. Seriously."

"I do. I want to meet your friends and come to your school events. And that's not a request."

"I know."

After we totally stuffed ourselves with pancakes, I paid and we headed out. On our way to the door, Ash stopped in front of the refrigerator case.

"You want a piece of pie?" I asked.

She dug into the little purse slung across her chest. "No, I'm gonna buy a piece for Mom."

"I'll buy it. What does she like?"

She raised an eyebrow. "You know what she likes."

"One piece of chocolate cream and a piece of peanut butter to go," I said to the woman behind the counter. She bagged it up and handed it to me, and I led Ash out of the diner.

Ash and I talked about music the entire way back to her house. It was no surprise that Ash had great taste and vast knowledge across genres. We agreed that we would see Radiohead together the next time they played in New York.

I wondered how many times Grace had played Radiohead or Jeff Buckley to Ash over the years. I hadn't been able to listen to either one since college.

I followed Ash up the steps. She swung the door open wide, turned around, and kissed me on the cheek. "Thanks for dinner, Father." She left me in the open doorway, holding the pie, as she ran up the stairs and called out, "Mom, some dude is at the door with pie!"

I swallowed, frozen in the doorway.

Sneaky little thing.

24. Once, We Were Lovers

GRACE

Every time I laid eyes on Matt, I'd instantly be overcome by two conflicting feelings: shock at how handsome he was—lean, strong, defined, and somehow sexier with age—and total disbelief that he was even there. I was convinced I would wake up and things would be back to the way they were before.

But I wanted to be strong around him. I had spent a week crying over how he took the news. I'd done enough falling apart for all of us. Frankly, I was getting tired of mulling over all this shit; I had been doing it for a decade and a half. If he wanted to blame me for what his psychotic ex-wife had done, then so be it. I was done crying and I was done apologizing.

Strutting toward him, I watched as his eyes scanned me from head to toe. I was wearing a short, silk nightgown and a devil-may-care look in my eyes. I took the bag from his hands. "Chocolate and peanut butter?" I asked, drily. He nodded. "Thanks."

"You're welcome."

"Okay, well, it's late." He just blinked at me then looked down at his slippers.

"Um . . . all right, I'm gonna head home."

"Okie dokie."

He headed for the door and I followed to close it behind him. But just before he stepped out of the doorway, he turned, placed his hands on my silk-clad hips, and kissed me right below the ear.

I whimpered.

"Night, Gracie," he whispered, and then he was gone. I stood in the doorway for several moments, trying to catch my breath. Just when I was learning to hold it together . . .

AFTER SCHOOL THE next day, I went to Green Acres, which didn't remotely embody its name. It was a subpar convalescent facility in the Bronx, where Orvin's daughter had placed him after his wife died a few years earlier. The place really needed renovation. The walls were painted that heinous shade of vomit-green from *The Exorcist*, and the whole place smelled of putrid yeast from the bread-making factory next door. Green Acres was awful. There was a small yard in the back for residents to get exercise, but not a single blade of grass. I broke Orvin out of there at least once a week. We'd go to a nearby park and play chess, and even though he couldn't remember my name anymore, I was fairly certain he knew who I was.

As we sat in the park, we listened to the wind whistling through the trees. "Do you still listen for it?" I asked.

"For what, doll?"

"The music."

"Yeah. I do. I always hear it."

"What do you think it means that I don't hear it any-more?"

He took my second knight. "Check. I don't know what it means. Maybe you're not listening hard enough."

How does he beat me every time? I moved my king. "I'm listening."

"No, you're too busy feeling sorry for yourself."

"I've never felt sorry for myself."

"Maybe not before, no, but you are now. Checkmate."

I reset the board. We played with a cheesy plastic-and-cardboard chess set that folded up and fit into my purse. "I'm not feeling sorry for myself. I'm just tired and kind of sad."

"Why are you sad?"

I studied Orvin's face. It was hard not to feel like Orvin didn't belong in Green Acres because he seemed so spry and alert. Yet oftentimes he would forget everything and ask when he had to be at the shop, which sadly had been closed for more than a decade. This was one of his good days, but he could slip easily into forgetting.

"Do you ever wish you weren't stuck in Green Acres?"

"My darling Grace, let me share a proverb with you."

I was startled. He hadn't called me by my name in . . . I didn't know how long. "Okay."

"'I used to think I was poor because I didn't have any shoes, and then I met a man with no feet.'"

I smiled sheepishly. "I am feeling sorry for myself, aren't I?"

"More than that. You're being ungrateful. You have the man you always wanted in your life again, a beautiful daughter, and a great job."

"Yes, but that man doesn't want me."

"He will. Just be yourself. Find the music."

ASH AND I ended up at Tati's for dinner that night. Tati was trying her hand at being domestic; she had met a man she actually wanted to date, and was bound and determined to impress him. It wasn't the first time Ash and I had been guinea pigs, though I can't say we enjoyed it. Tati was a terrible cook. Period.

Tati came to the table with a large platter. "Lamb tagine and Moroccan couscous!"

"Oh Tati, I hate eating lamb."

She looked affronted. "Why?"

"They're just too cute to eat."

"Well, this one's not cute anymore."

I shook my head and took a small serving. Ash wrinkled her nose and took an even smaller one while Tati ran around, looking for a wine key.

"Can I have some wine?" Ash asked.

"Nope," Tati and I said simultaneously.

"Just a sip? Dad said he'd let me have some wine at his house when he has me over for dinner."

"You call him Dad now?" Tati asked.

"Well, not to his face, but what else am I supposed to call him? Matt? It wasn't his fault that he didn't get to be my dad."

"Does he want to be called Dad?" I asked her, carefully.

"I don't think he cares. He wants to come to all my school stuff and meet my friends."

"I think it would make him feel good to hear you say it. The poor guy has been robbed of your childhood," Tati said.

I bristled. "What happened to the man-hater in you?" I shot back.

"Turning over a new leaf. You should, too."

"Call him Dad, if he wants," I told Ash. I handed my glass of wine over to her. "Just one sip."

She took a tiny sip and scrunched up her nose. "Ew."

Tati looked up at the ceiling wistfully. "I loved the way he used to dress."

I rolled my eyes.

"Did you and my dad get along when you guys were in college?" Ash asked Tati.

"Of course. Your mom and dad were inseparable. If I wanted to see Grace outside of class, then I had to see your dad, too. But we got along well, so it was all good fun back then." Tati turned to me. "Speaking of the good ol' days, I think you should come down and practice with us this week after school."

"What on earth for?" I said through a mouthful of couscous.

"We're looking for a cellist."

"You should totally do it, Mom. I can go to Dad's after school. He's working from home now and invited me to come over after school whenever I want."

"I don't know, Tati. I don't think I'm good enough anymore." I was also worried that Ash was embracing Matt a little too eagerly. It made me realize how desperately she was missing Dan. "And Ash, how is it that you're already so comfortable with your father? You barely know him?"

"I don't know," she said.

"I'm afraid you're doing this to displace your grief," I said.

"I think you're overanalyzing this, Mom. I look at him and I see myself. I'm just comfortable around him. Plus, he's so nice and wants to be a part of my life. Don't ruin that for me because of your screwed-up relationship with him."

"I'm going to pretend like you're not being sassy right now." Though she was probably right.

We continued to push the lamb and couscous around our plates. It was as terrible as it looked. Finally, Tati put down her fork.

"So, you guys wanna get a burger or something?"

Ash and I nodded eagerly.

"You should stick to spaghetti," Ash said. "You're good at that."

"That was takeout, Ash," I said, as Tati burst out laughing.

"Oh," she squeaked, blushing.

"C'mon," Tati said. "Let's get those burgers."

AFTER SCHOOL, FOR the rest of the week, I went to practice with Tati and the New York Philharmonic. Ash went to Matt's each day, and then each night, before she went to bed, she would recap every detail of their time together. She was falling in love with him, the way daughters do with their dads. How could she not? I was happy about it, but still, I felt this ache over my own relationship with Matt.

On Saturday, Tati offered to take Ash to a movie, and I went to dinner alone at a small Italian bistro, where I let the waiter talk me into ordering a bottle of wine.

"You can have a glass and take the rest home with you. We'll wrap it up," he said.

I agreed, but ended up staying for two hours and drinking

at least three quarters of the bottle. From under the little twinkly lights that hung from the awning, I watched people walking along the street, holding hands, kissing on the corner. *The Godfather*–like music and warmth from the outdoor heater was soothing me right to sleep. "Ma'am?" said the waiter as he reached for the bottle. "Can I wrap this up for you?"

That must be my cue to leave. Time for the tipsy lady to scram. "Yes, that would be wonderful." There was only about a glass left, but I took it anyway.

After I paid, I walked back the four blocks toward my house, but when I passed Matt's street, I turned onto it.

From the other side of the street, I could see inside his loft. There he was, sitting on his couch, staring straight ahead. In the darkness below, I stood watching him, thinking it was weird that, between he, me, and Ash, none of us were together that night. He was sipping wine and looking pensively at something, or maybe nothing at all. I wondered what kind of music he was listening to. He stood up and walked to the window. I backed up farther into the shadows so he couldn't see me. He was completely still as he stood there, watching the occasional car go by.

What is he thinking?

Finally, I said, *Screw it.* I darted across the street and rang the buzzer to his apartment.

He answered quickly. "Who is it?"

"It's Grace." My nerves were terrorizing my stomach.

"Come up."

When the elevator doors opened, he was standing there, waiting. I looked down at his bare feet and up to his black jeans, his belt and white T-shirt, up farther to his mouth, his neck, and his long, yummy hair, tied back. I shivered. "Hello." I held the paper bag out to him and he took it.

He pulled the bottle from the bag, laughed, and then looked up at me with a wry smile, "Thank you, Grace. I've never been given an almost completely empty bottle of wine before."

My face was expressionless. "It's really good. I saved you a glass."

He looked at me carefully, probably to gauge my level of inebriation. "Where's Ash tonight?"

"With Tati. Oh shoot, I need to find out when they'll be home."

He removed his cell phone from his back pocket and handed it to me. I dialed Tati's number. The movie was probably over by now, and I didn't want Ash to come home to an empty house.

"Hello?" Her voice sounded strange, and then I realized that she wouldn't recognize the number.

"Tati, it's me. Where are you?"

"We're getting ice cream. Everything okay? Whose number is this?"

"It's Matt's."

Without responding, I heard Tati pull the phone away from her ear and say to Ash, "Hey, let's rent movies and get a bunch of junk food and hang out at my house? Your mom says it's okay."

"Okay," I heard Ash say.

Tati came back on and whispered, "You're covered. See you in the morning."

I hit end and handed the phone back to Matt. "What did she say?"

"They're fine. Ash is staying over at Tati's tonight."

"Is Tati a good influence?" he asked, looking at me sideways.

"We're not twenty-one anymore, Matt; she doesn't sit around smoking pot all day. She's a world-class musician and an independent, educated woman. What do you think?"

"Yeah, you're right," he conceded immediately. I felt guilty for a second, realizing he was just trying to do what he thought dads should do. "So, to what do I owe this visit?"

Things were not going as I planned. "I don't know . . . I just need . . ."

"What?" He set the bottle down and moved toward me. "What do you need?" I couldn't tell yet if he was being seductive or annoyed or both.

When he stepped closer, I could feel his warmth and smell the cardamom-and-sandalwood scent of his body wash. "Did you just shower?"

He blinked. "Why?" He wasn't budging, wasn't giving me any clues with his body language as to how he felt about me, but I thought I could still detect a quiet anger or resentment beneath the surface.

And I was just drunk enough to call him on it.

"Who are you angry with, Matt?"

He didn't hesitate. "You. Elizabeth. Dan . . . Myself."

"Why on earth would you be angry at Dan?"

His voice was restrained. "I'm jealous of him." He looked into my eyes. "He got everything I wanted. He got what was mine."

"But it wasn't his fault. I've accepted that, and you should, too."

He moved a fraction of an inch closer and looked farther into my eyes. "Maybe. How much wine have you had?"

"I feel sober."

"You want me to walk you home?"

"That's not why I stopped here."

"What do you need, Grace?"

I leaned up on my toes and kissed him. The kiss felt fragile at first, like we would break into a million pieces if we went too fast, too hard. But it only took seconds before we were removing each other's clothes, our hands in each other's hair.

We collapsed onto the bed naked, kissing and tugging at each other. When he sat up, I crawled onto his lap and guided him inside me. He moaned from his chest and gripped my waist, my back arching involuntarily, my breasts rising up to meet his mouth. "So beautiful," he whispered between kissing and sucking and twirling his tongue around my nipple. He was patient but urgent, and he somehow knew where to put his hands, where I needed pressure, where I needed to be kissed.

He had ruined me for all other men. He was ruining me now.

He turned me around on my hands and knees, yanked my hips toward his body, and thrust into me. I felt like he was taking his anger out on me, but for some reason I wanted him to.

"Am I hurting you?"

"No. Don't stop."

I wanted to feel it. I wanted to feel like he was sending all the bad stuff far away.

The moment we came, he wrapped his arms around

me, and I could feel his heart beating against my back. He didn't say anything; he just held me like that until our hearts stopped racing. When he released me, I was suddenly self-conscious and scurried away to collect my clothes.

"Wait, come here," he said as he moved to sit at the edge of the bed. "I want to look at you." He pulled me toward him. Even in the dimly lit room, I was nervous. He used his index finger to trace circles in the soft skin of my belly. There were some faded stretch marks on my hips that he leaned in and kissed. "What was it like?"

"What?"

"When Ash was born?"

I laughed. "You don't want to know about childbirth right now."

"I mean, were you both healthy?" He ran his hand up the inside of my thigh and looked up at me. I nodded. "You're a good mom, Grace."

"Thank you." Isn't that all we need to hear sometimes — that you're a good mom or friend or daughter or wife?

"Were you happy?" His voice was shaky. "The day you had Ash, were you happy?"

"It was the happiest day of my life," I choked out.

He started to cry quietly. "I wish I was there," he said, and then his body was wracked with full, powerful sobs as he buried his face against my belly.

I held him, running my hands over his shoulders, through his hair. "I know, everything's okay," I said over and over, but I feared there would be no healing us. The scars were too deep.

"I feel like I'm living in a nightmare, like I've just woken up from a coma to discover that fifteen years of my life have gone by. Everything went on without me. I missed every-thing."

I continued to hold him all through the night and told him about the day Ash was born.

"We were in Venice when my water broke. They took me by water taxi to the hospital. I remember looking out onto the canals and thinking about you, hoping you were safe. It was uncharacteristically warm for that time of year, so warm that you could feel the heat radiating off the surface of the water. When I think about that day, it was like the sun was kissing the earth, like God was making his presence known.

"I was lucky. My labor was easy—everyone said so. At first, all I could do was stare in disbelief at her trembling little body, covered in blood and white stuff as she flailed around on my chest. I couldn't believe that you and I had made her. When she quieted down and began nursing, Dan said it was beautiful, that she and I were beautiful."

"I know you were," Matt said, and then sighed as he gazed out the window. Maybe he was imagining it and finally feeling a part of it.

"We didn't have a name for her when we arrived at the hospital. Dan was just a friend then, so I was making all of the decisions, even though I felt totally clueless. But somehow, in the hospital, I knew what to do. When I saw her, I could think of nothing but us—you and me—and how she was the evidence of what we'd had together. After that day, I never looked back at our time in college without joy because I had Ash to represent it for me, and she was perfect . . . poetry in motion—the evidence of a life burning well and bright. Everyone knew why I named her Ash. Tati was furious for a while—she hated you for not getting back to me—but she got over it. Dan understood.

"Ash was a fussy baby for the first few months, and we were traveling a lot. It wasn't easy. I was a new, young mom, trying to figure everything out. Eventually, we came back to New York and settled down. Dan insisted that we live with him in his brownstone, so we did. It was a godsend because it gave Ash some consistency and structure, and she had two adults to look out for her."

Matt made a sound in his chest like that last sentence pained him, but I went on.

"Ash's personality always shined. She was a rambunctious toddler with wild blonde hair and those sweet, cozy brown eyes, like yours. She talked, walked, and fed herself early."

"Of course she did."

I laughed. "Yes, she's your child, so things came easily to her. But soon she was her own person, and I thought less about what her name meant and more about her individuality. She's a beautiful soul, different from me and you."

"I know that. I knew it the moment I met her," he whispered. "Was Dan's death hard on her?"

"She was strong, but I knew it was hard on her. He was a good, patient dad, and he loved her more than anything. I was grateful that we had a little time to prepare for it. We took a trip and stayed in a beach house in Cape Cod for a month. That's where he died, listening to the ocean, with me and Ash by his side. He spent his last days sitting in a chair, watching us play on the beach. At night, we would make a bonfire and Ash would read us stories in the firelight. Dan seemed happy, even though he knew he didn't have much time left." I started to cry.

Matt moved up the bed and took me in his arms. "Keep going."

"It was a Tuesday when he died, just a boring old Tuesday. He was lucid in the morning. We had moved his hospital bed onto the back patio so he could look out on the water. A hospice worker was there. We wrapped ourselves in blankets and watched the waves crashing down as Dan took his last breaths. Ash cried for a few minutes, and that was it. It was over. I never saw her cry about it again."

"And you?"

"Well, you know me. I'm pretty much a blubbering mess all the time."

"You didn't used to be."

"I know," I said quietly.

Matt brushed my hair back and wiped tears from my cheeks. "Why didn't you have more children?"

"We thought we might, but then Dan got sick and it just didn't make sense. Ash would have been such a good big sister."

"Yes, she would be," he said drowsily.

We fell asleep in the early-morning hours. I got a text from Tati around eleven saying that she and Ash were going to lunch and then she would be taking her home. I quietly snuck out of Matt's and made sure I was home before Ash got there.

Neither of us texted or called for days after that.

25. Come Back to Me

GRACE

Over the next week, Ash got into the habit of making plans with her dad and not telling me. When I would scold her for it, she would say, "Parents are supposed to communicate with each other. Even nonmarried ones."

That was Ash, always being the grown-up.

I knew Matt and I couldn't go on like this, conflicted and torn. We deserved more from each other, but I wasn't sure if either of us was ready.

Finally, one afternoon, Matt came by to pick up Ash. I answered the door and invited him in. He stood in the doorway of the kitchen, watching me as I dried the dishes.

"How are you?" he asked, a little formally but not uncomfortably.

"Good. I've been practicing with the Philharmonic after school. I might be sitting in for their cellist, actually, but I would have to leave for two weeks in the summer. I'm not sure if I want to leave Ash behind for that long."

"That's fantastic, Grace. I could take Ash; maybe we could plan a trip to California for then."

Ash called down from upstairs, "Give me five minutes, Dad!"

"Okay," he called back.

"Where are you guys off to?" I asked without looking up.

"We're going to the Met and then dinner."

I glanced at the clock; it was five fifteen. "You'll never make it up there before it closes."

"They're open till nine on Fridays."

"Oh, that's right." I suddenly realized we were having the most normal conversation we'd ever had: just two people discussing the quotidian details of our lives.

Ash came into the kitchen wearing a crop top, and my eyes bugged out. "Excuse me, do you have a sweater to go with that?"

Ash rolled her eyes.

"That eye-rolling business has to stop. Your mom just asked you a question," Matt said sharply.

Whoa. I hadn't had that kind of backup in a long time.

"I know, Dad, I just . . ."

"Nope. Go upstairs and get a sweater."

Ash huffed and left the room. Matt and I stared at each other for a few seconds before he walked over to me. "You look different. You seem happier."

I hadn't realized it before, but I think he was right. "Yeah, maybe."

"You're welcome to come with us, if you want."

"That's okay. I have some papers to grade."

He looked at me steadily for a couple of beats and then

shrugged. "All right, see ya." He leaned in and kissed me on the cheek, as if he had done it a million times before.

Once Ash came down the stairs, I followed them out of the front door and watched as they walked toward the subway. They were laughing . . . and it sounded like music. A part of me wanted to join them, but another part told me to stay. As much as I loved seeing Matt, and as much as I loved spending that night at his apartment, the endless rejections over the years—and the way he had taken the news about Ash—had scarred me so thoroughly that it was hard to believe he was there with us, like I had always wanted.

I never really doubted his love for me, but it scared me that he was keeping a safe distance. I needed to protect myself.

WE BEGAN SPLITTING our weekends up. Ash would go to Matt's on either Fridays or Saturdays, and we alternated Sundays.

The New York Philharmonic officially offered me the cellist seat for two weeks, so I spent my time away from Ash practicing the music and preparing for my two-week trip abroad.

Ash finished her freshman year of high school with phenomenal grades and received an award of overall excellence. Both Matt and I attended the ceremony, and he was beaming the entire time, like the proud dad that he was. When we left the auditorium that day, he hugged me for a long time and whispered, "You did good with her. Thank you. I'm so proud of my girls."

My heart ached at his words. I didn't know if anyone had ever told me they were proud of me, and there was no one in the world I wanted to hear those words from more than him.

The summer began and I knew Ash would get bored, so I signed her up for a summer photography workshop. As soon as Matt caught wind of it, he signed up, too. I knew he could have taught the class himself, but he just wanted the time with his daughter. Ash told me that once all her classmates found out who he was, he became a rock star to everyone, including the instructor. Ash told me he was even dabbling with a more artistic style from the documentary style that had made him famous.

It was strange how Matt and I were finding ourselves again; it was like we were picking up where we had left off, with both of us exploring our passions with renewed energy. Part of me felt like I was living the life I'd been meant to live. The only problem was that Matt and I weren't exactly doing it together. We were running on parallel tracks.

One night, Ash seemed down.

"What's wrong, honey?" I asked.

"Nothing," she said in a flat voice.

"Talk to me." I sat next to her on her bed.

"Dad told me that he was offered a job in Singapore for *National Geographic*. He's supposed to transfer in the fall."

My eyes widened in shock. "What? When did he tell you that?" I could not imagine Matt leaving now after he and Ash had become so close and everyone was finally healing.

She started crying. "A long time ago. Like, right when we met, but now the thought of it makes me so sad."

"What? I can't even . . . when did this . . ." I barely knew how to respond. "I'll talk to him."

She wiped away the tears and stood up. "I'm so sick of you guys dancing around each other like you're in junior high. I actually have friends with more mature relationships than the two of you."

"That's enough," I said, sharply.

She stomped her foot. "No, I'm sick of it. You guys need a push."

"Ash, that's not for you to decide."

"Well, maybe if you'd get over yourself, Dad wouldn't leave."

She ran out into the hall and into the bathroom and slammed the door.

"Ash, come back!"

I walked to the bathroom and pounded on the door, but she wouldn't open it. After a few minutes, I gave up and went to my own room. I was angry. Upset. Confused. Was he really leaving? *How the hell could he do this to us? To me?*

Eventually, I heard Ash leave the bathroom and go to her room. When I went to check on her an hour later, she was fast asleep.

I called Tati and asked her to come over.

"It's ten o'clock," she said, flatly.

"I need to go to Matt's and I don't know how long I'll be there."

"Can't you just call him?"

"No, because I need to punch him in the face."

"Oh, Jesus. What happened now?"

"Ash said he might be taking a job in Singapore. We just had a big fight about it, and I don't know what the hell to do. Just come over, please."

"Got it. I'll be there in twenty minutes."

After Tati got to my house, I stormed several blocks to Matt's house, raging with anger. I rang the buzzer over and over again.

"Yes?" Matt said over the speaker.

"It's your baby-mama. Let me in."

I heard him laugh. "Come right up."

When I got to the loft, he opened the door wide, smiling. "Gracie."

"Don't Gracie me, you bastard." I shoved past him, threw my purse down, and crossed my arms. He looked scared. "What in the fuck, Matt? What is wrong with you?"

He leaned against the wall, perhaps to get as far away from me as possible. "What are you talking about?"

"Our poor daughter was in tears tonight because you told her you were moving to Singapore. Is that true? Because if it is—"

"Grace, stop. Listen to me." It looked like he was searching his mind. "I mentioned to her that I got a job offer a long time ago, when we barely knew each other."

"Well?"

"I told my boss I couldn't take it."

I narrowed my eyes at him. "When?"

"After that night you came here. I never would have left anyway; I was just in a daze. I had requested a job in the field before I reconnected with you and met Ash." He was sincere, pleading. "I feel bad that she's been dwelling on it."

"Yeah, well, kids do that."

He came toward me and reached out for my hands and held them between us. "I'm still learning, Grace."

I looked down and shook my head. "I know, I'm sorry.

I overreacted. She was just in so much pain. I just couldn't watch her go through what I went through . . ."

His eyes looked haunted. "I'm never gonna leave you guys. You have to believe me, Gracie. You have to."

I stared at him hard. "Make me believe."

He ran his thumb over my lip. "I will, even if it fucking takes me forever." And then his lips were on mine and we were in it, pulling away from the past and rushing fast into the future.

26. Our Time

GRACE

Matt, Ash, and I had dinner together every night for the next few nights. Things were finally starting to feel right.

On Friday of that week, I found Matt waiting for me at the front gate after school. Ash had told me to dress nicely that morning, and I could see she had given the same direction to Matt. I didn't know what was going on, but I decided I would go with the flow.

"What are you doing here?"

He smiled and then bent and kissed my cheek. "Nice to see you, Gracie. I think our daughter has something planned for us."

"Of course she does." He was in dress pants and a button-down shirt. I looked down at his gleaming black Converse. That was about as dressy as I ever saw Matt.

"You look good," I told him.

His eyes took in my casual floral dress and sandals. "So do you. You look lovely."

I grinned. "So what's this all about, you think?"

"Not a clue." He held an arm out to me. "Shall we?"

"How do you know where to go?" I asked.

"Ash told me to meet you here at the gate and escort you to the auditorium."

I nodded. "Let's go."

Inside the auditorium, we found Ash, Tati, and my orchestra students waiting for us, along with a few familiar faces from the Philharmonic. With the exception of Ash, they were all arranged in chairs with their instruments, as if they were about to play.

Ash came skipping over to us. "I thought we could do something fun today. All of us."

I waved to everyone. "Did you put this all together?"

"I had help."

Tati came over and I felt my throat tighten with emotion. "Are you two ready for this? Your daughter has worked very hard to plan something special for you today. Come and have a seat."

We sat on the two guest chairs set up in front of our own private orchestra. Tati was the conductor, which I found especially entertaining. Matt grabbed my hand as the music began. I knew it from the first note: "Hallelujah." He squeezed my hand and held on through the entire song.

At the end, I stood up excitedly and clapped like a maniac, yelling, "Bravo!" Matt whistled and clapped and then Ash came running over to us again.

"Wasn't that amazing?" she said.

"Oh, Ash, thank you, sweetie. That was so thoughtful of you."

"Wait, it's not over yet; this is just the beginning." She

handed us a manila envelope. I opened it and pulled out an eight-by-ten black-and-white photo of Matt and me in college. It was of the two of us in the lounge at Senior House. Tati had taken it, and I remembered it vividly. "Read the back." Ash said.

Matt stood behind me and watched as I turned it over. We both read the lines out loud:

> *"Hallelujah, you two found each other here . . . / Now head to the place you first met, just before senior year."*

Tati came up right behind Ash. "Give us a ten-minute head start," she said.

Matt laughed. "Okay, we'll see you over there."

We said our good-byes to the musicians and thanked them for a beautiful performance. After Ash and Tati took off in a cab, Matt took my hand in his. "Do you wanna walk?"

"Yeah."

It was a warm and sunny day. The neighborhood felt more laid-back than usual. Matt swung our hands back and forth as we walked down the street.

When we got to Senior House, the moment felt surreal and beautifully nostalgic. The building looked a little different but still felt the same. Tati and Ash were standing in the stairway. "Come up!" Tati yelled.

On the third landing, we peeked into my old room. It was empty except for my cello, propped on a chair near the window. I looked at Ash and she smiled. "Play for Dad, Mom." She handed Matt an old camera that I recognized from college. "It's loaded and all set for you."

He smiled. "Thank you, Ash."

"Okay you two, there's an envelope for you on the windowsill," Tati said.

"How did you guys get into this room?" I asked.

"We told the summer RA your story and he gave us the key. It's the summer and no one was using it anyway," Ash said, laughing.

"How much time do we have?" Matt asked.

"Be at the next location in an hour." She leaned up on her toes and kissed her dad on the cheek and then turned to me. "Have fun, you guys."

After they left, Matt closed the door behind us. Almost immediately, I heard the shutter on the camera clicking as he photographed me from behind. I went to the cello and sat down. "Any requests?"

He pulled the camera away from his face. " 'Fake Plastic Trees'?"

"You remember?"

"How could I forget?" His gaze was heavy. There was warmth and desire in his eyes, but there was also a tiny bit of regret that I knew would never go away. I felt it too, especially in that room.

I played the rather difficult song, alternating between vibrato and the bow. Matt stopped photographing me and just watched in wonder. When the song was over, I looked up to his smiling face. "You stopped taking pictures?"

"Some things are better to keep up here." He tapped the side of his head.

"I agree," I whispered.

He was at my side in two strides. As I stood, he gripped my face and kissed me hard. We broke away from each other for just a second. Matt set the camera on the windowsill and pressed the shutter release. The timer was on and he was back to kissing me as it clicked down and snapped open and shut, capturing the moment.

His hands crept under my dress, and before I knew it he was peeling my panties down. "Take these off," he said, breathily.

"There's no bed here."

"That's never stopped us before."

I pulled my panties down and kicked them off. Matt's belt was undone already when I looked back up. He picked me up to straddle him and set me on the chair. He was inside of me in two seconds without ever breaking the kiss.

"I love you, Gracie." His voice was so smooth near my ear that I practically fell apart in the first few moments. He told me he loved me but I already knew. We moved slowly and gently and it was enough. Our moans were quiet and soothing, and I didn't want it to ever end. Afterward we held each other for a long time.

Inside the envelope on the windowsill was a picture. It was an old color photograph of Matt and me in our pajamas, with the traffic blurred behind us. "This is cool. I've never seen this."

"I just got it developed when we got back in touch. Turn it over, let's see the clue."

Go east one block to Avenue Seven
And then south three more
To a little slice of heaven

We left Senior House with big smiles on our faces. "Gosh, I hope Ash doesn't think we . . ." I started to say.

"Honestly, Grace, she sort of set it up."

"Not for *that*."

"Well, we don't need to tell her everything."

About halfway down the block, I stopped. "Full disclosure?"

"Always."

I looked down at my feet. "I almost had an abortion."

He looked at my steadily. "What stopped you?"

"I couldn't do it." My eyes started to well up.

"Please don't cry. This is such a happy day—the happiest I've felt in a long time." He kissed me.

"I know. I'm just so happy I made the right choice."

"Me too," he said, quietly, as he held me on the street.

We found Ash and Tati standing outside of a building. "Come in, this is so cool," Ash yelled.

We walked in, and upon entering we realized it was a gallery, with a man standing in a suit. Tati introduced him as the owner of the gallery. "He agreed to let Ash put up these photos, and he loved them so much that he wants to run a show for the next two months."

I looked around, stunned. They were all Matt's photos of me blown up and mounted professionally. The first one was a color photo of me playing the cello in the old dorm room—a picture I had never seen before. The title tag next to it read "Grace in Color." I started to cry then, big, happy tears.

"These are beautiful. God, Ash . . ." Matt was emotional, too; he could barely speak. We both hugged her between us as we walked through the gallery, staring at all the memories, admiring Matt's talent and seeing his reaction to the photos, each so precious to him. It wasn't long before all of us, including Tati, were crying.

Huddled together near the door, Ash said, "There's just one more place. I have to go first, so give me a few minutes."

"No clue?"

"No, this one is a surprise," Ash said.

We all hugged and then Tati walked Ash to a cab. Just before Ash got in, she called back, "No more crying, you guys!"

"Okay, kid!" Matt called back.

Once Ash was gone, Tati walked up to us and put her hands on her hips. "Listen up. That little girl has been planning this for a long time. I told her it wasn't a good idea and she promised me that if things don't go her way, she won't be heartbroken."

"What is it, Tati?" I asked.

"I told her I wouldn't tell." She turned her attention to Matt. "Now, I don't know what's going to happen with your weird little family, but I have something to say to you personally. You saw how handy I am with a bow, right?" He nodded, with an amused smile on his face. "I will shove that thing so far up you-know-where, my friend, if you hurt either one of my girls."

He immediately threw his arms around her shoulders and pulled her into a hug. "I would never. They're my girls, too," he said quietly.

They pulled away and Tati pointed to the taxi behind her. "He knows where to take you. Go find your daughter."

In the back of the cab, Matt and I held hands. I don't think either one of us expected to pull up in front of City Hall, but that's where we ended up. "How did she know?" Matt asked.

"Tati must have told her the story. Look, there she is."

Ash was sitting on the steps, waiting for us. "Clever girl," Matt said.

"Our clever girl."

"Well, Gracie, do you feel like doing something crazy?"

"Always. But before we get out, I need to know if it's for her or for us. I'll do it either way, but I need to know."

He took my hand in his. "Graceland Marie Starr-Shore-Porter—whatever your name is—my life wasn't real without you. It was just a series of days all strung together by a bunch of regrets. But then I got you back. This is the right time, I promise; this is our time. You're the love of my life. I fucking love you, Grace. I've always loved you. I loved you when I wasn't with you, and before that, and right now. Marry me?"

"Fuck yeah," I whispered. I took his face between my hands and kissed him. "Let's go put on a show for her."

He pulled me out of the cab and we stood hand in hand, staring up at Ash. "What's this all about, kid?" Matt said.

She stood up and threw her arms out. "Come on, you guys. You know I'd make a way better witness than Gary Busey."

Matt looked over at me with arched eyebrows. "She doesn't smell like salami." He shrugged.

"'She doesn't smell like salami' will go down in history as the weirdest marriage proposal ever," I said.

"Graceland, are you calling me weird?"

"Yep, it's what I like about you."

Ash walked down the steps and stood near us. She was beaming.

"I should do this right," Matt said. He got down on one knee and took my hand in his.

"Grace, I love you and you love me. Now, will you marry me forever this time?"

"Yes. Forever."

FOURTH MOVEMENT:

EVIDENCE OF A LIFE BURNING WELL

ASH

My parents got married by the justice of the peace with me as their witness. In fifteen years, I never saw my mom look so full of life and love and happiness as she did on that day. I can't imagine what would have happened if they never saw each other on the subway. Would they have carried on with their lonely lives, living like two halves of one heart, just out of reach of each other? Who knows? All I know is that I'm glad they found each other again.

That summer, we all ended up going to Europe with the New York Philharmonic and then to California. It was like a grand honeymoon/family vacation. After we got back, Dad moved in with us. My parents were like teenagers in puppy love, with their faces attached to each other all the time. When I would roll my eyes at them, my dad would laugh and my mom would whine that they deserved it, that they were just making up for lost time. I liked giving them a hard time. It was actually really cool to know my mom and dad liked each other so much.

Dad kept his loft a few blocks away and we converted it into an art studio/office. We called it the Louvre. Mom loved to watch us at work in the studio, and she would play music or bring us food when she wasn't teaching.

I became a big sister a year after they got married. Finally, someone else to shoulder the burden. Actually, I really kind of adore my little brother. Leo. He's just a baby, so how bad can he be?

I know my mom and dad made mistakes and that connections were missed, but somehow I feel lucky because of it. Who knows what might have been if everything went perfectly for them? I know I got two awesome dads who loved me like crazy, and I got to see my own parents fall in love. How many people can say that?

Acknowledgments

To the readers: thank you for believing in this magic and allowing Matt and Grace into your hearts.

To family and friends who support me, encourage me and make me feel like what I'm doing matters in some small way: thank you.

Hey, Ya Ya's! Thanks for being proud, solid friends.

There is a big place in my heart for some special teachers and professors I've had who inspired me. For this book, I thought back to the many hours I spent in a darkroom in high school and college and how hard I tried to tell a story with one image alone. Now I get to use thousands of words. I'm still not sure what's easier; I just know I love both mediums, and I'm grateful to the people who opened my eyes to these art forms.

To the roomies, who have been waiting patiently: your enthusiasm has kept me going all these months.

Melissa, thank you for assisting me in New York and for the great music recs.

Thank you, Angie, for your undying support and enthusiasm.

Heather, you know your part in all of this and how important it is. You have a gift, truly.

To the author friends out there who continue being awesome sounding boards and support systems, you are so appreciated.

To Christina, my agent, thank you for always bringing me back to the work and to the writing. It helps me feel inspired when I find myself distracted by other aspects of the business.

Jhanteigh, I feel like this is our baby together. You brought so much to Matt and Grace's journey. Thank you from the bottom of my heart for believing in this story and allowing me to have at it.

Anthony, look at all of our evidence. How lucky, how blessed I am to have you in my life.

And finally, to Sam and Tony: my poetry. I can't wait to see you grow. I can't wait to know you more.